ALSO BY LAURA MOHER

BIG LOVE FROM GALWAY

Curves for Days

What She's Having

Hard to Get

a novel

LAURA MOHER

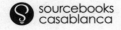

sourcebooks
casablanca

Copyright © 2025 by Laura Moher
Cover and internal design © 2025 by Sourcebooks
Cover design by Stephanie Gafron/Sourcebooks
Cover images © Naddya/Shutterstock, September Sonata/
Shutterstock, GreenSkyStudio/Shutterstock
Internal design by Tara Jaggers/Sourcebooks

Published by Sourcebooks Casablanca, an imprint of Sourcebooks
P.O. Box 4410, Naperville, Illinois 60567-4410
(630) 961-3900
sourcebooks.com

Cataloging-in-Publication Data is on file with the Library of Congress.

Printed and bound in the United States of America.
VP 10 9 8 7 6 5 4 3 2 1

To Dora, Pam, Kelly, Petra, Jana, Wanda, Joni,
and everyone else who advocates for survivors
of domestic abuse…

And to all the men who would never dream
of abusing anyone and who would speak up
and intervene if they witnessed abuse…

And to all the people in relationships that
show how love can and should be done…

Thank you. Keep up the good work.
I give thanks for people like you.

This book contains themes of domestic violence. Please check my web page (lauramoher .com/cw--resources.html) for specific triggers. My website also contains resources and links for those dealing with or wanting to know more about domestic violence.

CHAPTER 1

Andi

IT TAKES A VILLAGE TO keep this place afloat. Thank heavens Galway's a good one. July, donating leftover food from the restaurant. Rose, always managing to find funds from somewhere in emergencies. Tisha at the high school, and all our dedicated staff and volunteers, with their hard work and community contacts. Me, juggling spreadsheets and grant applications and worry.

It's going to take a village, four mules and a wagon to drag me out of my head tonight.

But it's almost five and I've been here since six this morning when I came to survey the storm damage and I've at least got to get out of *here*.

A few songs from my pep-talk playlist and maybe I'll have my shit together enough to walk out of this office and head for home without eagle-eye Pattie at the front desk asking if I'm okay.

I'll be okay. I am an island.

I'm the one who's always okay.

And anyway, if today showed me anything, it's that I'm not

really as alone as I sometimes feel. Between Bett at Bett's Coffee coming around the counter to give me a hug along with my daily Tall, Dark and Deadly order—Bett had loved Gram too—and Pattie having a vase of bright zinnias from her garden on my desk when I got to work, and July and Rose showing up with breakfast and Angus in tow so he could take stock of the damage last night's storm did to the shelter's backyard play-area fence, I've been surrounded by kindness all day.

Doesn't make me forget that I've got one former resident in the hospital and another who seems likely to go back to her husband. Doesn't make me forget this anniversary, either.

I jam in my earbuds and tip my head to the back of my chair. The low, rumbling buzz of The Chicks' "Sin Wagon" rolls through my ears straight into my brain, and I turn up the music without taking my feet off my desk. Without even opening my eyes. Just crank it up and let it pour in to fill my aching soul.

I am in desperate need of a stress outlet, and for the life of me I can't come up with one. My gym's closed indefinitely—two trees came down on it in the storm—so I can't go kickbox the shit out of anything. Can't pump my weight in iron. Can't even do a yoga class.

Softball season's over, so no pounding things with a bat, either.

It's ninety-eight degrees and wicked humid, so if I go out for a run before dark, I'm likely to die.

Tension boils like magma in me, but The Chicks pierce my thoughts with fiddle and banjo and the defiant snarl of a woman absolutely sick of a bad man's shit.

I don't know if The Chicks invented the term *mattress dancing*, but they've certainly brought it to my attention with this song. Sex—hot, energetic sex—now *there's* a stress outlet.

I could go out tonight—maybe down to Greenville... It's across the state line in South Carolina but not a bad drive—and find me a nice guy with good hands and a big, hard—

The image of my grandma rolling over in her grave interrupts that thought. As always.

God, I miss Gram.

Miss her crack of laughter in the evenings as we swapped the stories of our day. Her thoughtful pauses and slow, careful questions as she'd try to see a clear path for us through the tangle of life. I even miss her piercing see-every-damn-thing eyes.

Two years and one day ago, I'd have been calling her at the end of a day like this to ask if she wants me to build something new on the patio this weekend. She'd come up with some back-breaking project, and I'd lift and haul and sweat the stress out. And then later we'd have something nice to show for it. That's how we got the patio in the first place. And the low wall edging the ravine, and the firepit.

But today I can't think of anything new to build and Gram won't be around to enjoy it with me anyway, or to cook up a feast to give me energy, or to gripe at me to peel my filthy body off the patio pavers and go take a shower before my muscles "lock that way."

She loved to squeeze my biceps in passing. To settle beside me at the dining table and knock on my quads with her bony little knuckles. "That's my girl," she'd say, all smug. She took my ability to build stuff as assurance that I'd never need a man.

But tonight, despite all the times I've agreed with her pronouncements that "Salazar women are cursed—we're better off on our own," I'm starting to wonder.

This is the fault of my sickeningly-happy-with-their-new-partners friends.

I was *definitely* a fifth wheel last night at the roadhouse. Used to be I could count on July to be up for a spontaneous adventure at times like this, but now most days you can't get a piece of paper between her and Joe. And Rose has been with Angus ever since I first met her. With those two couples, every smile and every touch is foreplay. I don't want to think about it…but I can't look away.

So yeah, I am 100 percent sure a decent man and some mattress dancing are exactly what I need tonight. What else am I going to do…jump rope on the patio until I'm dehydrated? Drift around inside the cottage, drinking tea out of Gram's mug and staring at the empty chair that still holds the shape of her little butt? I'd lose my mind.

Now that the idea has occurred to me, I *cannot* stop imagining a nice guy with good hands and a big, hard—

My phone vibrates in my pocket.

I hit Pause on my fantasy and on the music.

"Andi. How you doin'?" From Lenny's voice and his occupation, you'd expect him to be a three-pack-a-day, whiskey-chugging guy but no, he has an occasional beer and a whole lot of sweet tea. Doesn't smoke at all. Trying, like me, not to reenact family mistakes.

"So-so, Lenny. How 'bout you?"

"Rashad ate bad shrimp and Chris has laryngitis or some such shit." Lenny's playing soft chords as he talks. Dude can't stay away from a keyboard for more than a few minutes without getting twitchy. "I'll be doin' a lot better if you can help us out this evenin.'"

Hmm. Singing beats the hell out of sitting in the cottage talking to Gram's empty chair. "You're in luck, Len. I am free as a bird. Lindon's?"

"Yes, ma'am. Thank god. Practice with us at six thirty?"

"I'll be there. Thanks, Lenny." Hallelujah. Band gigs offer a different kind of release than sex, but I love it and I'll take it.

Six-thirty practice leaves me just enough time to pick up dinner at July's and doll myself up.

I tell Pattie goodbye. "Tell everybody to be careful this weekend, okay?"

She nods. "You too. You're not going running tonight, are you?"

I shake my head. "Nah, too hot."

"Good. You should find somewhere better to do it anyway. It's not safe to run those roads up near your place." Pattie mothers me whenever she can.

I check the cameras at her desk to make sure there's no one suspicious in the parking lot. Make sure the latch clicks behind me as I leave the building. Walk quickly to my car, head high. Check under the car as I approach, and the back seat before I get in.

It's my routine, a really sucky routine, similar to the routines women all over the world develop for themselves just to try to be safe in a world that views us as prey or appropriate targets for rage.

Thank heavens for Lenny's call. I don't know why the hell I considered, even for a moment, trying to find a man for the night.

———

Kevin

"You gotta hold your end up higher or it'll spill! No, up! *Up!*" CeCe's voice is full of urgency.

I'm doing my best but I'm new to these controls, and then a cloud of gnats or mosquitoes or whatever these critters are rises up around me and I can't see what I'm doing. I lose control of the pipeline and it crashes down on us, spewing thick, shiny oil everywhere.

CeCe sighs. "You really suck at this, Uncle Kev. You just destroyed an entire ecosystem."

I rein in my laugh. I do hate letting her down, really. "It was my first time, CeCe. Besides, this is a really terrible game. Who needs this pressure?"

"*You're* the one who told me about it!" She's faking her outrage. She likes teasing me as much as I like giving her a hard time.

"Oh. Right. Why'd I do that, again?"

"Because you said our shooter games make you 'queasy.'" I can hear the air quotes in her voice. She sighs again, deeper, with the disgust only a fourteen-year-old can muster. "Face it, Uncle K—you're a bigger wuss than Great-Grandma. You're even a bigger wuss than *Great-Grandpa.*"

"Oooh, low blow." Great-Grandpa has the softest heart in the Midwest. "Hey, that boy in soccer camp still bothering you?"

"Nope. I did what you said. S-I-N-G. He hasn't messed with me or anybody else since. Thanks!"

Excellent. "Thank *Miss Congeniality.*" And my unrequited crush on Sandra Bullock.

In the background I hear my brother. "C'mon, CeCe. Time to go. What're you doing in there?"

"Losing another game with Uncle Kevin. He's what the French would call *les incompétents.*"

She gets bonus points for the *Home Alone* reference. At least she didn't call me a filthy animal this time.

"Hey, Kev!" Pete hollers. "Too bad you can't come to Mom and Dad's with us for dinner. It's steak night."

Another low blow. Not only do I have to tell my niece good-bye, but I also have to spend the rest of the evening wishing I were there with them all around the big table my folks set up on their screened porch. Or maybe they'll move it inside, if it's as hot there as here. Either way, all my favorite people will be there, talking at the same time so you can't help but follow three conversations at once. It's a toss-up whether there'll be more food or more laughter.

It's hard to be away, even though it means I can sleep in instead of dragging myself up before daylight to help whoever Mom or Dad promised I'd help with some backbreaking task. I mean, not that I mind helping. I'd just like to be *asked* first.

"See ya, brat. Give everybody a hug from me."

"Bye, Uncle Kev. Love you. Miss you."

"Love you too. Miss you too."

Then she's gone. I take a deep breath and blow it out.

Galway's a nice little town, it really is. It's just that every time I try a new-to-me restaurant or see an interesting shop or catch sight of somebody doing something athletic, the first thing that pops into my mind is, "I'll have to bring Mom and Grandma here," or "Pam and Cathy will love this," or "Dad and Pete could hook them up with better equipment." And my family lives 1,100 miles away. My whole family. Everybody I know and love.

The realization always sends me into a tailspin. Was this a giant mistake? What was I thinking? I don't even like change on my *good* days.

What full-grown man pulls up all his roots and leaves a decent job and everybody he cares about to go someplace he's never seen, all because he had his feelings hurt?

Okay, true, being dumped by a fiancée counts as more than

hurt feelings. It's more like...an identity fracture. *You're a nice guy, Kev, and I love you, but I'm bored to tears with you. You're so...vanilla.*

All I could think when Cheryl said it was "Vanilla's a valid flavor."

But I never saw it coming. And I just don't understand how niceness could be *bad*.

It's hard not to feel like this move was a mistake. Hours and days and evenings and weekends stretch empty in front of me with no end in sight. Trying to pass time, I've gotten settled in my apartment and finished my lesson plans for all my classes for the quarter. Yesterday I came in and got my classroom fixed up just the way I want it...bright colors and interesting math facts and trivia and challenges, websites for practice and math games, capsule bios of mathematicians from all over the world. Careers that make use of a strong math background. Today I came in and couldn't think of a single thing to adjust to make it better, so I sat here for hours making basic workout templates for different fitness goals for students. I haven't actually met any students yet—not till tomorrow, bright and early—but by god, I'll be ready.

School doesn't start until week after next, and except for a few hours I'm expected to work with kids on the fall teams, I've got nothing to do between now and then. So it felt like a gift from heaven when my niece called a little while ago. A respite from the loneliness I brought on my own damn self.

I'm a pitiful excuse for a grown-up man.

"Hey, Farm Boy. What you got going on tonight?"

It's Steve Jackson, lounging in my classroom doorway. Of all my new colleagues, he's the biggest. Biggest guy, biggest joker, biggest personality.

I roll my eyes because he expects it. "Still not a farmer, dude. Nobody in my family is a farmer."

He shakes his head, unconvinced as ever. "Don't know that I believe ya, man. Nebraska sounds mighty farmy to me."

"I'm from Lincoln. Population almost 300,000. Not as big as Asheville, but *many* times the size of Galway. And there's millions of acres of farmland right here in North Carolina."

Steve drops his bag. "Oooh. Somebody's been studying." He saunters into the room and squints at one of my bulletin boards. Absently rubs his right shoulder.

"You betcha. *Some*body's gotta know what they're talking about around here." I watch his fingers press deep into his skin. "You know I can give you some exercises for that shoulder."

He shakes his head. "It's not too bad. Just a little ache. Got plans tonight?"

I wish. "Nope. Please say you've got an idea."

"Always, man. Bunch of us going to dinner and then to Lindon's for the band. Wanna go?"

"Yep." I would *pay* for company tonight.

He tells me to meet them at July's—"southwest corner of the town square"—at seven to eat and after that we'll head a few blocks north to the bar. Then he strolls out, scooping up his duffel and waving without turning around.

Hallelujah and thank the Lord for bighearted social science teachers.

CHAPTER 2

Andi

JULY'S IS HOPPING, AS ALWAYS. I was planning to order carryout, but Rose and Angus wave me over to their booth.

"Sit with us!" Rose nods to the empty bench seat across from them. They always sit on the same side, holding hands or playing footsie or god knows what under the table. It would be sickening if it weren't so fascinating.

I've known Angus forever, but Rose has only been in town for a year or so. I've only gotten to know her well these past few months. When I'm with them, I have trouble noticing anything but their interactions. The scary-looking wall of a man and the short, smiling bouncy ball of a woman, the way they tease and pretend-gripe at each other, the naked adoration in their eyes when they look at each other. His big, scarred thumb so gentle, rubbing the nape of her neck. The way she'll put a hand on his chest and pretend to push him away...but then just let it linger there over his heart.

I watch them and wonder how they're different when they're

alone rather than in public. For the life of me, I can't picture them changing. There is absolutely nothing in their gaze suggesting broken trust or fear or pretense...just warmth and contentment and delight in each other.

Hard to believe. Hard to even imagine.

"I can't stay. I'm just ordering carryout. What're y'all up to tonight?" I perch on the edge of the bench and give Sonya my order while Rose makes up some ridiculous story about Angus needing to get to bed early because "he hasn't slept well the past few nights."

"I'm okay," he protests. "I think we should go hear Lenny and the guys."

"We can do that tomorrow night. Tonight you *need* your *sleep*." She turns the full force of her big brown eyes on him and he visibly melts.

"*Oh.* Okay." Dude's finally figured out he's about to have a very, *very* good night at home.

Whew. I am *not* up to explaining to Rose my occasional—and, from what I hear, shocking—transformation into someone who wears sexy clothes and knows her way around an eyeliner pencil and a pair of stilettos. She probably doesn't even know I sing.

"Damn, Andi!" Lenny pretends to stagger back when I walk into the practice room.

Not entirely unexpected; when I'd first modeled this dress with its built-in push-up bra for July, she'd said, "Damn, Andi! You're gonna put somebody's eyes out with those things!" And then when I'd turned to show her the rear view, she'd actually whistled.

Chris laughs. "Watch out, Andi, you're gonna make David

jealous. He's not gonna be the prettiest one onstage tonight." He's raspy, barely louder than a whisper.

David rolls his eyes and shakes his head in good-natured disgust. "Lookin' good, Andi."

"Thank you, David. The rest of y'all act like you've never seen cleavage before." I give them the evil eye, although I've gotta admit, the new dress is magnificent. And so are my boobs.

"Gonna teach those white boys to appreciate a thicc woman." James plays a funky bass line and Chris follows with a rim shot on drums.

Lenny whips out a pencil for the set list. "Whatcha wanna sing tonight? Bonnie? Etta? Nina?"

"Yeah, and how 'bout that Hannah Williams one we practiced last time?"

He nods, his pencil flying over the page. "Nice. You'll bring down the house."

Next best thing to good sex is bringing down the house.

I wish Gram could hear me sing tonight. Even though it would scare her to see me dressed up like this, she'd be proud.

At home, before I got ready, I'd stood in the living room staring at the pictures on the mantel. Gram with my mom in Asheville when Mom was little. My mom with my sister, Lola, in Charlotte. All three generations together: Gram, Lola, Mom with me in a baby snuggle carrier, at Biltmore.

Nothing with the sperm donor, of course.

Gram was a small and beautiful woman. Mom was medium-sized and beautiful. I'm big and usually I do my best to be plain, thanks to a few decades of Gram's tutoring. *If they don't notice you, they won't try to hurt you, Andi. You can live your life better if you don't let them see you.*

I've never doubted her love or her desire to protect me. Haven't had much reason to doubt her advice either, what with my line of work, until recently after watching my friends in their new relationships.

Well, July and Joe aren't exactly new to each other, but they were apart most of the time since they met. Watching them find their way back to each other these past few months has been touching. Mesmerizing. For the first time in my life, I found myself wanting to cheer on a romantic couple. Wanting to say to July, "What's wrong with you—can't you see how great this guy is? He obviously loves you and you love him! What's holding you back?"

The man would quietly move mountains for her and smile at her while he did it.

Even so, given family history and all the proof I've had for all these years that Gram was right, it doesn't seem right to be doubting her now.

––––––

Kevin

July's restaurant gets a definite "like very much" on my new List of Things I Have Opinions About. The food is wonderful, the portions generous, and I get to try something new: beets. Not my favorite, but not bad, especially roasted with sweet potatoes and chicken.

I'd like to have sat at one of the sidewalk patio tables to see what goes on in the square, but even with the heat, they were all full. We were lucky, coming inside just as a big family was leaving, or we would never have gotten to sit together.

The atmosphere's great, everybody talking and laughing and

calling out to people at other tables. If this were my hometown and I knew everyone, coming to July's would be like sliding into a warm bath on a cold night.

There's funky, bluesy music playing—"That's the Blue Shoes. That's the band we're going to hear later," Steve tells me—and July herself takes time to circulate between tables. She's a big, sunny blond who looks like she could give me some pointers in the weight room. A guy is with her some of the time, lean and sun-browned and mostly quiet, with a quick half grin and a glow in his eyes whenever he looks at July.

My group is made up of other teachers from Galway High, some with their significant others. I'd met most of them before and am learning names as fast as I can. I recognize Arlene, the cute little French teacher, and meet her wife, Hazel. The civics/government guy, Henry, is one of the football coaches. I've already had a few conversations with him. Pat, who teaches the honors and AP literature classes, is with their partner, Diego.

"Tisha comes sometimes too. She's a hoot. Her husband's in the band," Steve says after pointing everyone out to me. Tisha is the vice principal, the one who seems to run things at Galway High. Energetic, sharp as a tack, her all-seeing dark eyes and no-nonsense manner balanced by a dry sense of humor. I look forward to knowing her better.

Someone asks what I think of Galway so far. Others chime in with *have I been to the lake,* and *have I tried this or that restaurant,* and *I should go out to the roadhouse one night,* and *the best auto mechanic in town is…*

We take our time eating, laughing, talking, and I'm feeling good—hopeful again—by the time we stroll across the square and up a couple more blocks to the bar to hear the band. Galway is a nice town. I can make a home here. Just have to be patient, push past this first lonely, outsider spell.

I can do this.

Lindon's is just what I expected: narrow, old, with faded brick and a tinted window that stretches most of the width of the place. Inside, dark, with a little stage up front and a long bar down the left side, beer mirrors and neon signs and rows of bottles on shelves behind it. Scuffed wooden floors, well-worn furniture and the smells of beer and popcorn in the air.

We manage to snag the last few tables near the stage and push them together. A server takes our drink orders and Steve tells me about the Blue Shoes. "Three of them went to high school just a couple of years ahead of me, and they all played football. Lenny and James—that's Tisha's husband, he's the bass player—and Rashad. They had a band in high school too, in the off-season. Got serious with it later. The other two guys are newer. Drummer's a couple of years younger than me and I think the other guitarist is too. David. He's a songwriter—they do some of his stuff along with blues and crossover. Trade off on vocals. Every damn one of them can sing."

Okay, I guess tonight I'll find out what I think about blues and crossover music. And about the Blue Shoes. And this bar. I'll develop firm opinions. Some of them maybe even negative. *See, Cheryl? I can judge too.*

Steve and Henry and some of the others drift into a conversation about the upcoming season opener against Brevard, Galway High's arch-rival. I listen with one ear as I watch the band members trickle onto the stage, greeting people they pass, picking up their instruments, checking and fiddling with equipment in that mysterious way of musicians. The keyboard player is a big white guy with a wild cloud of red hair. The drummer is shorter, stocky, with sandy hair. Looks like he was born with a set of drumsticks in his hands. There's another big guy messing with a bass, his Afro even bigger than the keyboard player's mass of curls. Tisha's James, I guess. Another smaller guy has a guitar. He's maybe Latino?—with the kind of brilliant smile people always comment on. He mostly trains it on his bandmates.

The keyboardist seems to be the leader, the one making soft last-minute comments to the others, the one they turn to with questions.

There are only four guys, though. I thought Steve mentioned five. I'm trying to figure out who's missing when a woman steps up onstage, her thick, curvy legs long and tanned and bare. Stiletto heels. Her hair's a silky dark sweep almost to her waist. I can't see her face but something about her sucks the air from the room. From my lungs.

And then she turns and shrugs out of the long loose shirt she's wearing and I see red. A long streak of it in her hair. A gleaming swipe of it across her full, lovely lips. Fringed rows of it around the snug fabric hugging her astounding curves. Red filling the back of my vision and my brain like a tide of wet heat. A red you want to dive into. Drive into, again and again. My hands clench at my sides and my heartbeat thumps in my ears.

She murmurs something to the guys of the band and they all laugh, her wide smile gleaming brightest of all, her eyes flashing even darker than those of the guitarist.

Every last bit of me is suddenly standing at attention.

Beside me, Steve snickers. "Pull your tongue back in before you close your mouth, Farm Boy. Don't want you to have to get stitches."

I can't muster a comeback or any coherent thought at all. I'm busy trying to make sense of my response to this woman. I've never… Criminy.

The women I've dated have all been pretty. Many have been athletes. All smallish and slim and…pretty.

The woman onstage makes "pretty" seem like an insult and "slim" seem like "not enough." She is vibrant. Full. Vivid. Gorgeous. Larger than life, with warm glowing skin over generous, ripe curves.

She's dangerous, with long crimson fingernails and an edge to her brilliant smile. Mysterious, with tattooed vines and feathers and curling leaves peeping out from under the fabric of her dress on her rounded thigh and the full inner curve of her right breast. I want to hike up that dress. Trace those patterns with my tongue, see where they lead and what picture they form. I imagine her splayed, her smooth skin the canvas for some lucky tattoo artist's masterpiece.

I'm still not breathing. Nice Guy Kevin be damned; this woman makes me want to lick and bite and squeeze and grind into her. All of the blood in my body has gathered in my groin. My dick suddenly has Very Firm Opinions.

Steve pokes me with an elbow. Pretends concern. "You okay, Farm Boy?"

"You didn't, uh, mention—" My voice is raspy.

"Yeah, I didn't know Andrea was going to be here. She fills in every now and then. I don't see Rashad. He must be out tonight." He laughs again. "You look like you need to get you some." He glances from me to the stage, shaking his head. "Just not Andrea."

"Why—" *If I can't have her, I don't want anybody.* That ridiculous thought shocks me as much as if I'd said it out loud. I'm not sure I could even *handle* a woman like this, me being so vanilla and all. But every single part of me wants to try.

Steve shrugs, hands open. "She doesn't usually sing with them. Only shows up when they need someone to fill in. Steams up the whole place, then disappears into the night." He eyes the woman onstage. "You can look but you can't touch. I mean, you can dream, but that woman never goes home with anybody." He shakes his head regretfully. "Many have tried."

Up onstage, the band members step into position. The keyboard player—Lenny, Steve had said—swirls his hands over the keys and pulls the mic close. "Good evenin', Galway! How's everybody doin' tonight?"

If the answering roar is any indication, this place is full of fans and they're all doing fine.

Lenny smiles. "Good to be back with our favorite hometown crowd. If you see Rashad tomorrow, you tell him not to eat old shrimp, okay? But tonight our loss is also our gain, because we have the lovely Andrea joinin' us…" Another roar from the packed bar, with a fair number of whistles thrown in. The bandmates grin. Andrea drops a slow wink and a shimmy, setting all that fringe shaking, right along with my pulse. Lenny nods at her. "And she's leading us off with some Southside Johnny…" And the band rolls into a slow strut of a song with Andrea crooning about having a fever, her voice low and sultry, by turns velvet-smooth and sexy rough.

I'm melting in my chair even before she starts addressing each new line to a different audience member. And when her eyes land on me and she sings that when she thinks about me she feels all right, the fingers of her right hand just barely skim over the smooth, plump, top curve of her breast, and all that fringe quivers below, and I. Am. Lost.

CHAPTER 3

Andi

DAMMIT, I WISH WE WEREN'T in Galway, because there is a big. blond snack of a man—no, hell, he's a five-course feast of a man—at the teachers' table, right next to Steve Jackson. If we were in Asheville or Charlotte or Greenville, I'd be planning my after-party accordingly.

He's easily as tall as Lenny and James, with eight-foot-wide shoulders and biceps that strain the sleeves of his dark polo. No wedding ring or sign of there ever having been a wedding ring on the hand he has clenched around his beer mug. His expression is just right when he looks at me...sweet, poleaxed, and not real bright. A golden retriever of a man. Probably a coach, like Steve. All brawn and not too many brains, young enough to have plenty of stamina, and almost certainly up for a night of energetic, no-strings sex.

He's freakin' *perfect*.

And there's not a damn thing I can do about it because this is my hometown and you don't pee in your own pool, unless you're really gross and have no sense. I have a serious professional reputation to guard and no need for entanglements. So I divide my attention between him and all the other people in the bar who look interested, and just enjoy having his eyes on me as I sing and dance with James and David.

But ohhh, if we weren't in Galway, I could strip that polo off of him and gnaw my way across those big shoulders and up the firm column of his neck, bite that square jaw and his cute little earlobes, let him flutter those thick gold-tipped lashes against my skin...

No. Rein it in, Andrea.

So I channel my sadness over Gram's death and my worry over my clients and my rage at abusers worldwide and every last ounce of my sexual frustration into songs by Etta James and Nina Simone and Janis Joplin. I do a little dance sandwich between big James and pretty David, and I enjoy just being up here with these guys. I'm not the only one dealing with stuff; Lenny had a nightmare of a childhood and Chris is still in love with his remarried ex, years after their split. The stage is a place where they can let everything out too.

For James and David, it's different. James is a big flirt with a deep voice and a big belly-laugh. He acts like a hound dog when he's up here singing and playing, but offstage he's a devoted dad and husband, a master with a barbecue grill and surprisingly good at freeze tag. David might as well still be on his honeymoon, he's so besotted with his wife, and they're over the moon about the three kids they're adopting.

But onstage we all put on a show, wailing and flirting and sometimes raunching it up, singing our hearts out, playing to the crowd. And it's almost enough. By the end of our first set, some of the tension is leaving my body, replaced by the high of a good performance.

I speed back to the restroom while I can, not even glancing at Steve Jackson's table or his big blond friend. Not gonna go there. Too dangerous. Too tempting.

I use the facilities and check my makeup and my cheap fake nails, make sure everything's where it should be. I look into my eyes in the mirror for a long minute, hoping that no one else can see loneliness or sadness or fear in me tonight. Just in case, I reach into the top of my dress and adjust the girls to show a little more cleavage. Strategic tattoos, the girls, and a butt load of makeup... Those are the secret of the Andi-to-Andrea attitude shift.

I'm starting to get hoarse. Might have overdone it a bit on a couple of those songs. Gotta pace myself if I'm going to be able to do justice to "Late Nights and Heartbreak" at the end of the night.

Need to check Lenny's set list real quick before we take the stage again...

I'm out the restroom door, headed up the hall full speed, when out of nowhere I hit a wall. Not a metaphorical one—a solid wall of muscle and sinew and hard flesh, directly in my path. The force of the collision sends us careening through the curtain into the little alcove where Lindon's stores extra chairs. Knocks the air out of my lungs.

Alarm floods my veins with ice. I struggle to regain my balance enough to fight or flee.

"Oh, ma'am, I'm so sorry! Are you okay?" Voice like low, warm velvet. Big hands gentle on my waist, not grabbing, just steadying me.

Light glints off thick lashes above eyes that look dark in the shadowed alcove, but those cheekbones and that jawline are unmistakable.

I'm okay. It's Snack Man

Oh my god, it's my big blond snack man, his hard body still close to mine, his thumbs rubbing slow circles just below my ribs, his scent a little spicier and more mysterious than I would have expected. A faint glimmer of my lip gloss on his left pec.

And just like that, I take leave of my senses. Instead of moving back into the hallway, I step farther in. Tilt my chin up and aim my full Andrea smolder at him. Raise one long red fingernail and stroke it slowly across his chest, just below the lip gloss. His breathing stalls and his nipple hardens under my fingertip.

So do mine, under my dress. I feel a tug low in my belly, and instead of taking it as warning, I arch closer.

"I"—I rub my fingertip back the other way, over his nipple again—"messed up my lipstick on your shirt here. I should probably go fix that. You want to make it worth my while?"

His hands clench and unclench and clench again on my waist before his thumbs resume their lazy stroking. "Make it...worth your while?"

I stretch my arm up slowly, bringing my hand to the back of his hard, warm neck. His eyes sweep my arm and shoulder and chest before rising to mine. When I tug his face down, he doesn't resist.

Kevin

My idiot brain chooses this moment to remember every science concept I ever studied. Osmosis, as the heat of her body under my fingertips seeps through my cell membranes to set me on fire. Absorption as I soak up the hunger in her eyes, and reflection as mine mirror it back. Surface tension, as every freaking molecule of my body quivers and strains to hold it together despite the irresistible pull of her.

This wet dream of a woman—no, this mesmerizing, all-powerful *goddess*—is pulling me in for a kiss, her dark eyes glowing and a pulse beating fast in her throat just uphill of her amazing breasts.

Life shifts into slow motion. A delicious, see-every-detail, think-every-thought-fully slow motion.

My hands are on her, one at her waist, the other rising to cup the silky skin of her shoulder.

God, I've missed touching people. I've gone almost totally without physical contact with another person for the past three and a half weeks. That's unheard of in my big family, where physical interactions are constant. My last hug and kiss and hand-holding and arm pat and shoulder bump—really, any skin-to-skin contact—was in Nebraska when I was saying goodbye as I set out on my move to North Carolina.

I am starving for human touch and Andrea's smooth skin is a feast. I want to run my hands all over her, dip her back over my arm and press my mouth to her throat, her collarbones, the firm curves of her breasts, suck and nip and, just, *feast*.

Lord, she feels impossibly good. Warm, soft, firm, full... I try to get control of myself, but her dark eyes have me and she doesn't seem to want to let go. In fact, one of her hands is in my hair now, her fingertips swirling against my scalp in a way that never felt sexy before but that brings a low growl up out of me tonight. I'm about five seconds away from stripping her naked and taking her up against the wall.

And then our mouths meet in a kiss so hungry, so forceful it's impossible to know who is giving and who is taking.

Holy mother of god. It's like inhaling a flame. She's hot in my hands, hot against my lips, hot everywhere we press together. The slide of her tongue, the friction of her body against mine as she pulls me closer... Her taste and scent are irresistible. Salty, sweet, and spicy, warm and dark and captivating.

I ache to bury my face in her cleavage and breathe her in. Discover the source of that scent and that heat. Lick her, taste her, suck little marks into her skin there.

We devour each other, pleasure humming out of us, my hands smoothing up and down her back. I want to get closer, but all too soon she pulls away.

I let go, of course, but my hands and body scream a silent protest. I stand with her in that dim alcove, still on fire, waiting to see what she'll do next.

Her lipstick really does need fixing now. I've eaten most of it off of her. She puts one hand on my forearm as if to steady herself. "That was *def*initely worth my while. Thank you." Then she goes up on tiptoe, kisses my cheek, and disappears through the curtain and into the women's restroom.

I have to forcibly gather my wits and will my body back under control before I duck into the men's room to see if I have lipstick all over me. I do *not* want to have to explain to Steve or anybody else what just happened. I mean, not that I'm even sure what just happened, except me being hit by lightning in the shadowy back hallway of a bar.

No, kissing Andrea will be a memory I'll keep to myself and treasure. Because *damn*, what could I possibly say about it? "Well, one night I met this goddess..."

CHAPTER 4

Andi

STUPID, STUPID, STUPID.

I can't remember the last time I kissed a Galway man. But with the taste of him still on my mouth, the feel of his big hands still on my waist, I can't make myself feel entirely sorry. I can't find the resolve to not do it again.

Because, dammit, the man fits all my requirements. Every last one. I'd become very aware of that when we were pressed together in the hallway, consuming each other's souls. Every. Damn. One.

But I'm not a complete idiot so I shout down my internal clamorings as I do a lightning fix of my makeup, even as I ache in all the appropriate places. Shout them down again as I retake the stage, carefully not looking at the teachers' table.

Even if I wanted to follow up on that kiss with more heart-pounding nonsense with him, how would I go about it? I'm not taking a stranger home with me. The cottage is my safe spot. My refuge from the rest of the world.

But lord I need and want a man tonight. This particular man. Big, strong, passionate, and oh-so-gentle... That's my unicorn—an irresistible combination I wasn't sure really existed in a living man. *Jesus.* I'd wanted to wrap my legs around him and go at it against the wall in that alcove, risk be damned.

For him to be here on this night of all nights, as if I'd placed an order for him... Passing up this opportunity would be like stamping "return to sender" on a gift-wrapped package from God.

But if I *were* going to break my no-Galway-guys rule, where would we even go? Even if I were willing to take him to the cottage, Gram would haunt my ass for doing something so stupid.

He's not from around here, that much I know, so he probably doesn't have a place of his own nearby. I couldn't go with him to the house of whoever he's visiting, especially if it's Steve Jackson. And no way could I get through a hotel lobby without someone seeing me. Dressing up every now and then is pushing it. Galway doesn't need to be speculating about my sex life too.

I don't even know if he drove himself, so even car sex is out. And dammit, I'm not in high school anymore, anyway, even if he did have a vehicle big enough for the two of us to get up to something interesting.

There are *so* many reasons why this urge to spend the night with him is foolish. But still I think about it, all the way through "Chain of Fools" and "Damn Your Eyes" and Lenny's rendition of a Stevie Ray Vaughan song and James channeling Muddy Waters.

I wait for Snack to tell Steve Jackson about our kiss—because of course he will; he's a guy and it was obvious earlier that Steve was teasing him about watching me—but I don't see them talking much, at least not long enough for that story. And Steve isn't leering, isn't looking at me any different than usual, and Snack isn't doing anything gross or obvious. He's just watching and listening to us play, and damn, suddenly I'm wondering why I'd assumed he wasn't real bright, because now that light in his eyes looks an awful lot like curiosity. Like he's sitting there sipping his beer and listening and…thinking.

Goddammit, this is why I can't have nice things. I can't have a thinking man looking at me when I'm trying to talk myself out of sleeping with him.

And then, halfway through the second set, the teachers' table settles up with their server. They get up to leave, saluting Lenny and the guys on the way out. All except Snack, who waves them off, tugs one of their little tables closer to the wall and stays behind, his chair tilted back on two legs, his eyes still on me, still burning with interest.

And low in my belly I feel that tug again.

Common sense abandons me, replaced by thoughts of how I might actually be able to do this safely.

He was respectful of my wishes in that alcove. Steve Jackson knows him, so he's probably not a serial killer. Even if he has violent tendencies, he'd have to know he wouldn't get away with it. Lenny and the band know Steve. I could point Snack out to Lenny and make sure he knows Lenny sees him. That should make things safer physically.

I sing and think and watch him watching me, and every part of my body reacts to him.

Foolish or not, I'm going to see if it's doable.

Kevin

Never done anything remotely like this before, but when the rest of my group leaves halfway through the second set, I decide to stick around.

Steve laughs at me. "Man, you got it bad. I'm telling ya, you're wasting your time. And you're gonna be hurtin' in a few hours when the fall teams show up to meet Trainer Farm Boy."

He's probably right. And he's probably not the only one who will laugh at me tonight. But I wave him off anyway. "Guess that'll teach me, won't it?"

Then I sit by myself, tipped back to the wall, and I memorize everything about Andrea, from the curve of her cheek to the shape of her dark eyes to the length of her bare curvy legs, and I listen to the music and feel her voice like a cat's purr up my spine and down to my balls.

I don't know what I'm hoping for. Never hooked up with a stranger before, so I don't know how those start. Not sure what she's thinking after our kiss. But I want more of her, whatever shape "more" takes. Coffee? Another kiss? Sex up against a wall somewhere? I'm a yes, whatever.

After the second set, she pauses by my table and says, her voice husky, "Your friends abandoned you. You gonna stick around?" and I'm so overcome by the sight and scent and warmth of her so close to me and the possible implications of her question that all I can say is, "Yeah." And then I really *do* feel like somebody who should answer to the name Farm Boy.

But then she says, with a tiny frown, "They didn't leave you without a place to stay, did they?"

I don't know why she's asking and I'm afraid to hope. "No,

I've got my own place." My words come out careful. Let her make what she will of them.

"That's good," she says, and moves on to talk to somebody at another table, leaving me wondering if I'm losing my mind.

But no way am I leaving without seeing what happens, so I settle in for another set, which Andrea closes with the most amazing, gutsy rendition of a song I have *ever* heard. A faithless woman singing to the lover she knows she's not good enough for, breaking her own heart even as she's cheating. And damn, there's not a whisper of sound or a dry eye in the place as her voice fills the room, rising with the force of four people, tearing our hearts out, nothing moving anywhere but ghosts of past heartbreaks and the tremor of red fringe.

The song ends and there's a silence just long enough for us all to start breathing again, and then the bar explodes with sound: whistles and whoops and cheers. The bass player James shakes his head at Andrea and wipes imaginary sweat from his brow. The guitarist takes hold of her hand and raises it in a "the winner!" gesture. Lenny the keyboardist says into the mic, "First time we've done that one for a crowd. I guess it's a keeper..." and the drummer just sits back and grins. Andrea's smile lights up the room and it's a while before the noise dies down.

I'm leaning forward at the edge of my chair—when did that happen?—when Andrea goes up on tiptoe to whisper something in Lenny's ear. He turns and gives me a long, hard look I recognize as a warning, and my heart pauses in its rhythm. Before I can figure out what that's about, the band takes a bow. Then Andrea's down off the stage asking me to meet her in a few minutes at Lenny's van in the alley behind the bar.

And I may be a vanilla farm boy from Nebraska, but I throw

down money for my drinks and tip so fast you'd think I do this kind of thing every night. No way am I missing a chance to spend a little more time with this woman.

And when I meet her back there and she asks if I drove and if I'd like to go somewhere more private, I say yes. *Oh, hell yes. Yes, please. Thank you, God, yes.*

———————

The first thing she says after I start my car is, "You're single, right? There's nobody who would be hurt by you being with me, right?"

When I assure her I'm single, the next thing out of her pretty mouth is, "Do you have condoms?" She's angled herself toward me slightly, her back partly against her door, one smooth knee near where my hand rests on the gearshift.

Well, okay then. That clears up my uncertainty about her intentions. We are not going for coffee. "I–I'll stop for some." I don't know whether to be excited or disappointed that she doesn't want to get to know me better first. Well, okay, part of me is definitely, hugely excited.

We can get to know each other later.

I find a place that's open twenty-four hours. "Do you want to come in and choose what kind?"

She smiles faintly, her eyes glowing. "Surprise me."

I buy two different types in case she really does have a preference.

Back in the car, as I put on my signal to pull out of the lot, I glance over at her. "I was surprised you asked me to... I heard you don't ever do this."

Her face is beautiful even in uneven light. Even expression-less. "Do this?"

"Go home with anybody."

"Hmm." A tiny furrow appears between her dark brows. "Guess I was just never tempted before." She doesn't offer any further explanation.

So many things that could mean.

My apartment complex isn't fancy but it's decent. Well kept, and near the high school. She's out of the car before I can get to her door to open it.

My hand hovers at the small of her back as we head up to the second floor. I can feel the heat of her without even touching her.

The apartment's small but I keep it pretty tidy, thank god, except for a few partly unpacked boxes along one wall in the dining area. Andrea gazes down at all the University of Nebraska memorabilia and then grins at me.

"Yeah." I scratch the back of my head. "My family gave me every Nebraska product known to humankind as a going-away gift. Guess they were afraid I'd forget where I came from."

"Haven't had time to unpack?" Her eyes crinkle wonderfully at the corners when she smiles.

"Nah, that's not the problem… Turns out I hate the color red. I've never said that out loud before. Lightning would strike me if I said it in Nebraska." I toss my wallet and keys and the condom bag onto the counter that separates the kitchen from the dining area. "Are you thirsty? Hungry?"

"I'd love water." Her voice has gone from husky to raspy over the evening.

She follows me into the kitchen and I pour her a glass of cool water from the fridge. Her throat, when she drinks, is so smooth and lovely my own mouth goes dry. When she goes to put the glass in the sink, I take it from her and drink a few swallows myself.

Then I'm not sure what to do. Talk? Reach for her? Head for another room? Which other room?

She watches me, her dark eyes warm, as I shove my not-quite-shaking hands in my jeans pockets and lean back against the counter.

"So," I say, like an inexperienced idiot. I've had experience, just not...*this* experience. Nothing that would prepare me for an over-the-top sexy, gorgeous, talented stranger-woman asking to come home with me. And if I've got condoms.

"So." She's not smiling now. I can't read her expression.

Is she having second thoughts? Shit. But okay. "There's no pressure, you know? We don't have to do anything if you don't want to." I keep my voice soft, reassuring.

"Oh god." She drops her head back, giving me a whiff of her sweet shampoo and another view of her gorgeous throat. "Did I pressure you into this? I was really wanting...but it's okay. I can go."

That surprises a laugh out of me. Suddenly we're just two people here.

"Andrea." I reach out and trace a fingertip down her bare arm. Watch goose bumps form there. When she shivers, I feel it deep in my own gut. "I absolutely don't want you to go. I just wanted to make sure you're okay with a different decision than your usual."

Her smile blooms. She takes half a step closer. Rests a hand on my arm. "Tonight I *need* something different than my usual. So I'm really hoping you're okay with providing that." A tiny dimple appears in her right cheek. "I'm hoping you'll provide it really enthusiastically."

I cup her bare elbow. "I don't know if I can put into words

just how enthusiastic I am." The proof is right here, if she'd just look down.

Might as well be honest. "I've never brought home anybody I wasn't already dating. I'm not sure what—how—"

She steps closer. Puts her purse on the counter beside my keys. "What if… maybe if we recreate what we were doing at Lindon's? That was…nice."

"Okay." The scent of her makes me dizzy. "Do you want to crash into me like a wrecking ball again?"

She laughs. "You poor dainty man." She moves into me, placing one fingertip on my shirt. "Based on this lip gloss, I must have had my mouth right here." She presses her finger and then her mouth to my pec, leaving a full perfect puckered-lips print over the older smudged one I'd tried to wipe off.

My breathing stutters, just as it had at Lindon's. "I am never washing this shirt again." I clear my throat. Raise my hands to her sides. "I remember holding you…like this. And then I'm pretty sure you overpowered my dainty self and made me kiss you like this."

Her dark eyes shine and her arms come up around my neck as I lower my mouth to hers.

CHAPTER 5

Kevin

AND JUST LIKE AT LINDON'S, her mouth sets me on fire. I like kissing, in general—it's always been a nice way to show somebody I feel close to them—but with Andrea it's all-consuming. Blots out all thought of anything else, all awareness of where we are... It's just me and her and this astounding, electric connection everywhere we touch.

Under my hands she's all full, firm curves and enticing dips and, under that flirty fringe, hot skin like silk.

Next thing I know, we're in the bedroom doorway, her warm fingers sliding up my abs to my chest, leaving a trail of fire. She breaks the kiss, easing my shirt over my head, and drops it, panting. "I liked the way you looked at me at Lindon's. What were you thinking?"

My breathing is uneven, my body flooded with sensation and warmth, my brain short-circuiting. "I was thinking...'What a massively talented woman'?" My frantic fingers find the zipper tab at the back of her dress and pull it down, easing it over her shoulders.

She leans into me in the doorway. It feels incredible but prevents her dress from coming off as I'd hoped. "Funny man. Part of the time you were looking at my boobs." She leans back to see my face and the dress drops to her waist, leaving her breasts bare and me speechless.

The only way I can touch her is with reverence, cupping the heavy hot weight of her, groaning as her nipples harden against my palms. "To be fair...they're gorgeous... You're gorgeous..." I dip my head, take one of the dark peaks into my mouth, and now she's the one who groans.

"Thank you—ooh!" Her fingers work at the button of my jeans. "I like that you looked...hungry."

I try to think, but I'm tracing the pattern of curling leaves and vines that leads down into her cleavage and halfway around the underside of her other breast. I press my face there. My lips. Trace them again with my tongue. "I was...jealous of your tattoo artist."

My fly is open. She's got her head back, her eyes closed. "Mmm?" She slides her hands around my waist and down into my clothes to clasp my bare butt.

I lose my mind a little more when she squeezes and presses her belly into me. "For getting to see you...all your private spots..." My fingers seek her nipples as I find her mouth for another long, drugging kiss.

She wriggles her hips and the dress drops to the floor at her feet. "Well, not *all* my private spots..."

I take her by the shoulders and just gaze. All this smooth skin...all these wonderful curves... My hands skim over every bit of her I can see, and some I can't, squeezing, caressing, worshiping her with touch.

Her eyes close again and she smiles, holding on to my waist. "Mmm..."

My turn for a question. I drag my mouth down her smooth, lovely throat. "When you were singing, when you looked at me, what were you thinking?" *Please please please let it not be, "What a boring, vanilla man"*...

"I was thinking...what a miracle that you were there, when I had been wishing so hard for somebody like you..." She slides one hand down into the front of my jeans, her fingers wrapping around me over my underwear.

I almost come right then and there. Nothing about this night has been typical or anything like I expected when I agreed to meet Steve and the others. Thank heavens.

Two can play that game. I pull her to me again, put my arms around her and squeeze her behind. Her big, lovely, amazingly curvy, almost-entirely-bare behind. "Oh lordy..."

She laughs. An amused, mischievous, throaty sound. "Don't they have thongs in Nebraska?"

"Don't know about the underwear, but I've never felt such a wonderful backside in my life." I keep hold of her. Keep squeezing, caressing, adoring her with my hands, groaning again. I might never stop groaning, because I know I'll never stop thinking about this, and groaning is the only response to such an experience.

She shoves my jeans and my underwear down, and this time her fingers wrap around my bare skin. "Oh my god, you meet *all* my requirements."

I kick off my sandals and pants and manage to let her play for a full five seconds before I pick her up—she's no lightweight but I have never had a more welcome task—and carry her the two steps to the bed. I'm just about to follow her down when, at the same second, we both say, "Condoms!" Takes me zero point two seconds to retrieve them and then she's tearing open one of the packets as I ask her what she'd like.

"You. In me. Hard." Her nimble fingers roll that sucker on, and I am on her so fast it's embarrassing.

A grown man with a fair amount of experience, with a woman he's been pretty much worshiping for hours, and instead of keeping my cool and going gentle and easy, I shove my way in like she asked, fast and forceful into the heaven of her body. And I like it.

She rises to meet every thrust, her dark eyes closing, her hands clenching my ass, her back arching and flexing, over and over. "Oh—my god—yes!"

Afraid I'll come before she's ready, I brace myself on one arm, slip my hand between us and find her with my thumb. Stroke her, put just a little pressure there with each thrust, and glory in the tiny gasps and sounds of pleasure she makes. Revel in her fierce smile and the wildness of the ride and the strength of her beautiful body's response to me. To this.

And she's close...so close. Her muscles clamp down on me. I bend to kiss her and then realize she doesn't know... Somehow we never got around to... Instead of kissing her mouth, I press my lips to her ear and whisper, "Andrea, I'm Kevin."

And she's coming, with my name on her lips. "Kevin!" Coming and coming, arching and laughing with what sounds an awful lot like relief and joy.

And I fall over the edge right after, laughing myself and whispering her name into her ear.

Afterward I slide to her side and we lie there together, my arm across her waist, her fingers twirling my hair as if she doesn't want to break the connection any more than I do. Eventually our breathing slows but I can't shed this big silly smile.

She turns her face to look at me. She's got a faint smile herself. "Kevin, that was… You were exactly who I needed tonight. Thank you."

I look into her beautiful eyes and trace one fingertip across her brow, down her temple, over her velvety cheekbone, and my mouth says, "You are the first person I have really touched since I moved to North Carolina. I don't think anything has ever felt this good to me before. So thank *you*."

Crap, why did I tell her that? She didn't need to know that.

Andi

I'm not sure what he's telling me. What it means. "You mean 'touched' like…?" I wave back and forth between us, nearly getting distracted by the beauty of his big, muscular body so close. So naked, except for that condom, which is in danger of falling off now.

Is…he *blushing*? Because I'm looking at him? Is there no end to the charm of this man?

"No"—he clears his throat and drops his gaze for just a second before meeting mine again—"'touched' like having any skin contact at all. Not a hug, not a kiss, no—Well, no, I guess I got a couple of handshakes my first day at school, but nothing… warm. Nothing personal. No, like, enjoying just being with somebody. You know. Leaning on them a little, touching their arm… nothing *close*. For, like, three and a half weeks."

"You keep track of the time between these things?" If I'm

going to tease him, I'm going to touch him to take any sting out of the words. I run my knuckle back and forth along his sturdy jaw.

He gives me a quick half smile and—more charm. Big, sweet dude actually has a *dimple* in his left cheek. Freaking *adorable*. "Ha! Not usually. Took me awhile to realize what was wrong. Why I was feeling so...off."

His finger moves down my throat to my collarbone. So gentle it tickles.

I see him watching my nipples tighten in response, but he drags his gaze back upward, clearing his throat again. "A couple of days ago I was in a restaurant and this older woman and little girl came in and joined a couple sitting near me, and they all stood up and hugged and were so happy to be together...and I thought, 'Okay, *that's* what's wrong. *That's* what's missing.'"

"So this"—I wave between us again—"helped make up for that?"

"No. Well, I mean, yeah, but...*so* much more." His eyes narrow, his focus shifting to my mouth. His fingers find my chin, tilting it to angle my face toward his.

"Yeah?" I say it just before his lips meet mine.

"I don't think I can describe it." His mouth is soft and warm now, his kisses gentle and so leisurely, like he's planning to do this for a long time.

My tongue brushes his and there's that belly tug again. I press my body into his. "Try." Everywhere I'm soft, he's hard. Everywhere I'm curved, he's got angles and planes. I'm smooth and he's dusted everywhere with curly, sun-bleached blond hair, soft and springy to the touch. I take hold of his hip and tilt my head back to let him answer.

"It's like...if everyday touches are meals—you know, basic

nutrition—this, with you, is…a prime rib dinner with a loaded baked potato and a side of jumbo shrimp. Homemade pumpkin pie with real whipped cream."

I feel a slow, satisfied cat smile stretch across my face. I almost purr. "Please tell me that's your favorite meal."

"Yes, ma'am, it certainly is." His hand is in my hair at the base of my skull now, putting just enough pressure to bring our lips together for another kiss. His half smile and dimple are back.

I could lie here and kiss this lovely man all night. All. Night. I slide my hands up over his shoulders so that every bit of his glorious naked front side is plastered to every bit of mine, and his hands find resting spots behind my neck and on the curve of my ass, holding me just the way I like, right where I want to be.

He's growing hard again already, Not-So-Little-Kevin rising up against my belly. Makes me want to laugh with pleasure, but he might misunderstand and feel hurt. I tilt my head and break the kiss, brushing my lips across his, admitting, "I too have found this a…an enjoyable meal."

His smile widens, deepening that dimple, and his eyes half close. The hand at my neck ghosts over my shoulder to cup my breast, his thumb making lazy circles over my nipple. "For you, the food equivalent would be…?"

"Mmm." My hips roll against him and he hardens more. I arch into his hand. "Barbecue chicken. Grilled veggies."

He leans in for a kiss.

"Warm, crusty bread with butter." I'm close to moaning again.

Again he steals a kiss, deeper this time.

"And some kind of deep, dark chocolate cake…"—I can't stop my gasp as he ducks his head and sucks my nipple into his mouth—"with just a hint of cinnamon."

"Mmm. You're making me hungry again." There's a rough edge to the words he mutters against my skin.

"I'm... Oh! Hunger can be good." Mine is approaching starvation. I fumble behind him for the open condom box and pull out another. Reach down between us and pull off the old one.

"Hungry can be very, very good." He catches his lip between his teeth and pulls back just enough to see what he's doing, opening the new packet, removing the rubber and rolling it on, taking the used one from me and tossing it to the nightstand with the empty wrapper.

I lift my leg to hook my knee over his hip and he slides right into me. Slides his arm under my waist to keep me close, holds my thigh in the crook of his arm, and starts a long, slow rhythm, rocking in, grinding, sliding almost all the way out. Rocking in, grinding, sliding out. This—he—is exactly what I need tonight. He's filling my emptiness in the best of ways. His warm eyes, his shy smile, his affection, his big hands, his—

He adds a little twist to his hips on the next thrust and I moan my appreciation. He squeezes my ass and laughs. He holds my gaze, his eyes telling me I'm pleasing him too. Our pace is such a good match, the contact so perfect, that I come even quicker than before, and this time he's right with me, holding me close as he shudders into me. My release is so total—physical and emotional—that it brings tears to my eyes.

And when he kisses me and says again that nothing has ever felt so good, his words and his vulnerability feel like gifts, and I want to give him something in return.

"Today...was the anniversary of my grandma's death. I was really sad. Being with you helped me too."

I fall silent, thank heavens, as he kisses me, his fingers toying gently with the little wisps of hair at my temple. "I'm glad." His voice is husky. "And I'm sorry about your grandma."

It's delicious—almost too comfortable—lying here in his arms, tucked against his big body. Another woman might get used to this lovely feeling. This lovely man.

An uncursed, non-Salazar woman, anyway. But I'm not going to waste precious time thinking of that. His hair is soft in my fingers. I hold him and breathe him in.

But...if I'm not careful, I'll fall asleep.

I allow myself a few minutes more of this peace, then I nudge his knee with mine. "Kevin, can you take me home?"

His brown eyes are so warm when they open, when he smiles softly and pulls me closer. "Would you stay with me?" His voice is low. Hopeful. "I'd love to sleep holding you." He trails the backs of his fingers over my cheek, combs them through my hair, then does it again, slowly. It's magic. Hypnotic. "I have to be at the high school in a few hours anyway, so I could get you home early. Stay with me, please?"

And god help me, I don't want to leave either. I've never spent a whole night with a man, but here I am, snuggling right up to this big, gentle guy I just met, amazed at the way we fit into each other's arms so right.

CHAPTER 6

Andi

I EASE OUT OF BED to use the bathroom before I fall asleep. I find a washcloth and do a rudimentary washup while I'm in there. I don't bother with the fake tattoos. Or the hair product.

When I crawl back into bed, he reaches out one long arm and pulls me in close. Makes a satisfied sound and buries his face in the crook of my neck. "I smell soap," he mumbles, his eyes still closed.

"I washed up a little." Not sure he's really awake, so I say it softly, my voice almost gone anyway.

"Must investigate." And before I realize what he's talking about, he has slipped away under the sheet, where he proceeds to "investigate" me thoroughly. Leisurely. Delightfully, with lips and tongue and fingers, till I'm gasping, gripping his hair, rising to meet his mouth, my own eyes squeezing shut as he brings me to another climax.

I'm laughing weakly when he crawls back up beside me. "That was... Wow." I wrap both arms around him. "You are a lovely, lovely man."

He cuddles me close, his smile a little smug but mostly just sweet. We drift off to sleep in our warm nest together, and I'm not aware of anything else until his phone alarm goes off a few hours later.

His arousal is hard against my hip. The sheet slips, giving me a tantalizing glimpse when he reaches to silence his phone, and it's my turn to investigate. His breath catches and he strokes my hair with one hand, gripping the sheets with his other. I grope blindly for a condom on the nightstand, ease it onto him, and then crawl up to straddle him, taking him into me, riding him drowsily, slow and deep, to a powerful, shattering climax, smiling down into his eyes the whole time because I've so enjoyed being with him and he is such a nice guy, and because, okay, I'm not in a hurry to say goodbye knowing I'll never see him again after this. So I save up the feel of his touches—the press of his fingers into my hips, the scrape of his palms over my nipples, the delicate tracing of my cheek with one fingertip—and his expressions and every one of his pleasure sounds.

Afterward he holds me and kisses me with bone-melting sweetness until the alarm goes off again, and with a "Shoot!" he's throwing on workout clothes over those glorious muscles, zipping me into my dress, pressing one last quick kiss to the nape of my neck, and apologizing profusely for not being able to fix me breakfast in bed.

And then we jump into his car and I direct him to Lenny and Chris's apartment complex, because I rode to Lindon's with them. I say, "No, go, you'll be late!" to his offer to walk me inside, and I blow a kiss as he drives away.

My car's parked beside the band's big white van. I glance around for would-be assailants and then head home to the little stone cottage I shared with Grandma, a million feelings, good and bad, swirling through me.

———————

I have to force myself awake a few hours later when my phone rings.

Lenny, soft chords sounding in the background, as usual. I think he does all his thinking and communicating from the piano bench. "There something you want to tell me, babe?"

I shove my hair—which is reverting to its usual wavy state—off my face. "What? Lenny?" My voice isn't quite back to normal. Still a little hoarse.

"*Some*body got flowers today. Somebody who doesn't happen to live at my apartment. Hmm…let's see… The card is addressed to 'Andrea.'"

I sit up fast, both warmed and panicked. *Shit. This was supposed to have ended this morning.* I didn't want to involve Chris and Lenny. "Is the card sealed?"

"No, the envelope flap's just tucked in."

I squeeze my eyes shut and grit my teeth, knowing this is a risky move. "Would you read me the card, please?"

Lenny chuckles. There's a rustling of paper and then he reads, "'Andrea, I'm so glad I met you. May I take you to dinner and a movie? Ball game? Concert? Other date of your choice? Kevin.' Then there's a phone number."

Shit shit shit. Such a sweet guy. Such a big, sexy, warm, classy guy. I should've known he wouldn't write anything sleazy or embarrassing.

Why couldn't I be a normal, uncursed person with faith in men and love? I might actually say yes if I were.

But nope. One night is all I do. All I want.

And it was a hell of a night. Be tough to live up to that one.

Lenny's patiently waiting for a response.

"Is the florist's name on the card?"

"Yep."

"Call them, please, Lenny. Tell them there's been a mistake and there's no one there by that name."

He blows out a breath. "Ooh, cold. You sure, babe?"

No. Yes. I sigh. "Yeah. He seems like a good guy but I'm not looking for a boyfriend." There's silence as we think on that. I break it by asking, "Y'all need me tonight?"

"Naw, 'Shad called and said he's feeling better, so we're good. But thanks. Usual deal with the money?"

"Yeah. Thanks." I always split my cut with whoever needed the night off. That way I get to have fun and put a little extra in savings, whoever I fill in for doesn't lose much income, and the Blue Shoes have an incentive to call me again next time. "Tell the guys I had fun last night."

"Will do. We did too, babe. Good to see you. You know you missed your calling." Pause. "You sure you want me to…?"

"Yeah. Thanks, Lenny." I end the call and flop back on the bed, staring up at the ceiling, reliving my time with Kevin: his kisses, his big gentle hands, his low teasing voice, his brown eyes full of humor and warmth, his hard powerful body on mine…

When I hear my whiny moan of regret at giving that up, I roll out of bed and head to the shower. It takes a while to scrub away the temporary tattoos and all the hair product I'd used. I'd nearly shrieked when I got home earlier and saw the rat's nest that is my hair today. Good god, if that look is what Kevin likes, he really wouldn't want regular day-to-day me anyway. Which is too bad, because the girls and parts south are all begging, "Please, Mom, can we keep him?"

There's beard burn on my face and neck and breasts and thighs. I apply lotion with no-nonsense, not-thinking-about-Kevin-touching-me-there-at-all strokes. I'm glad to remove the fake nails. I like mine short and natural and clean. I pull my wet hair back in a thick braid, brush and floss, and when I glance in the mirror again, it's regular Andi looking back at me.

Kevin

"You look like shit, Farm Boy." Steve greets me with a big obnoxious grin. "What'd I tell you? Crashed and burned, didn't you?"

I flash him a middle finger and a grin and don't answer.

"That'll teach ya." He laughs his big belly-laugh all the way to the head coach's office as his football players begin to trickle sleepily into the locker room.

"Yeah." But I'm remembering the feel of Andrea in my arms, the scent and taste of her, the sound of her low laugh in my ear. The only thing I learned last night is that good things come to those who wait.

If I weren't so genuinely tired, it would be nearly impossible for me to hide just how good I'm feeling.

Or how good I'm feeling until I finish meeting with student athletes about my personal training program. Then I find a voicemail message from the florist saying I must've given them the wrong address but that they'll redeliver for no extra charge if I can provide them with the correct one.

She'd been out of the car and I'd been halfway to practice

before I realized I hadn't officially asked to see her again. And that we hadn't exchanged any contact information. I'd been just assuming that of course we'd get together again. We were good together, so why wouldn't we see each other again?

I'd remembered the name of the apartment complex—Galway Arms, very simple—and was pretty sure I'd read the number right on the door closest to where Andrea told me to let her off, so I'd used my phone to order flowers before I even got out of the car at school.

Guess I'll have to go by and recheck the address and hope she doesn't catch me doing it. Don't want her to worry that I'm some creepy stalker type.

I go to the apartment she'd directed me to and verify the number and the building and the street, and then I call the florist, who says, "That's where we delivered it to, sir. Right after the driver dropped it off, the gentleman there called us back to say there's no one there by the name on the card."

The gentleman? She'd told me she was single, hadn't she? Or had I just assumed, because of her question to me about it...

She hadn't mentioned a roommate. Then again, we didn't spend much time talking.

I find the mailboxes and check the one for the apartment I'd thought was hers. The box has two last names and first initials on it. Neither initial is *A*, and I don't know Andrea's last name. *Another first—sleeping with someone without knowing her last name.* The only *A* on the whole row of mailboxes is a last name—Alexander—for a couple, Mike and Leah.

I don't know whether she has a vehicle, much less what make or model it might be, so looking around the parking lot wouldn't help. I walk back to my car and sit staring at the apartment door for a few minutes, out of ideas. Is it possible she isn't really single? Or that Andrea isn't really her name?

Yeah, either one's possible.

Crap, I hope she's not in a relationship. I really like her, and I'd be really disappointed if she lied. It would suck even worse if I unknowingly helped her cheat on her partner.

I'm stumped. I can't go knock on that door. If the people there don't know Andrea, they've already been bothered once today. And if she has a significant other here, it might get her in trouble. Dangerous trouble. I don't want to endanger her.

If she didn't get the flowers, then she didn't get the card, so she doesn't have my number. And I have no way of finding hers. I pull out my phone and do a search. Three Andreas in Galway on social media, but none are the right age or look anything like her.

Maybe she didn't go inside after all.

I may be boring, but this is a real first. First woman I get interested in in North Carolina. First woman to use me for sex and then ghost me an hour later. That's not fair though; I didn't ask for her information either.

Is there a chance she might still want to see me?

She might remember where I live and what color my Toyota is. If she wants to get hold of me, she could do it that way. Leave me a note on my windshield or my apartment door or something. And how pathetic is that, that I'm hoping she'll do that? *Dammit.*

But…I don't know for sure what she wants. Maybe it was just a one-night thing for her, or maybe she thought I wasn't interested because I forgot to get her number.

Maybe I'm losing my damn mind.

My concerns yesterday about how I was going to get through

the long weekend seem laughable now. I'm going to spend it obsessing about Andrea, of course.

I give up on the flower delivery idea, head home and take a shower. Run errands, do laundry. Google the Blue Shoes. Read everything about them, view every picture of them, and learn absolutely no more about her than I already knew.

I try to talk myself out of the idea forming in my mind, but no. At 10:00 p.m. I'm at Lindon's, paying the cover charge and squeezing through the crowd to the bar where I take the last available stool and watch the Andrea-less band.

There's a second guitarist with them tonight. Must be the Rashad guy Steve mentioned. The band's got a different feel without Andrea but they're still great. I'm not here for the music, though. At the band's first break, I fight my way through the crowd to the keyboardist, who doesn't really look surprised to see me.

"Lenny?" I shoot for friendly but not too friendly.

"Yep." He looks me up and down and waits. I get the feeling he already knows what I'm going to say.

"My name's Kevin Mahoney. I met Andrea last night and got to spend some time with her"—gotta be careful with my words—"but we were in a hurry when we said goodbye and I didn't realize until later that I hadn't gotten her number or her last name or anything."

Lenny just looks at me.

"I'd like to send her some flowers. Ask her to dinner. But I can't, because I don't know how to get hold of her." It's already obvious this approach isn't going to work.

"That's a shame," Lenny says, deadpan. "Andrea's a fine woman."

I sigh. Cut straight to the chase. "You're not going to give me her number, are you?"

"Can't, man. Not a safe thing to do to a woman."

I nod, resigned. "Yeah. I understand." I fish in my pocket and pull out a little piece of paper from my wallet. Hold the paper out to Lenny. "Would you give this to her then? It's my number. That way she can call me if she wants. No risk."

Lenny stares at me for a few more beats before taking the paper and shoving it in his own wallet. "I'll give it to her. But I wouldn't get your hopes up."

I nod. "Too late. But I understand. Thanks." I take a step or two away, then turn back. "She's not going to be here tonight at all, is she?"

Lenny shakes his head.

I leave, unable to tell from any of his responses whether Andrea has a partner or whether she'd told Lenny anything about our night together or how she feels about it. About me. *Crap.*

CHAPTER 7

Andi

BY 1:30 P.M. SUNDAY I am so sick of myself I'd probably drive
full speed cross-state to the ocean trying to outrun my brain,
if I didn't have brunch plans. Spent most of yesterday and this
morning trying to work from home on the football team project but always dissolving into a puddle of whine. As in, "But I
waaant him!"

Not, like, as a significant other. Obviously. Just, like, as a fun
occasional other. Somebody to blow off steam with and fuck silly.
No more than that.

Not that the cuddling afterward sucked, because it didn't.

It's just that I am not a cuddling kinda gal. We Salazar
women...no cuddling for us.

So anyway, it's good that I have plans.

Rose is already there with Sabina from the B and B, and July's
just coming out of the kitchen with pitchers of fresh-squeezed OJ
and ice water. The restaurant closes at two on Sundays and things
have slowed enough that she can eat with us.

July slides in beside Sabina. They're both blond, cheerful women, but the resemblance ends there. Sabina is in her fifties and tiny, with a silvery pixie cut and bright blue eyes. July's got an inch or so on me and is built like an immensely strong farm girl. Maybe a dairy maid, with that long swinging ponytail of hers.

That leaves the brunettes, me and round little Rose, on the other side of the booth.

"Sabina's thinking of going lizardless," Rose says just as Sonya appears to take our order.

I'm about to make a crack but Sabina beats me to it. "I've been lizardless for years. I'm just thinking about removing them from my decorating as well."

July's eyebrows shoot up in comic shock. Rose and I laugh.

Sonya misses the double entendre, clutching her order pad to her chest. "Ooh, I've heard about your lizards! I heard they're really cute!"

The B and B is full of bright lizard sketches, ceramic lizards, lizards stitched onto pillows… Some kind of inside joke between Sabina and her late husband.

"Well, I'll save you some, then, Sonya." Sabina snaps her menu closed. "I'll never get rid of the photos Howard took on our honeymoon, but the rest of them are getting on my nerves."

Sonya, like almost all of July's servers and kitchen staff, cycled through the crisis shelter a while back. She's possibly the sweetest person on the face of the planet, and she looks thrilled at the prospect of decorative lizards, bless her heart. She's still smiling as she heads back to the kitchen after writing down our orders.

Rose frowns at Sabina. "You okay? I've never heard you sound irritated by anything."

Sabina waves her hand. "Oh, I'm fine. Just a little restless, I think. Maybe I'll sell the B and B and buy a motorcycle and some leather clothes and take off cross-country."

"Not alone! You have to find a biker boyfriend first. Or maybe a women's motorcycle gang." Rose and Sabina aren't related and hadn't even met before Rose showed up in town last year, but now they have a kind of devoted aunt–favorite niece relationship. They're protective of each other.

"Ha!" Sabina reaches across the table and pokes at my hand. "How about you, Andi? You're as lizardless as I am. Wanna biker-chick it cross-country with me?"

I guess I hesitate a second too long, caught in a flashback of Friday night and my nice guy who turned out to be so much more than a snack…

"Oh. My. God. Look at that smile." July leans across the table and peers into my eyes. "You devil. What'd you do?"

Now Rose is looking at me, her eyes huge with surprise and… glee? *Some*thing unholy.

I straighten and study my nails. "Oh, nothing, really. I had a nice time Friday night. I'm still happily lizardless. It won't happen again." Because it was *stupid*. I was stupid. And *weak*.

"Why the hell not?" Rose's voice is an octave higher than usual. "Treat yourself! God knows you need stress relief!"

That's a surprise. Rose is smart, but I hadn't realized my stress levels were obvious.

"Well, it worked. I am now entirely stress-free." What I am is a gigantic liar.

She looks skeptical. Also very, very curious. "Who was it? Anybody I know?"

"I don't think so." I turn to face her better in the booth. "I shouldn't have mentioned it. I don't want to talk about it. It was fun, and now it's done." There. Boundaries set.

"Spoilsport," she mutters. "You know, I missed out on an awful lot of gossiping with girlfriends over the years. The least you all could do is indulge me when I've got the chance." Then, "Ooh, yummy!" as Sonya appears with a loaded tray and slides Rose's eggs Benedict in front of her. Thank god.

Her attention's diverted from the Kevin situation, but he's still lounging around near the forefront of my own mind, usually naked, his brown eyes crinkling at the corners as he smiles at me, his big hands warm as they slide down my body and pull me close. Lenny's late-night text made sure of that, even though it only said, Magic Mike showed up at Lindon's asking about you. Name's Kevin Mahoney and a phone number. I stared at it for a long time before I finally sent a text: Kevin, Lenny gave me this #. I just wanted that one night, no more. Thx for a nice time. Take care. A

Then I lay awake for a long time, feeling like I'd kicked a puppy. Or myself.

I had no idea the guy would try to find me after the flower thing didn't work.

I had no idea I'd care.

When I checked my phone this morning I had a message from him. Well, several:

> Okay thx
> I had a nice time too
> I mean, not just
> Nvr mind. thx

Persistence in a man can turn to pushiness. This was just

sweet. Every time I think of it, I picture Kevin looking at me in his kitchen, shoving his hands in his jean pockets, unsure of what to do next. Respectful and thoughtful.

Sometimes I hate when people are unexpectedly nice when I was braced for...something different.

I take my first bite of quiche-so-good-it-makes-you-weep. "Mmm, July, this is fabulous. As always. Where's Joe today?"

Rose snorts and answers for July. "He and Angus were about to come to blows over some silly thing about Joe's building. I left them there to come meet you all."

Sabina laughs, swiping a bit of pork loin through peach chutney on her plate. "Oh dear. Joe doesn't stand a chance against Angus."

"Joe's not big, but he's wiry. And fast." July is loyal to her man. Sweetly, devotedly loyal. And Joe is a really good guy. And a good athlete. And wiry. And fast. She stops buttering her toast to look up at me. "That reminds me... He said he's not going to be able to do your volunteer training this go-round after all. He's really disappointed but he's got to be in Cullowhee for a required class."

Damn. Joe would have been the perfect volunteer to work with kids at the shelter. We don't have enough men volunteering, and it's crucial that the kids have an example of a good, loving, nonviolent man.

"Well, darn." I swallow another bite. "Tell him I'm hoping he can do it next time, then."

She nods. "How's the big project going?"

The project is a surprise I'll be springing on the high school football team next week with Coach Comstock's permission. Rose helped me get the funding and July provided gift cards as a thank-you to the people who participated, but they don't know the details and Sabina doesn't know anything about it. She's looking at me expectantly now.

"I'll be able to fill y'all in on it later, Sabina. It's…an experiment." I think back over the past few weeks and about the three interviews I still have to cram in over the next couple of days, if we're going to get it finished on time. "A really time-consuming, exhausting experiment. But it'll be worth it if it does any good."

It's been a labor of love for me, another staff member, one of our talented, dedicated volunteers, and lovely people like July and Rose and James's wife, Tisha, the vice principal. Everybody involved donated expertise, influence, effort, resources… On bad days, it's the thought of folks like them that keeps me going.

The football team's first game is this coming Friday night. Coach didn't want us to give our presentation to the team on game day, so we've scheduled it for right after practice Thursday evening. We'll go over to the high school while the players are still on the field, familiarize ourselves with the locker room's audiovisual setup and get the video ready to roll.

I'm pretty sure we'll make an immediate impression, but it'll take at least a year to get a sense of longer-term effects. I hope we haven't wasted hundreds of hours and a fair amount of grant money. I'm doing my best to make it effective. Success or not, I still have to keep the shelter and rape crisis center functioning.

Kevin

I'm just finishing up with my last student athletes when the football team heads inside. I follow everybody to the locker room, intending to talk to the coaches about how things will change once classes start on Monday. But instead of waving the kids to the showers, Coach Comstock tells them to take a seat. Waves the coaches and me in too. I settle in against the back wall, figuring we're in for some kind of pep talk or scouting report as a lead-up to their season opener. Not sure why I'm included, but okay.

"Huh." Steve's leaning beside me. "Andi Salazar's here. And Tisha. Wonder what's going on?"

I've got no idea who Andy Salazar is but I always enjoy my interactions with Tisha. Don't know what she might have to say to the football team, though.

It's another scorcher out there and I'm sticking to the wall. My shirt's soaked through, but it'd probably be rude to pull it off.

When everyone's found a seat on a bench or table, Coach Comstock steps forward. "We got some special guests to talk to us today. With the season starting, a lot of eyes will be on y'all. On us. On the school. Listen to what these ladies have to say so you can do us proud." With no more than that, he steps back and nods to somebody standing off to one side.

Three women step forward from the lockers, leaving Tisha in the corner.

"Thanks, Coach," the tallest one says. "Hey, guys." Her voice is low and pleasant and she knows how to make it carry. The talk dies down as everyone focuses on her. She's a pretty woman. *Very* pretty. As pretty as Andrea, in a much more subdued way. Not that I'm allowing myself to think about Andrea.

This woman is big, but she moves like a jock herself, loose and easy. Her fresh-scrubbed face is beautiful. Reminds me of Sarah Shahi. Reminds me of *Andrea*.

Wait.

What the—

Her big dark eyes don't need any ornamentation. She's got reddish-brown hair pulled back in a thick braid. Her clothes are as no-nonsense as her voice: black jeans, gray button-down shirt, and a boxy jacket that gives her a squarish look.

"For those who don't know me, I'm Andi Salazar."

Andi, not Andy. Andi as in short for Andrea.

This calm, serious professional woman is the woman who had me by the dick the other night, onstage and in that alcove and in my bed. The woman I'd stupidly and with lightning-fast idiocy begun to hope would be in my future…but who handed me my heart back with a *one night, no more* and a *thx for a nice time*.

I don't know why I'd heard Cheryl's voice when I read that message. Cheryl's voice and *boring* and *nice* and *vanilla*. Been trying to drag myself up out of that emotional swamp ever since.

Andrea—Andi—is still talking, and suddenly I need to know what she's saying. No microphones or makeup or red fringe or overwhelming glorious nakedness today, but…somehow she's every bit as compelling. I lean forward to hear.

"My colleagues here are Shannon Wolcott and Maria Perez. We're from the Galway Women's Crisis Shelter. Thanks for sticking around today. We won't talk long; mainly I have a video to show you. We'll tell you a little more in a few minutes. Right now, as you watch this video, think about that line from Spider-Man about how having power comes with a lot of responsibility."

She speaks with confidence, standing easily in front of this group of large young men, making just the right amount of eye contact. Then she turns to the side of the room where a handful of Latino players sit and, switching smoothly into Spanish, talks some more. Then she steps back and the woman she'd introduced as Maria hits a button on the projector as Tisha turns out the lights.

The video starts with a plain black background, an acoustic guitar playing a really distinctive melody. I've heard this song. It's by a band my sister used to like—band with a weird name. Frog something? No, Toad. Toad the Wet Sprocket. Song about rape. This is just an instrumental version, though, playing in the background as statistics flash across the screen for domestic violence and sexual assault: national numbers, then North Carolina numbers, then Galway numbers. The music fades to silence then and we see women of various ages and sizes in near-complete darkness in three-quarter silhouette so that just the edges of their faces are visible...brow line, curve of cheek, chin and jaw.

One by one the women speak, telling of an incident in which they were assaulted. Some women tell of abuse by high school or college boyfriends, others of abuse by strangers, others of all types of assaults in the workplace or by friends or acquaintances, some sexual in nature, others not. The video shows each woman three times, first to say what they were doing when the assault occurred ("I was at a party," "I was at work," "I was making dinner," "I was on a date..."), then to say a little about the assault itself, and finally to tell of the effects the assault has had on their lives. Flashbacks, nightmares, lost jobs, breakups, dropping out of school, fear of certain places or smells or types of people or darkness...

None of the women speaks loudly or dramatically, but their pain is unmistakable and everybody in the room is riveted. It takes me a few minutes to realize that as each woman speaks, someone in the room straightens or stiffens. One by one, these guys are realizing that they're listening to the terrible experiences of their own loved ones. Even in the darkened locker room I can see shock on many faces.

This video was designed for maximum impact on this specific group of people.

Freaking brilliant, and executed perfectly.

To make sure everyone understands every single word, subtitles play across the bottom of the screen in English and Spanish.

The video ends with statements from men identifying themselves as former Galway High student athletes. One guy says, "If you're watching this, then you probably just had the same kind of shock I had right before I agreed to take part in this video—the shock of hearing someone you love describe a time when someone attacked them and hurt them."

One by one, the others speak, each voicing part of a powerful message: "You know from the statistics at the beginning of the video that these kinds of attacks are common." "You're probably beginning to realize that we all know someone who has experienced this." "Sexual and domestic violence are problems that hit Galway just as hard as anywhere else." "The victims can't stop this violence, no matter how often we try to lay the blame on them." "Only potential perpetrators can stop the violence." "The only way to stop it is…to stop it." "Don't abuse people." "Don't stand by while others abuse them." "Don't use drinking or other substances as an excuse." "Don't tell yourself you have the right to do whatever you want with another person's body."

"Everyone is as important as your loved ones." "And everyone's future matters just as much as yours." "Use your strength for good." "If you see one of your buddies behaving badly, stop them, for their sake and the sake of the person who would be their victim." "Use your power to stand up for others." "Because no one should have to go through what your loved ones have been through."

The video ends with a montage of headlines about good Samaritans who stepped in and stopped assaults, helped victims, and generally showed themselves to be decent human beings willing to stand up when someone needed help—true heroes who used their power for good.

The locker room is completely silent after the video ends. Andi Salazar lets the silence sit for a minute before signaling Tisha to bring the lights back up. Then Andi says quietly, in English and Spanish, "Each of you is a powerful young man. When you leave this locker room, you'll have a million chances to honor—or to dishonor—yourselves, your families, your team, your school, your community. What you do, good or bad, affects other people's lives, sometimes for many years. Each of you has the power to do great harm and the power to do great good. Your choices matter."

She falls silent for a beat and then says, "Thanks for listening. Coach let us slip cards and information for the crisis shelter in all your lockers. If you have any questions or if you know anyone who needs help, please call us. All our services are free and confidential." Then Andi raises a hand in farewell and she and the other women leave the locker room with Tisha.

Everyone turns to look wordlessly at Coach Comstock. He clears his throat. "Turns out someone I know was on that video too. I expect y'all to make the right decisions, on the field and off. Hit the showers."

Daaamn. I watch the team drift off, most of them still subdued. Even Steve is silent beside me. I bet I'm the only one in the room who didn't just hear a loved one tell her story of abuse. You can bet I'm thinking of it, though. Suddenly I feel a burning urge to call my sisters. My mom. Check in with CeCe again, and my other nieces and my grandmas, make sure everybody's okay. Talk to them about what I just saw. Let them know I'm there for them if they ever need me.

If that gut-punch video was Andi Salazar's brainchild, she is a freaking genius.

How could one person contain so much? Talent, and passion...and painful, unbearable-to-look-at beauty.

CHAPTER 8

Kevin

THE ROOM'S ALMOST EMPTY BY the time I shake off whatever fog Andi and her video laid down in my brain. I peel myself off the wall and head for the door. Down the hall a way, she's standing outside the coaches' office saying goodbye to the other women.

"Thanks, everybody. Y'all are the best." She puts her hand on Tisha's arm. "Please thank James and the guys again for me. They were perfect on that backing track." With a wave, she turns and ducks into the office.

Huh. Tisha's husband, James, and the Blue Shoes must have done that instrumental Toad the Wet Sprocket bit. That's a small town for you.

I've got a burning desire to talk to Andi—and absolutely no idea what to say. *Hey, great violence-against-women video! Hello again, I think you're amazing.* Maybe it would be enough just to stand next to her and soak up her presence. But she'd probably object to that.

I follow her into the outer office where Steve and I and other trainers and assistants stash our stuff while we work with students.

Andi's talking to Coach Comstock, half-in and half-out of his office, and I can't keep from lingering, trying to overhear what she's saying. Something about permission to run on the high school track after school. Something about a safety issue. Coach must wave her in, because she steps into his office and shuts the door behind her. I can't hear their soft conversation but through the window I see her dig in her pocket and hand him a business card. Coach must've been as moved and shaken by the presentation as everyone else.

I don't know what kind of spell I'm under. She's made it clear I served my purpose and she's done with me, but I can't leave, can't look away to find my stuff. I just watch, studying the curves of her cheek and lips and throat, the shape of her mouth as she speaks, the grace of her gestures, the gleam in her dark eyes.

And then Coach says something and she tilts back her head and laughs, the rich, throaty sound bubbling up out of her, and *holymotherofgod* every fiber of my being squeezes with that glorious sound.

I actually stagger a little, bumping my leg on the desk and dropping into a chair, which squeaks a protest at having to bear my sudden weight.

The differences between the other night and today are many. Andi's speaking voice, for one…but she'd been singing all out for a couple of hours by the time I talked to her at Lindon's, and she'd sounded hoarse.

Her gray blouse and boxy jacket don't give many clues to what they cover. If I were meeting her for the first time today, I'd assume she's kind of squarish—her outfit disguises her amazing

curves so well. Completely hides her waist. Her jeans, though...
Shit, now I'm staring at Andi's ass, remembering how her big,
lovely bottom had felt in my hands. Maybe I should just go shove
my tongue in her mouth, see if she tastes the same today. And...
oh, great, now I'm hard.

I have lost my damn mind in the space of a week.

She turns to the door, steps out of Coach's office and meets
my eye just as Steve comes in from the hallway. Before I can gauge
her reaction to seeing me, Steve says, "Damn, Andi, just rip everybody's heart out and stomp on it, why don't you?"

She gives him a tiny half grin. "Whatever works, Steve. How
you doing?"

"Doin' okay." Steve nods. "Crazy busy right now, o' course.
Hey, you meet Farm Boy the other night? Andi Salazar, Kevin
Mahoney. Kev's our new trainer."

"Nice to meet you formally." Andi ambles over and holds
out her hand.

I stand to shake and damn, there's a current between us that
shoots straight to my groin. No way could I ignore or deny the
connection between us. But she looks right at me, her dark eyes
sober, and doesn't blink away and shows no reaction. I am that
unmemorable.

"I didn't have any of your loved ones in the video, did I?"
she asks.

"Uh, no." I've reached superhuman levels of awkward. "I'm,
uh, not a football coach."

She nods. "Makes sense. Otherwise I'd have gotten someone
you know in the video too."

I have no doubt she's telling the truth. She probably would've
tracked my family to Lincoln and gotten them talking about

experiences it would kill me to hear about. "You do all those interviews yourself?"

She nods again.

"Damn." And then I'm back to speechless.

"Well." She straightens and heads toward the door. "Thanks, guys, for letting me talk to the team. If you see anybody you think we could help, refer them to me, okay? We do hospital advocacy, court advocacy, counseling...all free. Let me know if you need any more of my cards." She steps out and then pokes her head back in. "Oh, and good luck tomorrow night."

She and Steve wave at each other and then she's gone.

I stand staring after her, feeling completely invisible and useless.

Beside me, Steve laughs. "Seriously, Farm Boy, don't they have girls in Nebraska? You get that same look every time you see her. She already shot you down, dude. Have some pride."

"In my defense, she's really, really beautiful," I say when I can form words. "You two seem to know each other pretty well."

"Went to high school together. She's good people."

"That video was brilliant."

"Made her point, that's for damn sure. Andi's real smart. Always has been." He leans to reach around me, opening a desk drawer, grabbing a handful of manila folders he stuffs in his laptop bag.

"You ever date her?" My voice is as hoarse as Andrea's was the night I met her.

Without looking up, he says, "Nah. She's a fine woman— beautiful when she actually dresses like a girl—but she's too serious, you know? Always studying in school, work, work, work, and I think she's the same now, except when she's onstage. And that's not very often." He shakes his head. "I want a woman to laugh with me. Make me laugh. Not always be talking about depressing shit all the time."

Images flash through my mind: Andrea laughing and dancing with the band, singing her heart out, clearly enjoying every minute of it; Andrea grinning and teasing me in the bar and in my kitchen and in my bed; Andrea riding me slow and deep, pure pleasure on her face.

Steve finishes zipping his bag and smirks. "Besides, man, Andi's scary. She can fuck a guy up."

That's for damn sure. But I don't think he's thinking about what I'm thinking about. "What do you mean?"

He shakes his head, laughing. "Old story. Junior year. Dumbass kid asked her to the prom—no surprise there, she was real pretty, real nice—and she went with him. He made a move on her afterward with people right there and she said no, but he didn't listen. Tried to grab her again and she knocked him down. Knocked one of his teeth loose. He got up and started screaming in her face and she didn't even blink, just stared him down. Said, 'When a girl tells you no, you stop. Now back off. Your face already messed up my manicure once.' Dude backed off. Wise decision. She will Fuck. You. Up."

I laugh out loud. "Good for her!" CeCe would do the same in that situation.

"Yeah. Her grandma raised her. Tough, strict old woman. I guess a manicure was a pretty big deal." Steve's still grinning.

"Andi ever beat up anybody who wasn't assaulting her?"

He frowns. "Not that I ever heard."

"I won't attack her, then, and I should be fine."

Andi

Big, shallow jerk showed no reaction to seeing me again. To touching me.

Okay, that's not fair. He's the one who reached out afterward. I'm the one who rebuffed him. Still, my hand is tingling from his fingers, and he... Just, nothing. *You were inside me, you big jerk! I slept in your arms. I guess when you sent me flowers and said you'd like to see me again, you were only talking to parts of me that are hidden under my clothes today.*

Dammit. What is even wrong with me? His reaction is exactly what I should've expected after blowing him off. I went out that night wanting hot sex with a decent single guy, *not* looking for a deep connection, and certainly not for a relationship, and I made it clear later that's all I wanted.

Still, that zing when we shook hands... How could he not feel that?

Maybe he just doesn't find regular me attractive enough to be interesting.

If they don't notice you, they won't try to hurt you, Andi.

Me and my scraped-back hair and my blah work clothes. Another point to Gram.

I head for the parking lot, not knowing whether to stomp the rest of the way to my car in some kind of disappointment tantrum or to be relieved he hadn't said anything in front of Steve about our night together. Steve's a decent guy, basically, but there would have been something different in the way he looked at me if Kevin had told him. Which is exactly why I have the no-Galway-guys rule in the first place—and why it was so stupid for me to break it.

I shouldn't have been surprised to see him in the locker room.

He's a big muscly guy and he was sitting at a table full of other coaches and teachers in Lindon's.

Was it a bad idea to ask Coach if I can run on the track in the afternoons? The idea hit me after Pattie had said I needed a safer place to run. Self-defense experts always caution against running alone, running in isolated areas, and so forth. With my gym still closed, this seemed the safest place for me to exercise.

Surely if Kevin didn't react to me today, he won't bother me later either. In fact, it's probably *good* that he showed so little interest today. I'm in his head as Andi-from-the-shelter now, someone he met in a completely different context. Not as the woman who blew him off. This is probably *good*.

And no reason to worry he'll pursue me any further, especially after he gets used to seeing me in my baggy shorts and T-shirt and sneakers and my hair in its usual braid. And no makeup or tattoos. And oh-so-attractive sweat pouring down my naked face.

Don't think about naked.

"Hey, you." Tisha is unlocking her car in the next row over from mine. "Y'all did a great job on that video."

"Couldn't have done it without you paving the way with the families. Thanks, Tish. We appreciate you."

She waves that away. Tosses her briefcase onto her passenger seat. "Happy to do it. Anything that'll help." She leans her forearms on top of her door and studies me. She's a slim, elegant woman with smooth, gorgeous brown skin and sharp eyes that probably cause panic attacks in students trying to bullshit her.

Grown-ass professional woman that I am, she makes me a little nervous too, looking at me like that.

"James said something about you seeming interested in the new math teacher the other night at Lindon's. Kevin? Said he came around looking for you the next night." She gives me a smart-ass smirk that suddenly makes her look like her much-less-scary little sister Shay, Rashad's wife. "Y'all got something going on there?"

Well, hell. A math teacher. I was right to suspect he might be brighter than I'd originally thought.

I deflect. "Hell, Tisha, he flirted that night but barely even acknowledged me today. That's for the best. I'm not looking for a man."

She shakes her head. "That's a shame. He seems like a good one. I like him."

I snort. "One of those nice guys who's most interested when a woman's got her tits out."

She laughs and sinks into her seat. "Baby, most of them are like that."

Ain't that the damn truth.

We wave and part ways. I climb into my car and push all thought of Kevin—naked or otherwise—out of mind. Check the rearview mirror to make sure no one's following me and head home, replaying the video presentation in my head.

I'm pretty sure Tisha's right—it went well. I studied the players' faces as they watched the video. There wasn't a sound in the locker room, at least while we were in there. Some of the young guys sat stony-faced but others had looked shocked, sad, disturbed, sickened.

I know the video got through to at least some of them, and they can apply peer pressure to their teammates. And to other students who look up to the jocks.

If this project is successful, it'll lower rates of violence among the high schoolers, especially violence by the athletes, at least temporarily. I can write a paper, do a conference presentation, and maybe similar projects can be tried in other places.

It's hugely labor-intensive and time-consuming, tailoring a video to a specific gathering, finding and interviewing someone willing to share from the families of every member of the group, but if it works for a high-risk population like football players, it's more than worth it, especially if it helps change the culture.

I check my mirrors again before I take the turn onto the road to the cottage. Still nobody behind me.

I'm going to take the night off. Indulge myself with a kick-ass chick flick and a bag of Hershey's Kisses.

And I absolutely will not spend one more minute thinking of another kind of yummy kisses or the big, sweet, disappointing man who provided them.

CHAPTER 9

Kevin

I HAD INTENDED TO PICK up a pizza, head home, and take a shower. Instead, I end up turning onto the country road and then the state highway, aimlessly following its rises and dips and twists, my windows down despite the heat. I want to feel the breeze on me. Smell that air that's so different here than anywhere else I've been.

Her eyes today… There was something in her eyes today, and not just when she spoke to me. Something cooler. More reserved. Locked away. The seriousness of the presentation and her job probably accounts for some of it, but I can't shake the feeling that there's something else.

The night we were together, she seemed freer. Younger. Like her muscles were relaxed and her spirits lighter, especially after that first time we made love.

Well. Not made love, I guess.

The first time we'd—What?

What exactly was that?

I haven't done a lot of just plain fooling around. But I can't imagine it feels like that. I swear I thought we connected with more than our bodies. I know we gave each other comfort. We teased and laughed. Enjoyed each other.

I always figured a hookup would be a lot more impersonal than that. A lot less warm.

Not so immediately addictive.

As I'd pulled into the high school parking lot the morning I dropped her at the apartment complex, I was already looking forward to the next time I could see her.

Do other people take this stuff in stride?

How. In the *hell*. Could someone take a night with Andi Salazar in *stride*? How could it be possible for someone to experience that—her—and not walk away permanently changed?

And that was how I felt before I saw her work today.

Jesus.

How can one person be so amazing and talented in so many ways?

I get now why she was ready to move on from me after one night.

Must've crossed the state line a while back. I'm in downtown Spartanburg now. I slow down. Drive past Morgan Square, which is definitely not a square. Past some interesting-looking restaurants I am unfortunately not fit to go into in my wind-dried, sweaty state. Same for the little cute bookstore—Hub City Bookshop. I'll have to come back down here sometime when I'm clean.

There are couples strolling hand in hand. I can barely remember what that's like, although it's been less than a year for me.

I imagine exploring this place hand in hand with Andi Salazar. The Andi I met that first night, the one who could laugh and tease me and blow my mind in bed.

That serious-eyed Andi from today, though... It's hard to imagine her laughing. I *definitely* have trouble picturing her holding some guy's hand.

I get what Steve was saying about her now. If I hadn't been with her last weekend, I would never guess, based on today, that she could be like that.

As sad as it is to think I won't ever be with her like that again, there's a tiny part of me that views that one time as a gift. Something rare and special not many people get to glimpse. Yeah, I'm alone now, but one night she shared that with me... She trusted me enough to let go.

I don't know what led her to that grim line of work, but I can sure see how it would sober a person up fast. Make them view the world through cautious eyes. I'd like to hear that story. I wish I could know her. Even if she never invites herself into my bed again.

But I mean, there will always be a spot for her there. Because I'm not as stupid as people sometimes assume I am.

Main Street broadens. Changes names. I follow it till it meets the interstate where I turn north, toward home.

Galway's not the home of my birth, but it's the home of my choice, and I've got to build a life there, with or without Andi Salazar.

———

She's back on Tuesday.

School started yesterday and I'd briefly seen her out back on the track that afternoon, but I'd been heading inside for strength training with a couple of students and I only caught a glimpse of her before the doors closed behind us.

Today, though, I've just finished running some students through sprints and set others to do stamina work when I see her come in from the parking lot.

Like yesterday, she's in a baggy, oversized T-shirt and shorts, looking more like a kid than like a thirtysomething professional woman or a sexy could-be rock star. She walks to an out-of-the-way spot in the inner oval and sets her water jug and keys in the grass. As she raises her hands to fasten her wavy hair up off her neck, a breeze plasters the T-shirt to her torso, and just like that, I'm back in my apartment, my hands and mouth on her full breasts, my body tight with need. The sun catches reddish glints in her hair as she turns to do a few graceful stretches. Then she puts in earbuds and jogs onto the track.

I have a few minutes free and I can't stop myself. I catch her just before she finishes her first circuit of the track. "Andi?" I have no idea what else I'm going to say.

She gives a startled jerk, leaps to the side, and pulls out one earbud. "Ack! You scared the hell out of me!"

"Sorry. Sorry. I didn't mean to." We eye each other as she comes out of her defensive stance—damn, she must've really been feeling jumpy—and resumes her run.

She sets a good pace for a distance workout, her strides easy, no wasted motion.

I match her, running beside her around a turn before speaking again.

"I just...wanted to say what a great video that was the other day. I should have told you then."

"Well..." Her voice is wary. "Thanks. We worked hard on it to tailor it for the team."

I nod. "Your effort showed. I think it made an impression."

"Good." She doesn't smile. "It's a real problem, you know? Sometimes it seems like we'll never make a dent in it. So I'll try anything."

"Yeah. Lotta guys—jocks especially—need to hear they're not gods who can just take whatever they want."

She flicks a glance at me. "*You're* a jock."

I send her a grin but the sight of her flushed, pretty face does odd things to my gut so I shift my gaze back to the track. "Not anymore. In high school, at first. Got some pressure to continue, but…"

She lets the silence hang for a beat. "But?"

"Well, I grew up in Nebraska and I was a big guy whose older brother played football. Everybody assumed I would too. But sophomore year of high school, I saw one of my friends—a really smart guy—take a terrible hit, bad concussion, and I swear he was never the same. I didn't want to risk that. It was near the end of the season, so I finished but I told them I wasn't going to play anymore." Hardest thing I ever did was telling my family that. Seeing the disappointment in my dad's eyes, the disbelief in my brother's. I was shaking so hard my teeth were nearly chattering as I'd forced the words out. Remembering still makes me nauseous.

I feel her gaze on the side of my face.

She cuts straight to the point. "Why are you a trainer, if you think it's so dangerous?"

I shake my head. "My…job here is unusual. I didn't apply for a coaching position. I'm a math teacher. But when I showed up for my interview, Steve and a couple of the other coaches pegged me as an athlete and asked me about my training regimen, all kinds of questions. They could see on my résumé that I had a trainer's certificate. Only got that to help out in my folks' sporting goods store when I wasn't teaching.

"I could see where Steve's questions were going so I told them I wasn't interested in coaching football. But a week later an offer showed up in my mailbox for a position teaching math and acting as kind of a general fitness trainer to individual students. Not just football, and not just the kids on teams. I'm to help students work on strength, speed, endurance, flexibility…things that will help them get in shape, stay in shape, avoid injury."

She shakes her head. "How many of them come to you wanting to lose weight?"

I glance over at her, trying to understand her reason for asking. She's big…and clearly fit. She's moving easily and well, able to talk as she runs… Please, God, don't let her be wanting to change that gorgeous body. "Some," I say cautiously. "I tell them I won't work on that. I'm to help keep them healthy, not change their size."

She holds my gaze longer this time and nods. "Good for you."

We run in silence for half a lap, then I turn the subject back. "There've been some high-profile rape cases linked to football in Nebraska over the years."

She blows out a sigh. "Nebraska's not unique in that. I think you'd have a hard time finding a program that's *not* got a bad rape history. Or domestic violence."

I fear she's right. "I thought your approach was genius, with the video. Really bring it home to the players. Make 'em see how their choices matter, through the eyes of people they love."

She nods. "Yeah, that was my goal. Some people criticize that approach though."

"What? Why?"

"They say if we focus on people's mothers or sisters or wives, we're reinforcing the idea that women only matter in terms of their connections to men." She shrugs one shoulder. "It's a valid point. But sometimes I think we have to do whatever works. Baby steps."

I mull this over as we make another circuit in silence. She doesn't try to speak. Finally I gesture to the other side of the track. "Guess I should go check on my students." But suddenly I have to know. Have to ask. "Look, I don't want to make you uncomfortable or push you to talk to me about this, but could you let me know if I did anything to upset you last weekend? You're okay, right? We're okay?" I mean, not that there's a "we."

She meets my eye, serious as a judge, and I know that whatever comes out of her mouth will be the gospel truth.

"No, Kevin, you didn't do anything wrong. You were lovely. I just don't do relationships. I actively avoid them."

She holds my gaze and I realize she's not going to say anything more.

I nod. That's...good, I guess? At least I didn't do anything that bothered her. Maybe this one really isn't a "me" problem. "Okay, then. Thanks. Well, I'll get back to work. I just wanted to say hi and that I thought you did a good job on that video. A great thing."

She actually smiles. For a second I see that light in her eyes, the light I saw when she was with me the other night. It catches me like a punch in the gut.

"Thanks, Farm Boy."

She's actually teasing me. In another situation I might laugh. Tease her back. But I reach over and touch her elbow lightly. "I prefer Kevin." *The name you called me when I was inside you and you were coming.*

I leave her and go back to my students.

Andi

I don't know what to think or do about this damn man.

He's really pissing me off.

No, that's not true. I just wish it were true. My elbow still tingles where he touched me. I want to go grab him by that damp, clingy T-shirt of his that does nothing but accentuate the muscles underneath—just grab him and drag him into that shadowy corner where the main school building meets the gym. Kiss him until he begs for mercy. Except I know he won't beg. He'll take hold of me and kiss me till my knees are weak.

But I also want to yell at him to stop being so freaking nice. Stop tempting me in multiple stupid ways.

It was just supposed to be one night. It wasn't supposed to leave me wanting more.

When he suddenly popped up beside me on the track, I leapt halfway into the grass oval. My own damn fault. We're supposed to always be aware of our surroundings and not wear anything that would impede our sight or hearing, but there I was, running with earbuds in and music blasting as if I didn't have a care in the world. Damn Chicks are making me crazy too. Well, no, today it was Chinchilla. My "Women Rage" playlist.

But I feel safe enough to have earbuds in here at the high school with so many people around. And, really, I am safe here. Kevin Mahoney's only a danger to my composure and my libido. Maybe a little to my stupid heart, if I'm not careful.

I thought I'd erected a taller wall between my libido and my heart.

Don't think about erect.

I can hear Gram's voice in my head now. "Andi, I've only been dead two years and already you've forgotten a lifetime of my teaching? Salazar women need to Stay. Away. From *men*. The more we want them, the more damage they can do. Act like you've got some sense."

———

The rest of August passes quickly. I'm up to my elbows in all the usual fundraising and personnel and public relations stuff for the shelter, as well as gearing up for Labor Day and volunteer training next month. It's a sure bet that, between heat and alcohol consumption, the shelter will be full to bursting over the holiday weekend. We'll need to have extra emergency lodgings lined up, so I'm busy finding locations and available funding for that too.

The gym is still a construction zone, but I know Pattie's right about running on those winding mountain roads so I keep going to the high school for my exercise and stress relief.

The side benefit of getting to see Kevin working with students, sometimes running sprints or longer distances with them himself, is purely that—a side benefit. I would never go anywhere specifically to ogle...but lord, do I enjoy seeing him in motion. Something about his powerful thighs and calves and his beautifully shaped knees as he digs in for a burst of speed... It makes me feel a little faint. A little fluttery, and warmer than my own easy pace justifies. And on the hotter days, when sweat makes his T-shirt cling to his skin, I remember the feel of every one of those ridges and hollows under my fingertips as he surged into me. *Mercy.*

It's like I'm turning into somebody else. Somebody without a sense of self-preservation.

The students seem to like him. Some of the girls flock around him, of course, but the boys do too. I can never hear what he's saying to them, but whenever he explains things, they look attentive. From a distance I see what has to be teasing or good-natured trash talk. Nothing the least bit flirty or inappropriate on his part, just an easy grin and laid-back instruction. The kids don't seem resentful, even when he sets them to doing truly grueling tasks.

But I'm not here to ogle. I'm just a mildly interested observer who happens to be running in ovals around him with nothing much else to look at.

Salazar women are known to be delusional.

Sometimes he joins me, matching my pace and asking about my day. He's never disrespectful or flirty with me any more than with the kids, so I don't really know how to take his attention. Is his interest just polite? Purely platonic now? Obviously he's aware enough of me to know when I'm on the track—he always waves hello and goodbye—but he seems like a genuinely nice and outgoing guy, so maybe he's just being friendly.

He might even be trying to set an example for the hetero kids of how it's possible for men and women to be just friends. That's admirable, I guess, but also, if I'm honest, kind of a downer. Despite my own wishes and Gram's constant voice in my head, my interest in him has grown.

Despite what I *want* to want, I don't want to be platonic friends with him. I want to be flirty, frequent-and-energetic-mattress-dancing-between-two-healthy-young-adults friends. Not, like, "Let's have a nice intimate dinner together and talk about our secret dreams" friends; that would be too much, and my grandma would haunt me and shriek a lot.

I just want something more than an impersonal, occasional running companion.

But either he's amazingly good at honoring my stated wishes or he doesn't think Everyday Andi warrants more of his attention. I've learned Gram's lessons well. Tamped down any beauty I have and fastened it tight, except for those rare occasions when I'm with the Blue Shoes.

I'd thought that was the way I wanted it. Kevin Mahoney has me rethinking things. I'd thought Singer Andrea was my costume and Drab Andi was the real me. But if the real me wants him, knows how to get him, and is also in the way...who's real and who's a disguise?

I am hoist with my own petard.

CHAPTER 10

Kevin

SOMETIMES I CAN TELL WHEN she's on the track without even turning around. I feel it in the back of my neck.

I love to watch her run. I remember how those long, strong, smooth legs felt around my waist when I was inside her. My fingers itch to sift through her shiny hair—wavier and lighter than the night I met her—to free it from that thick braid...

I do my best not to get distracted from my work, but the students must have noticed something because they're always teasing me.

"Isn't that Ms. Salazar over there, Mr. Mahoney? Think you ought to go say hi?" Or "You're killing us with these sprints, Mr. M. Go run with your girlfriend." Or, one day, from one of the mouthier kids, "I see what you see in her, Mr. M. She's big but man is she a MILF." That earns him a pointed finger and a dead serious, "Cut that out. That's no way to talk about a woman." Which earns me a bunch of widened eyes among the circle of students around me. Kid apologizes, and they never make the mistake of talking like that around me again.

Thing is, I *want* to go run with her. I want to ask her to have dinner with me tonight. I want to get to know her better. I just can't justify pestering her for a date when she's told me no. What I want is moot.

If she still finds me attractive, I sure can't tell. That first night, she was completely up-front about her wishes. Since then, though, she's barely even cracked a smile at me. I can't see any renewed interest on her part at all. And every day I feel a little crazier, a little more desperate to talk to her—really get to know her. A little sadder that we will never be a "we."

But one hot afternoon in algebra class when some of my students are having trouble, I decide to ask Andi for help. I watch for her after school, and as soon as I can, I join her on the track.

"Hi." I'm a freakin' conversational genius.

She gives me the infrequent little smile I've actually grown fond of. It isn't the big, wide grin that melted my knees that first night, but it's…cute. Playful. "Hey."

I turn my eyes to the track in front of us. "Got a favor to ask."

"Yeah?"

"I couldn't help but notice your Spanish language skills during your presentation to the football team." I toss her a quick glance.

She nods. "I was raised bilingual."

"Any chance you'd help me with something for one of my math classes?" This is a ridiculous, unreasonable, too-big, hopeless request. I'm an idiot.

She raises her pretty brows. "Like what?"

"I have these sample problems I always give out." I'm wishing I hadn't brought this up. Maybe I should've stayed over in the shade with students. But I'm in it now, so... "I make them to supplement the textbook. The samples lead the students through each kind of problem, start to finish, explaining exactly why we do each step and what it means." I look over to gauge her reaction.

She just nods. "Okay..."

"So the sheets have really seemed to help students understand the process...*but*..."

"They're in English and you have some students whose English isn't strong yet."

"Exactly."

"You want me to translate them for you?"

"I think it would really help them. And I'd owe you big-time."

She arches one brow and a tiny bit of Singer Andi shines in her eyes. "Owe me?"

God help me. Suddenly I'm way more breathless than this easy run calls for. I'm going to burst into flame right here on the track. "Yeah. Favor of your choice." I make a heroic effort not to hope too hard for a candlelight dinner or something requiring condoms.

"Hmm." There's an undercurrent in her voice but I can't pin it down.

We run in silence for a hundred yards before she glances at me again. "Is this a good-sized translation job that might require ongoing time or effort?"

Bigger than I have any right asking her to do, that's for sure. "Well, I do it for all my classes, for each concept we cover...so yeah, I guess it *could* be. I was originally thinking about the particular sheet my algebra students were struggling with today."

Her gaze captures me. "That's actually good, because the first thing that came to mind as a return favor is ongoing too."

"Yeah? What's that?" *Marriage is ongoing. Marry me. We can call it… What's the phrase? Marriage of convenience. Let it grow from there.*

"We have a volunteer training session coming up in a couple of weeks. We always need volunteers to do all kinds of things including playing with the kids or helping them with schoolwork."

"Okay…?"

"The kids in the shelter have often not had many good male role models. So we're always on the lookout for male volunteers who're good with children."

Makes sense. "I like kids. What's involved?"

"Any kind of work with minors involves pretty extensive background checks, but I'm assuming you've already passed those as a teacher, right?"

"Yeah."

"So you would come to our volunteer training sessions every night for a week in September, and then after that you'd donate time each month to volunteering at the shelter. We don't allow adult men inside the residence part of the building, but we've got an outdoor area with picnic tables and a bad weather playroom."

I'm surprised by how much I like the idea. I love kids. I like being useful. And I have way too much free time. This would connect me to my new community *and* maybe let me see more of what Andi does in her work.

I'm nodding before the words even come out. "Sounds good to me."

"Excellent!" And damn if she doesn't flash that blinding first-night smile.

I almost trip over my own feet. "Yeah?" I'm smiling back, warmth blooming in my chest.

"Yeah." There's that light in her dark eyes.

I could stop and kiss her right here on the track in front of the whole world. Instead, we arrange for me to email her the next few worksheets I need translated, and for her to send me the volunteer training info. But I'm still thinking about kissing her.

Andi

The dinner crowd is thinning out as I push through the door to July's. July always packages leftovers for the shelter and it's my turn to pick them up. I'll treat myself to a nice dinner while I'm here, to celebrate my deal with Kevin Mahoney.

As usual, Blue Shoes music is playing, big James channeling Muddy Waters's "Mannish Boy," the rest of the band shouting the response to each line.

I love those guys. It's all I can do to keep from strutting across the dining room in time to their music, but I manage to walk normally to the booth closest to the kitchen.

Sonya brings me water and a menu.

"Hey, you're here late." From what I remember, she doesn't drive and she's rarely out after dark.

Her smile is a fraction dimmer than usual. "Yeah... We have a couple out sick on the night crew. I said I'd stay till eight." Her voice wavers and I see the effort she makes to firm it back up. "July said she'd give me a ride home after, but I told her it wouldn't kill me to walk a few blocks at night."

More like a mile and a half. And her knuckles are white, she's gripping the order pad so tight.

"I'll be done eating by then. My turn to take leftovers to

the shelter, so I'll be going right by your place. Let me drop you off."

"Well…" She nibbles her bottom lip. "That'd be great, if you really don't mind." Her pretty smile widens and her brow clears as she writes down my order.

It takes some former shelter clients a while to feel safe again. A few of them never really seem to. I'm glad Sonya's going home to a big, lively houseful of warm, strong survivors—Donna, Tina and two of July's other employees, plus their kids, all in a modified fourplex.

I rack my brain trying to remember the details of Sonya's particularly terrible boyfriend experience. It had culminated in a famous-about-town incident in this very restaurant, with several townspeople intervening before July sent him away for good…

"Hey, you." July appears with my food, interrupting my thoughts. Instead of dropping off my meal, she puts down dinner for both of us and slides in across from me, her smile as warm as always. She shakes open a napkin and drapes it across her lap, even though she's still wearing her sturdy kitchen apron. "What you up to tonight?"

I lean in and inhale the spicy, comforting aroma of Smokin' Joe's Peppery Pasta. "Oh, you know. Just sitting here hating men."

"As one does." Nothing fazes July.

"Not you." I blow on a forkful before putting it in my mouth. The flavors explode on my tongue. "Damn, July, that man can cook as well as you and Donna! This stuff's better every time I eat it. Where is he tonight?"

"Cullowhee. First week of classes. I'll tell him you said so." She's eating the same thing as me, only topped with chicken instead of shrimp. She takes a bite and leans back as she chews, studying me. "You're glowing. Something good happening in your world?"

Woman has an uncanny way of sizing people up. Sussing out what they might be feeling. Probably can't tell I nearly dragged a big, sweaty, delicious man into a shadowy corner to have my way with him at the high school earlier, but she's right, sexual frustration aside, I'm feeling good. "I pulled off the volunteer coup of the century."

"Oh? Tell me about it."

Between bites of pasta I tell her about the translation-for-volunteering arrangement.

She listens as she eats, her head tipped like she's considering something. "This guy was running with you at the time? How'd that happen? You know him from somewhere?"

Ah. Of course. Trust July to pull the pieces together.

"Yeahhh…from that last time I sang with the Blue Shoes. He runs with me sometimes at the high school, ever since I did the presentation there."

Her eyes go round and her brows shoot up. "Ohhh. *That* guy." She picks up a blistered shishito from her plate, grins, and bites into it. "Well, isn't *that* interesting?"

Gray eyes don't usually look so wicked.

"Don't jump to conclusions, goofball. It's not like we're dating. This is a business arrangement. I told him it was only a one-time thing, but I think dolled-up singers are more his type anyway."

"Oh, please." She scowls, raking me with an up-and-down glance. "You're delusional if you think you can make yourself unattractive enough for him to not still want you."

"Worked with everybody else. Why should Kevin Mahoney be any different?"

"No. No." She wags a finger at me. "They're scared of you, not oblivious. There's a difference."

Doesn't matter, really. No point in thinking about it.

But of course I spend the night doing so anyway.

CHAPTER 11

Andi

THE NEXT WEEK IS EXHAUSTING. Holidays are always extra busy but this Labor Day is especially bad, with off-the-charts humidity and brutally hot dog days. I make the arrangements for overflow shelter with local motels, which means I also have to squeeze the budget extra hard to foot the bill for those rooms, and there's still not enough without having to choose some other bill to pay late. Thank god for Rose and her work at the new Galway Brown Foundation. She's saved our asses in more than one recent emergency by scrounging up funds from somewhere. She does it again this week.

But then there's the ever-present volunteer shortage. We have an amazing bunch of volunteers—we couldn't keep afloat without them—but understandably, except for handing out goodies to the shelter kids on gift-giving holidays, most people want to be with their own families at those times. I can't blame them—it's always devastating to see the injuries and hear the stories and have proof of people's ugliness in the emergency room, and it's heartbreaking to see the dazed, tearful expressions—or worse, the stoic ones—on the faces of kids as you try to get them settled into the noisy, chaotic space of the shelter.

So making sure the volunteer shifts are covered for Labor Day takes extra time too. I put myself on the on-call list for hospital runs all weekend. It's not like I've had family or holiday plans anyway since Gram died.

It's a long, difficult weekend, and then the next few days I carve out extra time to huddle with our volunteer coordinator and a couple of other staff members, making sure we've got everything ready for volunteer training next week. We do trainings twice a year, but they always require some tweaking.

I manage to get to the high school to run most weekdays, but I don't have the energy to do my usual distance. It's easiest, of course, when Kevin runs with me, because I'm too busy ignoring his stupid charm to pay attention to how tired I am.

Pretty sure his charm is pure niceness, not any kind of flirting. He's been completely respectful about my "no" to dating. If he *is* flirting, it's the subtlest, lowest-key, lowest-pressure flirting I've ever experienced. An extra twinkle in those brown eyes when he smiles at me, the appearance of those dimples, brief bursts of laughter at things I say.

I've had guys look at me with hunger and calculation when I'm onstage. I've had them look at me with caution in my day-to-day life. But I've never had a man look at me the way Kevin does, with something like delight. Something like anticipation for what might come out of my mouth next. Something like pleasure for just being with me, hot, sweaty me, running ovals around a high school track in the sweltering heat.

On Friday he walks me to my car.

I check my surroundings the way I always do and see a bunch of kids watching us from the track area. "We've got an audience." I nudge his abs with my elbow and almost get distracted by my urge to put my hand there. I rein that in quick. "Or you have a fan club."

He shakes his head, dimples deepening. Turns to the field and yells, "Get back to work!"

There's a flurry of activity as students pretend they hadn't been watching, but a few giggles float to us across the grass.

Kevin laughs. "Pains in my backside."

"You know you love them." He hasn't said so, but I've watched their interactions. He may have only recently met these kids but he's invested in them.

I click my lock and he steps closer to open my door for me, his other hand cupping my elbow.

"Thanks again for those translations you sent last night. You should have seen the relief on some of the kids' faces when I passed them out."

I toss my keys and water bottle onto the passenger seat and turn to face him. "Good. I'm glad to help."

He's still touching me. "I couldn't help but notice the time stamp on your email. 12:01 a.m. Pretty late for you to be up working."

I shrug, careful not to dislodge his hand. Because I am a glutton for punishment. "Oh, you know. You gotta fit stuff in when you can. I went to bed right after."

"Well. Thank you." He gives my elbow a little squeeze, then turns me loose and reaches up to catch a flyaway bit of my hair and tuck it behind my ear, his fingertips barely brushing my skin.

It takes all I have to suppress a full-body shiver, despite the heat. I wait half a beat to see if he moves closer. Holding my breath, praying he moves closer. Wanting to grab hold of his damp shirt, sink back into my car, and tug him in on top of me.

Which would be *very* uncomfortable if we'd even both fit, but still, wishes are persistent little suckers.

But he doesn't step forward, so I slide into my seat and fit my key into the ignition. "You ready for next week?"

He nods, his expression serious now. "Looking forward to it. It'll do me some good to feel like I'm doing somebody else good, and I figure I've got a lot to learn first."

"I'll see you Monday evening, then. I won't be able to come run during training week. Just email me the next batch of worksheets whenever."

He nods, closes my door and pats the roof of the car, holding up one hand in a wave as I back out.

I drive away, trying to be glad he hadn't kissed me back there. If he had, it would have been a *bad* thing.

Kevin

I'm moving slowly when I leave the shelter building after the first night of training. The air feels different around me, like there's more to it—more to the world, more to life—than I'd known. Like there's a whole invisible universe full of activity going on around me and I ought to be able to peer between the molecules and layers and catch glimpses of things I'd not known existed before.

Survivors of domestic violence have taken on a whole new dimension in my eyes.

I'd walked in tonight with my head full of the question so

many people ask first thing whenever they hear of a domestic violence incident: Why doesn't she just leave? By the time I walk out after the first session, I know a whole lot more about that— enough more to make me embarrassed I ever even thought that was a valid question.

"But you know," one of the trainers said, uncapping a marker as she stepped up to the whiteboard, "that's how we've been *trained* to think about it. Even our language about domestic violence protects the perpetrators. Let me show you what I mean."

On the board she wrote, *The battered woman had serious injuries to her face and ribs*. She stepped back and pointed to what she'd written. "How many people in this scenario?"

As we opened our mouths to answer, I could see other trainees come to the same realization I had: that although *someone* must have done that damage to the woman—caused those injuries—they are nowhere to be seen in that statement. The focus was entirely on the victim.

The trainer wrote another sentence: *The woman was severely battered, sustaining injuries to her head and ribs*. She turned to look at us. "How about this—how many people appear in this version?"

Not much better. Yeah, it hinted at some unnamed person or force, but the language was so passive and vague that we couldn't say who.

"Exactly," the trainer said when we expressed this. "So how would we need to write a description to clearly show who was there and who did what?"

The man beat the woman, injuring her head and ribs, was what we came up with.

It was like watching a shadowy evildoer become solidly visible before our eyes as we adjusted the wording to reflect the reality.

Then we learned that "just leave" is a ridiculous oversimplification. Not only is leaving dangerous, with abusers desperate to regain control, but also abusers have often isolated their victims from access to money and loved ones, and there are often children involved whose needs for food and shelter and uninterrupted schooling have to be considered. And finally—this one made my blood boil—many families and faith communities have a history of suggesting that victims must have done something wrong to "bring this on" themselves.

One exercise that really got me, though, was when a staff member took a seat in a straight chair at the front of the room as another staff member told us her supposed life story, which included elements that have been shown to increase a person's vulnerability to domestic violence. Things like growing up in a family with a strong the-man-is-head-of-the-household vibe.

The story led up to the woman finding herself in a relationship with an abusive partner. She looked for help and was blamed or turned away. With each statement, a staff member came forward and put a blanket over the woman's head until, by the midpoint of the story, we couldn't see her. I'm not sure how she kept from smothering under there.

Then the story began to change. The woman reached out and someone actually provided something useful: the shelter hotline number. A staff member removed one of the blankets. Through the rest of the story, a blanket was removed with each bit of help, each action helping her to break free, until finally the woman on the chair was visible again.

Shannon, the trainer, asked her what it felt like under all those blankets. The woman gave a short laugh. "Lonely. I was with y'all, but not, you know? I couldn't reach you. I felt invisible. Cut off, after the first few blankets. It was getting hard to breathe or move. Hard to think. I couldn't see y'all, and I was having trouble hearing you, so I knew you probably couldn't see or hear me either."

The other trainees were leaning forward like I was, trying not to miss a word she said. I could see on their faces what I was thinking—that she was also describing life in an abusive relationship.

I don't remember the drive home. I can't get her words out of my head.

After that first night, I set my alarm for earlier, to get my class prep and grading done during the day to free my evening brain for the training.

I'm the only man out of ten volunteers-in-training. It's not a problem for me, but it stinks for the kids who need decent male role models.

It's a life-changing week. Each session flies by and I drive home with thoughts and feelings and questions whirring around in my mind. Some nights I lie awake thinking about things I never really understood before. My survival didn't depend on me knowing.

If any of my family and friends was in an abusive relationship, would they have the resources they need to break free? If they reached out, would I be able to help? Would I sense they needed help without them asking?

Later in the week, we cover relationship red flags and

characteristics of abusers, and I'm horrified at how many guys I've known who fit the profile. Toward the end of the week, one of the court advocates goes over the legal options available to survivors, and the difference between court-issued protection orders and actual physical safety.

The presenters do a great job. They're clear and knowledgeable, and they gently guide us newbies away from myths about the dynamics of domestic violence. Shannon's the official trainer but Andi is so good, so compelling, with such fire in her eyes that even the shelter staff are on the edge of their seats when she talks.

I don't try to seek her out during any of the sessions. It doesn't seem appropriate and my head is always spinning anyway. I need to get away and think about the things I've learned.

Each night I find myself on my couch with a cold beer, staring at the dark TV screen and rethinking every relationship I've ever observed. Every day I go to school and study the dynamics I see there. As a teacher, I'm a mandatory reporter if I see or suspect abuse. Am I going to be suspecting it everywhere now?

After training on the last night, Friday, I lie in bed squinting up at the ceiling, wondering if this is how Andi lives her life: in constant awareness of the danger in seemingly ordinary relationships, in fear for people she passes on the street. I wonder if she loves her work. I wonder how she can bear the weight of it.

CHAPTER 12

Andi

SHANNON AND I AND THE others are pleased with how the training goes. Friday night after we've thanked the new volunteers, issued them their training completion certificates, signed them up for their first volunteer shifts, and ushered them out the door, we clean up the training room, break out our traditional sparkling grape juice and freshly rewashed plastic wineglasses, and collapse into the chairs recently vacated by the volunteers.

"Too bad we can't have alcohol in the building." Shannon holds her wineglass up to the light and watches the bubbles rise.

"You say that every time." I tilt back in my chair to put my feet up on the table. Every single part of me aches with tiredness.

"I liked this bunch a lot," says one of the senior volunteers who helped tonight.

"Yeah," somebody else says. "This bunch didn't have that one know-it-all like so many groups have."

Everyone nods. I close my eyes and rub them. As I'd figured,

I hadn't gotten to slip away for any afternoon runs this week and my energy level reflects it. I'm satisfied with the training… and ready to go home to crawl into my bed. I'm not going to do a lick of work this weekend unless I get an emergency call. Might just sleep until noon tomorrow and Sunday both. And then take afternoon naps. Hell, I might go home tonight and sleep until my alarm goes off Monday morning.

But first…nose crinkling, I right my chair and look around. No trash cans nearby, and no visible trash, but something's really smelly. I open the drawers of the desk next to me against the wall. Peer in, poke around… Nothing.

Shannon nudges my foot with her own without getting up. "What're you looking for?"

"Whatever stinks. Somebody eat lunch in here and forget to clean up?"

"I don't smell anything." Shannon looks to the others and they shrug.

"How can you not smell that? It's…weird. Unpleasant. Kinda…mildew plus something else icky." Nothing in this desk, though. And no other furniture nearby.

"You hallucinating again?" Shannon turns away to refill her cup.

One of the senior volunteers holds her cup out for more too. "This was the first time I've seen a man in training."

"Kevin seems like a good guy." Shannon pours for her. "Quiet. Nice. Asked good questions."

I abandon my search for stinky stuff and resume my near-napping position. I nod without opening my eyes. "I think he'll be really good for the kids." My mind stays on him as the others discuss the strengths of the other new volunteers. Kevin seemed really interested in each part of the training, listening carefully, nodding his head occasionally, taking lots of notes.

I missed getting to talk to him this week, which means it's probably good that I didn't. I am far too interested in the man. I'm glad he didn't seek me out here at the shelter. I need to be completely professional during trainings. Not sure how easy that would have been if he'd been right there where I could feel his body heat and see the warmth in his eyes.

———————

As September passes, I wonder if I might be getting burned out. Or maybe a little depressed. It's harder and harder to get out of bed in the morning. Some days the only reason I run is to see Kevin. I ignore Gram's yelling. Try to convince myself it's okay to enjoy his company as long as we're not dating.

When we run, though, I rarely feel up to my usual distance or speed. Some days I even have trouble making myself go back to work afterward because I can feel my bed calling me home. I do always go back, of course, but it's difficult.

Wouldn't be my first go-around with depression. Had a couple of episodes when I was little, and again as a teen. Gram was ready for it. "Perfectly normal," she'd said. "To be expected, even." She'd gotten me the help I needed. I didn't realize until years later that therapy must have put a real strain on her budget. During those periods she didn't buy as much meat. We ate more rice and pasta and beans and didn't go out as often. After my therapy sessions, we'd hit the McDonald's drive-through as a treat, but she wouldn't get anything for herself; she'd say she wasn't hungry.

I miss that stubborn, giant-hearted little woman every damn day.

I still have a therapist in Asheville I see occasionally, as needed. Maybe I should make an appointment with her? But... something about that doesn't fit quite right. Yes, I'm exhausted all the time and tiredness is a symptom of depression, but I don't have any of the other red-flag symptoms. I'm not feeling blah about work or life in general; I'm just tired. No real changes in appetite or loss of interest in my regular activities. If the way my body and mind react to the sight and scent of Kevin is any indication, my sex drive's functioning just fine. I'm just...really, really tired.

Maybe I need more iron in my diet.

But also, okay, I've been a little emotional lately. I cried over a very sweet yogurt commercial the other night, which is a purely ridiculous thing to do, and I got a little weepy last Saturday when I dropped by work to get a file I needed and glanced out to the patio to see Kevin sitting at one of the picnic tables with a little guy who's fairly new to the shelter. The little boy was staring miserably at a workbook open in front of him on the table. His head was propped on the hand that held his pencil and he was twisting a short lock of his own hair tightly around his finger. He looked up and said something to Kevin and I could see a sheen of tears in his eyes.

Kevin said something in return, pointing to the lower part of the page, his gesture mimicking an explosion, a dimple showing in his cheek as he almost—but not quite—smiled as he talked. The little boy listened carefully, laughed once, looked back down at the worksheet for a long moment, and suddenly straightened as if hit with an electrical shock. He got his pencil into writing position and scribbled something on the page, then pushed it toward Kevin. Looked up at him with eyes full of hope. Kevin peered at the sheet, then reared back grinning and gave the little boy a high five. Then they both got up and joined some kids who were kicking around a soccer ball in the grass. The little guy's face was wreathed in smiles.

And I stood at the window crying. *Dammit.* I'd better make that therapy appointment soon. But…they felt like happy tears.

I don't know what the hell's going on with me.

———————

"I think I'm halfway in love with our new volunteer," Pattie says idly late Friday afternoon, putting the day's mail on my desk and wandering over to peer out the window.

"Oh yeah? Which one?" I've got papers spread in front of me and a different spreadsheet open on each of my monitors, comparing last year's shelter expenses to this year's for one of the reports required by the state.

"Kevin. I think probably a few of the residents are too."

That gets my attention. That could be a problem. "You teasing?"

Pattie gives me a half smile. "Well, can you blame them? He's nice to them, he's sweet and gentle with their kids, and he looks like…*that.*" She waves her hand at the window, at Kevin playing soccer with a mixed-age group of kids in the fenced backyard. "Some of the residents have started hanging out at the picnic tables whenever he's outside with the kids."

"Do you think they're worried he'll do something inappropriate with their children?" *Shit.*

Pattie rolls her eyes. "I think a couple of them would like to do something inappropriate to *him.*"

"He's not flirting with anybody, is he?" This is dead serious. My own misguided interest in Kevin aside, I can't let a volunteer mess with the emotions—or the bodies—of residents who are more vulnerable than usual during a stay in the shelter.

Pattie shakes her head. "Nah. He treats everybody the same. Nice, friendly, respectful, platonic." She injects a butt load of drama into her sigh. "Including me, unfortunately."

I snort and turn back to my spreadsheets. "We haven't had this come up before. I should probably talk to him about it. Will you send him in here when he's getting ready to leave?"

"Sure." Pattie takes one last look out the window and heads back to the reception desk.

———

Kevin

I don't know what to think when Pattie catches me on my way out and says Andi wants to see me. My heart gives a stupid little leap of hope, and then my brain mocks it for being dumbass enough to think that she's going to change her mind about seeing me.

I cross to her office and tap on the doorframe. She raises her gaze from the ocean of paper on her desk. She's so darn pretty, her face bare of makeup, her dark eyes shining, her wavy hair as always fighting to escape that braid. She's got a red pen in her hand and a pencil tucked in over one ear... Wonder if she's forgotten it. Freaking adorable.

Also, immensely capable, fully grown, and not in need of my schoolboy adoration.

"Oh, hey. Come in." She puts down the pen and waves me to one of the chairs in front of her desk. She gets up to close the door most of the way, then takes a seat facing me in the other guest chair instead of settling back behind her desk in the seat of power.

Today she's wearing jeans and a loose black shirt with bright woven sandals. Her toenails are the color of sunset. That should not cause any uproar in my body. Definitely shouldn't make me want to ease off those shoes and nibble on her. Undo a couple of her buttons, slip my hands inside, and warm us both with the friction of touch.

I'm an idiot. A lust-struck, confused, juvenile idiot.

"How are you doing?" Her eyes are friendly. Her smile is faint.

"Good, good. You?" I'm not comfortable enough to cross my legs. Instead I lean forward, elbows on my armrests, my fingers interlocked.

"I'm fine." She leans forward, just slightly, too. "First, thank you so much for all the good work you're doing here. I've heard that some of the more traumatized kids seem a little calmer and happier after playing with you out in the yard. Some of them are acting out less. And one boy was thrilled with a grade he got on a math test after you helped him prepare for it."

Well, that does my heart good. "Great!" I can feel a big, silly grin spread across my face.

"So I hope you're liking it enough to keep coming?"

I nod. "Definitely." I like younger kids a lot, and the kinds of play and tutoring I do here are different enough from my work with the high school students that I'm not in danger of getting burned out. Some of the little ones are so sweet I can almost hear my biological clock ticking when they reach for my hand or snuggle up next to me at the picnic tables. It's all I can do not to hug them, but as a volunteer I have to be real careful about stuff like that.

But I'd be lying if I said I didn't love it. Besides my general, pathetic need for companionship of all kinds, my knees go a little weak whenever I imagine a child calling me "Daddy." Makes me want to kill whoever made these kids' homes unsafe for them.

"Good, because we—they—sure need you." She leans back in her chair, suddenly looking less comfortable.

I brace for whatever's coming.

"We've got kind of an unfamiliar situation I need to talk to you about." She pauses, frowning down at her hands for a second before meeting my eye. "We've only ever had one male volunteer here before, and he looked like a little old Santa Claus and always worked the same shifts as his wife. So he was like a shelter grandpa, you might say."

"Okay...?" So, suddenly, after recruiting me, she has a problem with me being a man?

"Somebody mentioned to me today that maybe one or two of the women in shelter are developing kind of a crush on you."

That presses me back in my seat, gobsmacked. "What?"

She tilts her head, flashing me a tiny, brief grin. "Well, think about it. In this country we raise our little girls on princess stories, right? Stories with Prince Charming. So imagine you're a woman here, and you've grown up with that culture but you've had to seek shelter because your Prince Charming turned out to be not so charming, and then voilà! Here comes a big, sweet, good-looking man who's great with kids and always kind to you. What's not to crush on?"

What the hell? Is it true that women here are interested in me? It makes sense the way she describes it, but...I hardly even interact with the women. Just the kids.

Or...is she only talking about the residents? Could she be telling me something about her own feelings? *Down, stupid heart.*

There's zero evidence to support that hope, and almost two full months of words and clues refuting it. But she did just call me a big, sweet, good-looking man, so...

I resist an urge to shake my head like a wet dog to see if it'll help me make sense of this. "I—Wow."

She's watching me closely. "So it occurs to me that you might have some experience with this from your teaching. You've probably had parents show interest in you every now and then, haven't you?"

I try to focus on the question and not on the way the late-afternoon sun through her window edges her smooth cheekbone with gold. I clear my throat. "A couple of times I did wonder about messages I was getting, I guess. It's a thing teachers have to deal with sometimes."

"What's a teacher supposed to do if that happens? Is there, like, an ethical code you're supposed to follow?" She looks a little more comfortable in this less personal territory.

"I think some schools have policies about it. You know, forbidding relationships between teachers and parents of their students. A lot of teachers have strong feelings about it themselves. Some say they'd never do a relationship with a parent, period. Others are okay with it as long as the parent's child is no longer in their class and there aren't any younger kids coming up in the family who are likely to be in their class."

"How do *you* feel about it?" She cocks her head, studying me.

"I... Gosh. Haven't had to make that call." I blow out a breath, looking at the ceiling. "I think I'd probably fall in that second camp. I wouldn't see anything wrong with it if the child was no longer in my class and didn't have siblings who would be later."

"Okay." She plucks the pencil from behind her ear and turns

it over and over in her fingers. "Now think about the women here. You meet them when they're at a crisis point in their lives. Things have gone really wrong, and lots of things are up in the air for them. If they have kids, that's a whole other layer of worry and responsibility at a time when they might not have many resources. Some are recovering from physical injuries, and they almost all have psychic wounds, at very least."

She pauses to let that sink in. "We haven't had any attractive young guys volunteer here before, so we don't have an established policy. Which isn't good. Really, we need one for all volunteers, not just men. I need to write one, I guess. But I thought we should talk about it today. Come to an understanding. I'm sorry to embarrass you."

It's true, my face is hot, but I'm not sure it's from embarrassment. Did she just call me an attractive young guy? I'm the thirty-five-year-old man she turned down months ago.

"So knowing what you know now about our residents, what do you think the policy I write should say?" She's abandoned the pencil. Now her fingers are intertwined in her lap.

Distractions aside, I'm solid on the ethics of this issue. "It would be wrong for a volunteer to get involved with a shelter resident. Absolutely wrong while they're in residence, and probably also wrong after they leave shelter. There's just a, I don't know, power or resource difference that would probably never go away. The relationship would always be unbalanced. I'd make a policy prohibiting it." *Darn, she's good.* She didn't have to tell me to do—or not do—anything. She got me to state it myself.

She nods. "Your instincts are great. That's the policy I'm going to write." Her dark eyes settle on me. I can see faint shadows under them. Fatigue? Stress? "Some volunteers come in with a rescue fantasy, and I'm thinking any possibility of romance would only tangle that up more."

I nod. "Yeah." Teachers know a lot about rescue fantasies.

She slaps her hands on the arms of her chair and stands up. I catch her scent; today it's soap and something spicy, like cloves. I want to tug her down onto my lap, cuddle her curvy body to mine, and nibble on her, but instead I stand too.

She smiles up at me. "Okay, then. Thanks for talking to me and for understanding. It seemed important that we...have this talk since I know you're still pretty new to town and were feeling..." Her voice trails off and she looks less comfortable again. "...lonely not too long ago. It would be easy for you to be tempted... Well. Never mind. You doing okay?"

Awkward. Wow. I'm probably bright red again. That's such a good look. I sigh. "I've met some really nice people. Mostly through the high school. Been Steve's wingman a couple of times."

She laughs. "That dog. You should make him be your wingman too sometimes. It's only fair."

"Yeah...no. I'm not...really interested in that." And I sound pathetic. "I do some exploring. Drive around, try new places. You know, trying to get used to being here."

She searches my face, serious now. "Does it help make up for being away from your family?"

I can lie to save face, or I can be honest. "Well, I don't mind having a little more time to myself than I did in Nebraska. But I eat more meals alone than I'd like. Steve's not much for just hanging out and talking."

She nods, looking more sympathetic than pitying. "I know that feeling. My best friend recently got into a really great relationship. I'm glad she has this guy—he's the love of her life, for sure, and a really great person—but I miss having a dinner-date friend."

Ohhh, crap. This is a Very Bad Idea, but I can't hold the words back. "Look, I know you said you don't want to date, but if you ever feel like grabbing dinner or doing something on a weekend, let me know. I'll probably be free." My hand, which for some unfathomable reason I'd raised as if to reach out to her, hovers in the air before I force it back down to my side.

I've never made a first move before. Even as a friend. It's awful. Terrifying.

Suddenly I see back into my past, through a long line of friends and girlfriends—all the way back to second grade—all of whom approached me first. Vanilla Kevin never risked rejection by being the first to signal interest. That realization feels pretty awful too.

I can't read her expression as she studies me.

"Are you asking me as a date or as a friend?"

"Friend. I heard what you said. I know you don't want more."

CHAPTER 13

Andi

SHIT SHIT SHIT SHIT SHIT. *Why* did I have to ask him about being lonely? He didn't need to know how much I remember about...every damn thing about our time together.

I don't want to sit back down but I have no choice, what with my knees melting out from under me. From excitement? Disappointment? Relief? I don't have a clue.

Unexpected tears press at the back of my eyes. What kind of weak-ass bullshit is this? Gram would be bellowing at me to get back up. Assume defensive position.

I can handle almost any situation when I know what the goal is.

What's my fucking goal here? My body and my brain are at war. My softer feelings have chosen a really inconvenient time to make an appearance.

"You okay?" He's back in his seat across from me, leaning forward as if to catch me if my pathetic ass faints.

It's hard to think when he's looking at me like that, his brown eyes worried, his forehead crinkled in concern.

"I'm just...realizing how long it's been since I ate. Not sure if I had lunch." It's true; I've been buried in paperwork since my morning meetings ended. But also...I shouldn't be surprised or disappointed that he said "friend." Aside from a fleeting thought every now and then that maybe he was flirting, I've had no clear sign he's attracted to me. At least not to my regular, everyday self. And dammit, why do I have to keep reminding myself that I don't *want* us to be attracted to each other. It's *good* that he's respected my wishes and not pressured me.

But here I am, my stupid lust unrequited. Just me silently ogling his beautiful body, remembering how he'd felt and looked naked against me. It's just been me, swooning over how good he is with young people, approving how serious and respectful he was at volunteer training, and eating up his gentle teasing when he runs on the track with me. Just me, silently crushing on him like a damn teenager.

"If you wanna remedy that, you've got a willing dinner partner right here. If you want." His mouth tilts up at one corner but his dimple is nowhere in sight. His eyes are guarded.

You know what, why the hell not? I've gotta eat. "Have you been to Woollybooger's? The roadhouse?" I've had a powerful craving for barbecue lately, and Woollybooger's has the best.

"Heard about it. Was thinking about trying it this weekend." He leans back, his shoulders relaxing a fraction.

"Wanna follow me out there?" I have lost my damn mind. My mouth just keeps...saying things.

There's that dimple again. His smile is slow, and sweet. "Yes, ma'am, I do."

Oh, my heart is in trouble from this one.

That's a first. And it totally sucks.

I retrieve my purse, lock my office, and tell Pattie and the nighttime receptionist relieving her to be careful and have a good weekend. Do my usual visual sweep of the parking lot as we walk out. Check under my car and in the back seat. Buckle in and lead the way to the roadhouse.

This is all right. It's nothing but dinner. If tonight goes well, I'll have a single friend to do stuff with again.

I flip on my turn signal and make sure Kevin stays with me. I'm not sure I like having a man follow me. I'm not sure I don't. My stomach and brain are in an uproar and Gram is yelling and shaking her fists in my head.

Calm down, Gram; I'm not gonna marry him. It's just a platonic dinner. Guys are fine as friends. It's only romantic relationships I need to avoid. I mean, *sometimes* they seem to work okay for other people. Rose and July and their adoring partners have put a chink in my belief that romance is *always* doomed to fail. Not that this with Kevin is romantic.

Anyway, would I ever be able to set aside everything I've seen and everything I know about my own family history and all of Gram's training and everybody I've ever worked with and take a chance, if it were? Unlikely.

I'm not superstitious, not really. I don't think Gram meant it literally when she said the Salazar women are cursed. I just think she believed we'd be better off without men. So she was preparing me for that. Making sure I'd know I could handle that. And thrive.

Have I thrived, though?

I'm still debating that as we park side by side in Woollybooger's gravel lot at the edge of town. It's not full yet, but it will be soon, with Friday night happy hour. It's already noisy as we make our way to a booth in the far corner. I slide in and he sits across from me. For a second I flash on Rose and Angus and their inability to sit on opposite sides of a booth.

Kevin and I will never have a Rose-and-Angus-level relationship. That thought brings a wave of...wistfulness? Regret? Nah, why would it? That would be silly.

I'm thinking too much. I just need to chill and enjoy dinner with my new friend.

It smells different in here—not as good as usual—but I'm so hungry I don't even care. If I don't eat something soon I might die. It's probably rude of me to immediately bury myself in the menu, but I'm not sure how to open a conversation with Kevin tonight anyway, so.

"How y'all doing? What can I get you to drink?" Our server is a past client. She pretends not to know me and I take my cue from her.

Kevin orders a local beer. I don't really want anything but food, so I go with water and immediately point to the pulled-pork meal on the menu before she can leave. Kevin proceeds to order the exact same meal he'd likened me to when we were naked in his bed. Minus the pumpkin pie.

I don't think he hears my stupid dreamy little sigh. I hope not.

Once our server's gone, he faces me and looks me square in the eye. "So." He folds his hands on the table, his long, beautifully shaped fingers reminding me of how gentle his touch can be. How insistent. How much good he can do a body with those hands.

"So." Another little sigh escapes with the word. This would be a lot easier if I could stop thinking about taking him to bed.

Kevin

I was not expecting her to hide behind the menu like that. She's usually fearless. Now she mirrors my hands-clasped position, takes a deep breath…and stays silent.

A million thoughts and fears and wishes stream through my brain. She's going to say she's changed her mind about dating me. Or, she's already deciding this is a mistake and she's sorry she came. Or she's—

"I don't usually have dinner one-on-one with my guy friends."

I'm sure she means nothing special by it, but my heart leaps at her words anyway.

She tips her head. "But I guess I don't have one-on-one dinner with men in any capacity, really. Dates or anything. My work tends to scare people off. Maybe they think I hate all men. I don't know. People are weird. But also, the women in my family have a history of choosing…losers." She taps her fingertips on the table, pressing her lips together. "So my grandma raised me to not need or want a partner. Another friend would be nice though."

Well. That was a lot. But it's pretty cool that she just laid it all out there, instead of making me wonder. And I can lighten the situation for her so she doesn't spend the evening with that little furrow between her brows. "Don't get ahead of yourself. First you have to pass the friendship suitability quiz."

She arches one brow and looks at me sideways, but she's smirking now instead of looking unsure, so yay, me.

"Eleven questions. Number one: Did your family car have a name when you were growing up?"

Her answer is prompt. "Rusty. Rusty Bucketobolts. But I

think Gram might've had some other names for it she didn't want to say in front of me."

I nod. "Number two: most embarrassing middle school incident."

That sideways look is back. "Dude, you are pushing the boundaries of both privacy and friendship here. But it would have to be when I got caught pulling the fire alarm because it was too pretty a day to stay inside. My grandma made me bake cookies for every teacher and staff member in the building and deliver them personally with handwritten notes of apology."

I wince in sympathy, manage not to laugh, and lead her through nine more increasingly silly questions I make up on the spot. Then she makes me answer them all too, because "this friendship audition thing works both ways."

I ask her about growing up in Galway, and she asks me about growing up in Nebraska. Our food comes and we talk through the meal. She tears into her barbecue like she hasn't eaten in years, but then after three bites, pushes her basket away.

"Full already?" I'm enjoying my steak, wondering if she remembers me telling her this is my favorite meal, but she just looks puzzled.

"Yeah. Weird, huh? I was starving and now I'm stuffed." She shrugs. "Oh well. Leftovers for tomorrow."

We talk about our families. I tell her about my sisters and my brother and my folks and grandparents and nieces and nephews, and how I spend part of every Sunday afternoon eating with them via video call.

She looks delighted when I tell her they put a laptop on a lazy Susan on a box in my old chair at the table so I can get my usual view of them, and them of me.

"You must really miss them, huh?" Her head is tipped as she studies me, her eyes warm.

"Yeah, of course." Mostly. I'm starting, every now and then, to get some little niggle of some kind of goodish feeling—a sense of possibility? Anticipation?—when I realize I've got a day free with nobody else's wishes to consider. When we talk on the phone and I don't have to worry that they've volunteered me for something without checking with me first. But that's new and unexpected and I'm still trying to figure it out.

I feel bad that she seems to have had no family except the one grandmother.

We talk until the lights dim and the music cranks up, and then I tug her out on the floor to wow her with my two-step, trying not to be overcome by the feel of her in my arms, of the deep curve of her waist, hidden under that loose shirt. Of the way her body moves so perfectly with mine, even our first time dancing together, even as just friends.

She's laughing and so warm and lovely that I have to keep reminding myself not to pull her close. It takes me a while to notice the smudges of fatigue under her eyes.

"You okay? Am I keeping you out too late?" It can't be much past eight thirty or nine but she looks dead on her feet.

"I'm fine. Just tired." She smothers a yawn. "Still catching up on my rest from training week, I guess."

Training was weeks ago. "You need to get home, then." *Or better yet, come home with me and I'll cuddle you to sleep.* "You okay to drive?"

She waves that away. "Oh, yeah. I'm fine."

It's almost October and the nights are finally turning cool. The parking lot is well enough lit that we can't see many stars as

I walk her to her car. "This was fun, Andi. I'd love to hang out again some time."

She turns to face me, leaning back against the car, one fingertip touching my hand. That single point of contact is a tiny furnace, heating me through. "I'd like that. I'll try not to be such a party pooper next time."

We pull out our phones and exchange numbers, standing so close I can sense her body heat as music leaks from the roadhouse and wraps around us. An old Collin Raye song about two people who aren't as incompatible as they appear to be on the surface.

A long, wavy strand of hair has come loose from her braid and I brush it off her cheek, wanting to reach behind her to unravel the whole soft mass. Plunge my fingers into it and feel the burn of her turning to fire in my arms again.

Her dark eyes search my face. "Good night."

I lean in, sooo slowly, wanting to sip the word from her soft mouth…and then I remember that this is not a date, that we're just friends, and that what she really needs is rest. I marshal all my willpower and step back. Force out my own "good night."

And then I open her door and watch her climb in and drive away.

She gives me a sleepy cat's smile before she turns out of the lot.

It's okay.

This wasn't really goodbye—we'll build a friendship.

And then see what happens.

CHAPTER 14

Kevin

"HEY, YOU." HER MORNING VOICE, when she answers the phone, is warm, roughened velvet.

It melts me. Makes me have to feel for a chair to sink into before my plateful of eggs joins me in a puddle on the floor. "Good morning. Barely." I've already done my Saturday training hours, come back home, and fixed breakfast. Lunch. Whatever.

"Mmm...I didn't sleep *that* late, did I?"

The sound of her, stretching and yawning, muffled in sheets, fabric sliding over warm, smooth skin, nearly does me in. I shove my plate aside and thump my head a few times on the table in front of me. *Get it together, Kev.*

"Oh my gosh! It's eleven!" Totally different tone now, alert and genuinely shocked.

"Is that bad? Are you late for something?"

"No... no. I just can't remember the last time I slept past nine. This is weird! I—Hang on a minute, will you? I need to check my texts, make sure everything's okay."

I wait, eating my toast and eggs and trying not to miss the warm, blurred, just-for-you voice she'd used a minute ago.

"You still there? Thanks. Sorry. No problems, so that's good. How are you this morning?"

"Fine. Look, I know we had dinner just last night, but I wondered if you might want to do something together this weekend." I'm really pushing it, calling her so soon, but heaven help me, I couldn't stop myself.

"I just got invited to my friend Rose's house for a pool party. She says it's a small one—just a handful of people—because some of the regulars are out of town. Want to go with me?"

I can hear her opening and shutting drawers. I wonder what's in those drawers. What she's wearing right now. "Uh, sure." Time with her *and* I get to see her in her swimsuit? You betcha.

She says she'll pick me up at two, and then I'm alone again with my breakfast.

———

I use the ride from my apartment to Andi's friend's house to get myself under control. It's not easy, with Andi so close, her flimsy swimsuit cover-up riding up her thigh as she applies the gas and brake, her toned calf flexing. Instead of a braid, she's left her long hair down and it shifts in the breeze from her open window, sliding across her smooth bare shoulder and arm, its flowery scent teasing my nose. It's not any safer to look at her graceful hands on the steering wheel, a silver ring on her thumb catching the sunlight as she keeps the beat of the Jason Isbell song on the radio. I remember all too well the magic in those fingers.

On the back seat there's a pan of something rich and chocolaty and warm from the oven. "My secret brownie recipe," she tells me with a private, pleased little smile. My body reacts like she'd stroked me. I'm so busy trying to calm myself back down that I almost don't worry about what her friends will think of me.

It's just six of us. The host couple, Rose and Angus, and one other couple I recognize: July from the restaurant and the guy who was by her side that night.

Angus could've played pro football, with his height and bulk. Says he didn't, but his massive strength is apparent as he shakes my hand and looks me over. He's got at least two inches on me. The other guy, Joe, isn't much taller than July, with a lean, wiry distance-runner's build, but he eyes me too.

I remember thinking July looked massively strong when I saw her before. Today, her sleeveless swimsuit cover shows off her impressive biceps and triceps. She too looks me over pretty closely.

Rose is a hoot. A round little ball of energy, everywhere at once, usually carrying some kind of food. Her eyes are full of mischief as she gives me a quick up-and-down visual sweep. "Wellll. Kevin. Nice to meet you! I've heard so much about you."

What?

Andi looks at her like she's lost it. "No, you haven't."

"Hush, Andi. I'm practicing the basic social skills I should've learned in my youth."

Big Angus shakes his head, not very successfully hiding a grin, and turns to me. "You know much about grilling?" Tips his head toward Joe. "Usually Toothpick Boy here is the grill master, but I'm up for a change if you are."

Joe snorts. "It's yours if you want it, Kevin, but I don't mind if you don't. The important thing is to keep the yeti here away from fire. Nothing spoils an appetite faster than the smell of burnt hair."

Rose frowns at him. "You hush. Angus always smells nice." She hands Angus a platter of raw chicken breasts and salmon steaks and skewers of vegetables, then pats him on the arm. "I did miss your eyebrow, though, sweetie, till it grew back in. Thank heavens you didn't have your beard then."

July and Andi are trying not to laugh. Angus just rolls his eyes. Leads Joe and me out to a fine huge grill on the covered part of a flagstone patio that stretches fifteen or twenty feet to a sparkling pool surrounded by gorgeous plantings.

"Wow."

"Pretty cool, huh? Rosie and I did everything but the pool ourselves."

Joe nudges me to keep walking. "He always has to tell everybody that first thing."

"I think I would too. This is great." I'm completely sincere. They've built a paradise back here.

Joe nudges me again, a little harder than before. "Suck-up."

Angus laughs.

Truth be told, Joe handles the cooking effortlessly and I'm the one being grilled. Where I'm from, and what brought me to town, and how do I know Andi. I tell them about her high school presentation, not our hookup, of course. When I mention the volunteer training, Joe's all ears. "Man, I wanted to do that this round. Had a class out of town, though. Couldn't make it. How do you like volunteering there?"

By the time I've finished telling him about working with the kids, the meat and fish and veggies are ready and the three women have got the patio table set up with everything else we need for a feast. Crusty bread with butter, thick slices of tomato with mozzarella and basil leaves and curling slivers of purple onion, pitchers of fresh-squeezed lemonade and iced tea—seems like it's always sweet tea down here—and a bowl of well-seasoned rice. I could learn some serious cooking tricks from these folks.

Andi touches my elbow and peers at me, smiling a little, as we settle at the table. I smile back. I like her friends and I like her checking on me.

We pass around platters and fill our plates, and then it's the women's turn to grill me. The guys answer the questions they've already asked me, which is good of them, because it lets me save my energy for the women's much more dangerous questions. I'm mostly ready for those; I've seen my sisters and sister-in-law in action enough times to know what's coming.

July leads off. "What'd you think of the shelter training? Did you learn a lot that was new to you about domestic violence?"

Damn, smooth. She's giving me a chance to say whether I've had personal experience with it, without being too nosy.

I nod, swallowing my bite of melt-in-your-mouth salmon. "I learned a ton. Andi and the other trainers were amazing. I kinda think everybody should go through that training." They're all quiet, eating and listening, so I go on. "Made me realize I've seen some of the red flags with my students. Also with people I knew when I was in school. Made me think real hard about what to do in the future when I see that stuff."

"What kind of red flags?" Rose pops a bite of grilled zucchini in her mouth, her big brown eyes on me.

"Oh, you know—lotta jealousy, or someone trying to isolate their partner or control how they dress or who they talk to." Naming these things, I think of a few more instances I've seen. "I see it everywhere, now that Andi and her crew made it visible to me."

July nods, her expression sober. "It is everywhere." She tears off a hunk of bread, butters it, and holds it up for Joe to eat it from her fingers. "It didn't bother you to hear about it? Lot of guys get all defensive when women talk about it. Like they're being accused themselves."

I shake my head. "No. I just feel bad for my ignorance all these years."

July nods and leans against Joe, who slides his arm around her sturdy back.

"What would you do now if you thought one of your students was abusing another one?" Rose's eyes are filled with intensity. This isn't an idle question for her.

I pause with a forkful of salmon and rice halfway to my mouth. "Teachers are required to report if we know about abuse. But if I wasn't sure enough to report right off, I guess I'd...try to determine whether it's an emergency situation first. You know, like, do I need to intervene *right now* to stop someone from getting hurt?"

She's very still, listening. Angus, on the far side of her, is watching her with what I think is concern. Maybe trying to make sure she doesn't need him to do something or say something.

I settle my fork back on my plate and wipe my fingers with my napkin. "If there seemed to be immediate danger, I'd step in." The privilege of being a big guy nobody wants to mess with, I see now. "But if there didn't seem to be an immediate threat, I'd probably ask Andi for advice. Or Tisha. The vice principal. She's great too."

There's a general murmur of agreement. They all know Tisha. Of course they do.

But enough about me. I want to know Andi's friends, too. Their protectiveness is subtle but clear. They love her, and the feeling is mutual. So I ask what they do, and whether they all grew up in Galway, and how the couples got together. And they answer with a lot of laughter and teasing each other, and the afternoon stretches into early evening. We carry the food and dishes inside and come back out to get in the pool, and I'm enjoying their company so much I barely lose my power of speech when Andi takes off her cover-up and dips a toe in the water.

Her suit is severe, almost—a plain navy one-piece cut high at the hip and low in back—but on Andi it's the perfect frame for the precious work of art that is her body. I wish I could preserve this moment. The sun is about to sink behind the trees on the west side of the yard. Andi's wrapped her hair around her wrist, getting ready to fasten it back again, I think, and the long golden light makes her glow, glinting off that hair, highlighting her amazing curves.

Some people would say she's too big, but they are ignorant asses who should not be allowed out on their own.

I feel like this is a holy vision. Like I should shield my eyes or drop to my knees and worship. Not just the way she looks, but the person inside that body. The serious, passionate, smart, amazing person.

Her eyes come up, find me where I'm standing by a chair, my hand clenched around my T-shirt, and she smiles. "It's perfect! Come in." She raises her arms and fastens her hair back, watching me as I drop the shirt and cross the flagstones to her.

I need to get in the damn pool before I embarrass myself.

We turn and jump, together.

The next couple of hours pass in a blur of laughter and teasing and, for me, pure, blinding lust. We play water volleyball—and damn, except for little Rose, these people are athletes! July makes me eat at least three spikes—and talk trash and just have fun. I touch Andi whenever there's the slightest excuse, and I could swear she does the same.

When finally the mosquitoes begin to bite, we climb out and dry off. I'm almost reluctant to say goodbye to these people, except that I know by leaving I'll have the drive home alone with Andi.

"Kevin, it was really nice to meet you. Come back anytime." Rose may think she needs work on her manners, but they're just fine. She's a great, comfortable host. "Be good to our girl."

I know better than to think she's teasing about that last part, and I catch the tiny nods the others give at her words.

"I will." Some mischievous part of me makes me add, "Besides, I hear if I'm not, she'll hurt me."

"What?" More than one person says it. They're all staring at me, including Andi.

I paraphrase Steve Jackson mimicking high school Andi. "'When a girl says no, you stop. Now back off. Your face already messed up my manicure once.'"

Angus bursts out laughing.

"How could I have forgotten about that?" July's laughing too as she towels her hair.

"Where—Ohhh. You've been talking to Steve." Andi shakes her head, grinning, not bothering to deny a thing.

Rose demands to hear the story, so July tells it while the rest of us gather our things. Rose seems delighted beyond all reason. "Damn, Andi. I wish you'd been my friend in high school."

Andi stops smiling and gives her a hug. "Me too, Rose." I don't know what that's about, but it's really sweet to see. The love is strong in these folks.

July hands Andi back her empty brownie pan. "I'm telling you, Andi, if you'd just share that recipe, I could sell the hell out of those. Name 'em after your Gram...?" She wiggles her eyebrows.

Andi laughs. "Lemme think about it."

July and Joe live close enough to walk home and they set off hand in hand, turning down our offer of a ride. We thank Rose and Angus again and climb into Andi's car.

The sudden hush is disquieting.

"I really like your friends."

She starts the car and smiles at me, then pulls smoothly away from the curb. "They're great, aren't they?"

I lean my head back against the seat, content to just be with her a little longer, but it seems like no time at all before she's pulling up in front of my apartment building.

I can't read her expression in the uneven parking-lot lighting, and I'm aching at the thought of saying goodbye so soon.

So for the second time in two days—maybe the second time in my life—I ask for what I want. "Wanna come in?"

She studies me for what seems like hours.

I touch her hand. "It's okay if you don't. I just didn't wanna say goodbye yet."

Her mouth quirks at one corner. "I don't either. I was...trying to read your mind to know what the invitation entails."

Fair enough. "Whatever you want. We can watch TV. Or talk. Or drink tea or do each other's nails. Or you can kick my ass in a video game. I promise I won't cry. Much. My niece can vouch for that."

There's that smile that turns me from a solid to a liquid. "Okay, then, sure."

CHAPTER 15

Andi

I AM TORN LIKE A piece of paper. Part of me wants to forego friendship, take him by the shirt and drag his fine ass straight to his bedroom—I know the way, thanks—but the Gram-voice part of me is shouting, "No, don't be stupid! Go home now!"

He fits right in with my friends. They're a protective bunch in general, and since I've never brought a man with me anywhere, I knew they'd look him over good.

They all seem to like him. While the guys were bonding over raw meat at the grill in that weird way guys do, Rose said, "Well, he's a fine big hunk of man, isn't he? Almost as pretty as Angus." And later, after the volleyball game, July said in my ear, "He's fun. Good sport."

And god help me, I really do like him too. Despite all of Gran's training and ghostly hollering, I haven't stopped wanting him.

I turn off the ignition and follow him up to his apartment. Brush past him when he holds the door open for me. And try not to be awkward about the very different circumstances under which I was last here.

"Thirsty?" He shuts the door behind us, tosses his keys on the counter—déjà vu—and walks around me into the kitchen, flicking on lights as he goes.

I kind of am, actually. "Would you happen to have any juice?"

He opens the fridge and holds up a carton of cran-apple. "This okay?"

"Perfect."

He gets out two glasses and pours me juice and himself milk. "I can't believe those friends of yours ate all the brownies. Buzzards."

I manage not to blow cran-apple out my nose but it's a near miss. "You ate four of them yourself, if I'm not mistaken."

He flashes that dimple at me. "I didn't think anybody saw me steal that last one." He rubs his flat belly. "Sure would like one now with my milk. They were excellent."

I follow him to the living room where we settle on the couch. He scoops up the remote, turns on the TV, then fiddles with his phone. In a minute, the TV screen becomes a fireplace, complete with quietly crackling logs.

"Nice." I reach out and nudge him with my non-juice hand. "Festive."

He shoves me back, gently, his fingertips brushing over my arm, raising goose bumps. "Use your imagination, Salazar. Pretend it's a campfire. That's where all the best conversations happen." He polishes off his milk and sets the glass on the end table. Grabs hold of the big, square ottoman upholstered to match the couch and positions it so we can both use it.

I kick off my sandals and cross my feet beside his. "Okay, then. What kinds of conversations does one have around a campfire?"

He snorts. "Deep stuff. Big questions. Like...which Star Wars movie was worst? Have we had visitors from outer space? And how'd Dolly Parton turn out so dang cool?"

I nod, staring into the flames. "Ahh. I see." I finish my juice, which was really good, and set my glass on my end table. This couch is comfy and that video fire is mesmerizing. For all the sleep I got, I shouldn't be in danger of nodding off again, but...

I focus on staying awake. "So how did a Nebraska boy end up in Galway, North Carolina?"

He slouches down beside me and drops his head to the back of the couch. "Biggest spontaneous thing I ever did. I mean, I've *thought* of impulsive stuff before but never—" He turns his face to me. "But this is a nice town. I like the people here."

His big brown eyes are serious. He's sincere. Not flirting.

I don't know what to do with whatever bullshit is going on in my chest, thanks to his words. "What do you think was behind the impulse?"

He turns his head back to the fire and folds his hands on his belly. Sighs. "I had a bad breakup at the beginning of the year."

Hello.

"Bad how? Are you still hurting?"

His brow crinkles. "Fiancée dumped me. I...guess I'm still hurting? My pride, anyway. I finished out the teaching year but it was...really hard. Everything and everybody around me reminded me of smashed plans." He shakes his head and meets my eyes again. "I felt like I had to get away or I'd lose it. Like I needed a new start somewhere fresh to be able to move on."

I study his face, trying to gauge his feelings. "Do you miss your family and friends a lot?"

"Yes...and no. Mostly yes." He taps his thumbs together. "But being here alone has given me more time to think than I've ever had before."

I wish I could take his hand, relax into his side. "What do you think about?"

He snorts softly. "Everything. Every darn thing. What I want in my life. What I don't. What I like. What I don't." He tips his head toward me and laughs. The sound is harsh though, like it hurts him. "My ex said I was too nice. Had no personality of my own—just went along with what other people wanted."

"Did you?"

His nod is slow. Thoughtful. "Kinda. I've always been a people pleaser, I guess. And it wasn't hard—I wasn't a rebel or anything. I wanted the people around me to be happy, and I really didn't care all that much about what we ate or watched or played or whatever when we hung out. I just wanted to be with them. But I can see where that leaves all the decisions to others. I guess that's not fair."

I can't see his expression. I think there's sadness in his voice. Maybe resignation? But also a little defiance.

"Do you miss her a lot?"

Long pause as the fake fire crackles merrily just beyond our toes.

"I miss...having somebody. Having a plan. Having a...known future." Another pause. "She was smart. Fun. Pretty." He sighs. "But not always kind, I guess. Not very patient. I don't miss that."

I can picture it. I know people like that. Kevin deserves better. "You spent a lot of time trying to please her, huh?"

He's silent for a half beat. "Yeah. Guess I wasn't very good at it."

This time I can't miss the defeat in his voice.

If I had a big lively family I loved—and let's face it, his family would be fun and lively—I'd have to have been one wounded puppy to be upset enough to pull up my roots and move halfway across the country from them.

I nudge him with my elbow. "Kevin. That doesn't mean you failed. It sounds like you two weren't a great match."

We watch the fire in silence for a few minutes. Then he draws in a deep breath and blows it out. "Thanks, Andi. Enough about me." There go those thumbs, tapping again. "Tell me how you ended up doing the work you do."

Well. Not going to dump the whole terrible story on him, but I can give him part of it. "I wanted to do work that would help somebody. And I think I mentioned that women in my family have not always picked good guys, right? So I...knew something about families in crisis." I shrug. "It just made sense to follow this path."

He nods, twisting enough to see my face. "Do you love your work?"

I think that over. "I...never really considered doing anything else. It's challenging. It's important. I seem to have a knack for it. I get satisfaction from doing the job well. As well as it can be done, anyway."

He's quiet, maybe waiting for me to go on, and when I don't, he says, "Is there a 'but' in there?"

And then I'm telling him something I've never said out loud before. "But sometimes it's exhausting. Every now and then it feels hopeless. And if by some miracle people stop committing domestic violence and rape forever, I would fucking *celebrate* being out of a job."

He doesn't pry. Doesn't offer advice. Maybe that's why I sensed I could tell him in the first place. He just turns his face back to the fire and says, "I can understand that."

We change to lighter topics then. Music. We agree on Jason Isbell being great, but not on which song is his best. He's never heard of Amethyst Kiah, so I pull out my phone and play him a couple of her songs. He has me send him the link to one so he can listen again later. We watch the fire and listen to music and talk about everything and nothing.

I wake up to find us still on the couch, propped up against each other, Kevin breathing slow and deep beside me. It's got to be the middle of the night. I'm stiff and sleepy and uncomfortable. I don't want to leave him and I don't want to wake him up, but I need my bed.

"Hey, sleeping beauty." I keep my voice low. Rub his arm. "I'm going to leave. Lock the door behind me?"

"Hmm?" He's upright, trying to look alert but obviously befuddled to find me beside him in his living room. "Ohhh. Andi." That sweet smile of his starts across his face but stops when I stand up and gather our glasses and shuffle toward the kitchen.

He follows me. Watches as I turn on the faucet to rinse the glasses. Reaches out to touch my shoulder.

"Don't go. It's three in the morning and you're too tired to drive." He turns off the water, upends the glasses in the sink, and tugs me to the kitchen doorway. "Stay here. You can have the bedroom. I'll take the couch."

I yawn. "Kevin, I'm not going to kick you out of your own bed. I'll stay but *I'll* take the couch."

"If I let you do that, every member of my family will sense my ungentlemanliness and we'll hear them yelling all the way from Nebraska." He slumps against the doorframe.

"See, thaaat's why I need to go home." I look around for my purse, drooping myself.

He heaves a deep sigh. "C'mon. We'll sleep better in the bedroom. The bed's big enough for us to build an impenetrable pillow wall down the middle to guard my virtue."

I'm not too tired to snort. "Impenetrable, huh? To guard your virtue?"

"I said what I said. Don't try to have your way with me. I need my rest."

Eyes half-closed, he leads me by the hand to the bedroom and pulls down the covers to his bed. He gestures me in but then his eyes sweep me, taking in my cover-up and swimsuit. "Wait." He goes to his dresser and pulls out a T-shirt and boxers. "Here, these'll be more comfortable. You can have the bathroom first. There's a spare toothbrush in the medicine cabinet."

I can't believe I don't even protest. But between that bed that I remember as very comfy and the charm of this big sleepy man, I can't resist. I take the clothes, go into the bathroom, unwrap the toothbrush, and get ready for bed.

He arranges the pillows before he takes his turn in the bathroom. I'm just awake enough to register it when he turns out the light and climbs in beside me. "Remember," he mumbles, "keep your hands to yourself."

I remember smiling and sinking back into clean sheets and then…nothing until hours later when the morning sun finds a crack in his curtains. I'm in his arms on his side of the bed, warm and relaxed and peaceful, impenetrable pillow wall demolished.

"Good morning, intruder." His rough morning voice has a smile in it. "What would you like for breakfast?"

He's keeping the lower part of his body angled away from me. I figure there's a reason for that. I breathe in and out slowly and then turn to face him, just the real me in his bed, without the protection of makeup or distracting tattoos.

"Hi." His eyes crinkle at me as he looks me over. "You sleep okay?"

"Yeah. You?" I'm not sure what to do with my hands. I fold them under my cheek.

"Great. I slept great."

He's filling my senses with his warmth, his scent, and the sight of morning sunlight glinting off the blond scruff on his jaw. Yesterday I got to watch him leap and stretch and twist in the pool during the volleyball game wearing just swim trunks, and he is purely delicious. That same deliciousness is here with me now, his face a few inches from mine.

And I can't do a damn thing about it.

Clearly I've died. I'm just not sure whether I've ended up in heaven or hell.

CHAPTER 16

Kevin

I CAN'T BELIEVE I'VE WOKEN up with her in my bed. In my arms. This dedicated, amazing, gorgeous, sexy woman who has agreed to be my friend.

Gotta stop thinking about this being a *bed*. But I'm not ready to get up just yet. Need things to…calm down a little first.

"So 'Andi' is short for 'Andrea'?" Oh, dangerous, bringing back those memories while we're…right here at the scene of the… events of that night.

"Andrea Valeria Salazar." She pronounces it "ahn-DRAY-uh."

This would be the time for me to bring up breakfast again but god help me, I can't make myself leave this bed just yet.

She's quiet, watching me from behind those dark eyes, her smile fading.

"It's a beautiful name. All of it." I catch a wavy lock of her hair and wrap it around my finger, then unwind it again when I remember that's not a friend gesture. "Are you Latina?"

She tips her head in a half nod. "Gram was. My other

grandparents were white. Gram didn't even teach my mom Spanish."

"Oh yeah? Why not?"

She settles in like she's willing to stay a while too. "When she first came to North Carolina with her family, she was young and they were poor and didn't speak any English and she saw how people looked down on them. She learned English as fast as she could in school, but..." She shakes her head. "I think it was a really tough adjustment. When she started high school, she found work as a part-time nanny for a wealthy white family, after school and weekends and vacations, and she memorized the way they talked. Tried to erase her accent. Or, I guess, replace it with a North Carolina one. I mean, she was still a little brown girl, but..."

Her mouth quirks up in a half smile but it's bittersweet and fades quickly too.

I stay quiet and nod, hoping she'll keep talking.

"She married a white boy right after graduation. They had my mom not long after, but he was...not somebody it would have been good for her to stay with. So she left him and moved to a different town to get away. His family didn't want him with her anyway, and he wasn't any kind of dad, so nobody even kicked up a fuss when she took my mom and divorced him."

"That must've been rough for her and your mom." Her skin looks impossibly smooth. My fingers twitch, remembering.

She nods. Shrugs. "Yeah. Well. Rough in some ways, easier in others. Gram was tough. And smart. And stubborn. She raised my mom to speak the English of the wealthy family she'd worked for, hoping people would treat my mom better. But later with me, Gram said she realized knowledge is power, so she made sure I got every kind of knowledge she could provide, including Spanish."

I'm about to ask more but she presses her hand to her belly. "Oh my god. I am *so hungry*. You ever suddenly realize you're so hungry you feel half-sick? Is your offer of breakfast still open?" She sits up and swings her legs over the side of the bed. Heads for the bathroom.

"Yes, ma'am." I'm decent now, just barely, so I head to the kitchen.

It takes us almost no time to whip up a feast of bacon and eggs and toast. Andi eats most of a little carton of yogurt while we're cooking and then says she's too full to eat anything else, but I fix her a small plate with a bit of everything and she nibbles at it as we sit in the dining room playing gin rummy and debating which sport is the most fun to play and which is the most fun to watch. It's the kind of thing I never thought about before. Usually I'd just agree with what everybody else says, but Andi won't accept that. She teases and prods and badgers me into thinking about it, and before I know it, I'm practically arguing with her.

I mean, she's trying to convince me that *kickball* is the most fun to play.

What a ridiculous woman.

What a fun, silly, entertaining, gorgeous, sexy, ridiculous woman.

I could learn to like arguing, if it's always like this.

Way before I'm ready to say goodbye, she says she has to leave.

I don't like it but I get it. If I'm not careful, I'll scare her off, wanting too much. I've already claimed most of her weekend.

Tomorrow's a workday for both of us. And I've got some grading to do.

Still, I stop her as she's reaching for the front doorknob. "Will you come run at the high school tomorrow?"

She's back in her swimsuit and cover-up, her hair twisted into some kind of loose, sexy knot. She gives me a lazy smile over her shoulder. "No, I've got to drive to Asheville tomorrow after work. Annual meeting for North Carolina women's crisis center directors. Two days. I won't be home till Wednesday night."

I try my best not to give her what my sisters call "Kev's Puss-in-Boots eyes." Mainly because they say it with a fair amount of mockery. If it worked, I'd use it for sure.

Andi

All the way home and all through my packing, my thoughts are full of him. His big warm body so solid behind me—still on his own side of the bed—when I woke up. His eyes smiling into mine. His thoughtful answers last night to my questions about his breakup. His gentle teasing...

This weekend was so unexpected.

Seems I don't want a casual occasional-hookup thing with him after all. I want a...companion, of sorts?

Being with Kevin is so...*easy*. Even out of my element at his apartment, I was perfectly comfortable. He made it clear I was welcome for as long as I wanted to stay. We had fun together; we talked... I could have happily stuck around longer if I hadn't had to come home to get ready for my trip.

I've never spent that much time with a lover. Usually I'm ready to say "see ya" after a couple of orgasms. But Kevin's company is addictive. His teasing, too.

I snort, remembering, as I fold a sweater into my little roller suitcase, him talking about protecting his virtue and telling me last night to keep my hands to myself because he needed his rest. He was letting me know, in the sweetest way possible, that he didn't expect anything—that he really just meant sleep. Dammit.

The man's got some serious communication skills.

He's got a giant heart and I'm going to have to treat him with the care he deserves. I'm liking our budding friendship a lot. My stomach drops at the thought of wrecking that by pushing for sex when I don't want to be in a relationship.

I add another pair of slacks and extra underwear and my toiletries bag and zip-close the suitcase. Roll it to the garage door so it'll be easy to grab in the morning. Then I fix myself a cup of tea and settle with it in Gram's chair, thinking about how Kevin is messing with my ideas of what I want and don't want.

Wondering whether there's a chance I might actually want more than sex from a man someday.

It would have to be an impossibly good man for that to happen.

––––––––––––

Work Monday goes fine until the mail brings a plain white envelope addressed to me in block letters. Inside is a note in bold, aggressive block print. It says SEND THEM HOME BITCH OR ELSE.

Some people have no manners.

It's not signed, of course, but I call the police like I always do with threatening mail. They come down to pick this one up for fingerprinting, but that never seems to help. They ask if I know who it's from and I tell them no. That's mostly true. I'm not sure. They ask for a list of current shelter residents, and again I say no, as they knew I would. Our client confidentiality rules don't permit that.

Thing is, if the writer is who I think it is, I couldn't send his family home even if I wanted to. Which I will never, ever want, no matter what happens. That sick fuck is a danger to his entire family—not just those little girls. There's not a doubt in my mind he'd kill his wife and disappear with those babies if he ever got the chance. Which is why they are somewhere far away now, and nobody here, including me, knows where. And nobody knows I helped.

I tell Pattie at the desk and send an email warning the staff to be extra careful, and I remind them all that I'm going to Asheville and won't be back in until Thursday. And after work I'm a little more cautious scanning the area and the parking lot and checking my car, and I drive a roundabout route to the highway to make sure no one follows me to Asheville.

I generally enjoy these annual gatherings. The staff of the Galway center is great—knowledgeable, supportive, dedicated to the cause—but there's something next-level about being with other directors who understand not just the issues and the dynamics but also the level of stress that comes from keeping the whole operation afloat. From knowing that lives really do depend on your ability to do your job well.

It's also fun to stay in a decent hotel in a downtown area with plenty of good restaurants and interesting things to see within walking distance. I've made plans to have drinks and dinner with some of the others who live close enough to get here in time, but

I'm so exhausted as I wheel my little suitcase off the elevator and down the long hall to my hotel room that I decide to squeeze in a tiny nap before I meet up with them.

The smell hits me when I open the door. Kind of mildewy? But the room is cute and has everything I need, including a great view of downtown Asheville, and I'm too tired to go back down that hall and downstairs to ask for another room.

It's probably not strong enough or bad enough to qualify as a stench, anyway. Maybe I'll get used to it. I'll just…take my nap, and maybe when I wake up I won't notice it any more.

I set my phone timer, undress and crawl between sheets which smell faintly, comfortingly, of bleach, and that's my last thought before I wake up an hour later to the gentle tones of the alarm.

Really, I could just stay here in this bed and sleep the rest of the night. Text my friends and tell them I'll see them first thing in the morning. Tempting. I sit up and pick up the phone…and I'm hit with a wave of nausea so strong I'm out of bed racing for the bathroom.

There's not much in me to throw up, so it's mostly dry heaves. I feel better after a few minutes. Why is my body acting like this lately? Could I have been poisoned by whatever I smelled earlier? But…I haven't eaten since breakfast. And realizing that makes me simultaneously ravenous and queasy again. Maybe I just need food.

I've often forgotten to eat, or eaten irregularly, and sometimes it makes me cranky but it's never made me *vomit*. Is this a sign I'm getting old and my body is changing? That would totally suck. I'm only in my thirties, for Christ's sake.

Or maybe… Could it be related to low blood sugar, some-how? Or…diabetes? I don't know much about that. I'll have to look it up. Because online health searches do so much to help people feel better.

I splash my face with cold water. Fetch my toiletries bag from my suitcase so I can brush my teeth. Try not to touch the back of my throat with my toothbrush.

Maybe I've got some kind of virus. Or maybe I need some stronger stress-relief techniques. Maybe my new friend Kevin will generously agree to help me work it out in bed.

I'm kicking myself for my mind always going straight to sex when a text comes through from him: You get to Asheville okay? Gonna have a wild night out?

I text back: Ha! Just dinner with friends

Nope, I don't think wildness or staying out late is going to happen for me this week. I've never been so tired for such a long stretch. Weeks now, seems like.

Maybe I'm anemic. Does that cause nausea?

I am overdue for my annual exam anyway, so on the way down to meet the others, I pull up my doctor's scheduling app and am able to grab an appointment for Thursday afternoon. I can't keep up with my responsibilities if I'm not at my best.

———

Three days later I am in an obscenely thin cotton gown at my doctor's office. She's already typed my answers to the basic questions into the little monitor on the counter. Now she swings around to face me fully. "So...your sheet says you've been tired lately? Nauseous? Any other symptoms?"

I shake my head. "Well, my appetite's been a little weird. One minute I'm starving and then after three bites I'm full. And...I've been smelling weird smells nobody else seems to notice. Is that a symptom of anything?"

"Not sure." She makes another note on the monitor. "Fatigue

and nausea are common symptoms of a lot of things. Have you been doing anything different than usual?"

I shake my head. "Just a real quick business trip to Asheville. Most of the symptoms started before that."

"How about food or exercise or sleep or exposure to chemicals—anything different there?"

I shake my head again. "Can't think of anything, no."

"Have your periods been any heavier than usual?" She reaches into her pocket and pulls out one of those little lights they shine in your eyes.

I barely notice. The air has gone very still around me and I'm paralyzed. Periods.

Last period I had came unexpectedly at the surprise birthday party Rose threw for Sabina.

In late July.

It will be October in two days.

I've always been irregular, but nothing like this.

"Andi, you okay? Steady now." Dr. Willis is on her feet, gripping my arm firmly. "What are you experiencing?"

"Doc, if I were"—my voice comes out rusty and I have to clear my throat before I go on—"pregnant, would these symptoms fit that?"

"Yeah. Let's check, shall we?"

Forty-five minutes later, I walk out of there so dazed I almost forget to scan my surroundings. My purse rattles when I toss it onto the passenger seat of my car—the sample bottle of prenatal vitamins, percussion to the echo of Doc Willis's voice saying, "Andi, I'd say you're about two months along."

CHAPTER 17

Andi

WHEN GRAM FIRST CAME TO get me, she brought one of those baby snuggle packs so she could carry me strapped to her chest. She took me almost everywhere she went, from packing up my stuff to packing up her old apartment to driving us to our new life in Galway to the nighttime cleaning jobs she'd wrangled from an accounting firm and a real estate office. I don't remember any of that, of course, but she told me the story every time I requested it, once I was old enough to ask questions.

When I started school, she studied for the real estate exam and got her North Carolina Realtor's license. Her old employer hired her on a commission-only basis and she built a solid base of clients. It was through one of them that she found the cottage. It had been sitting empty for three years and needed an intense cleaning and modernization. The tiny stone house had only one small bedroom, one cramped bathroom, and no garage. But Gram had been scrimping and saving, and when her lowball offer was accepted, we moved up into the hills above town. And as I got older and stronger, we started fixing up the little place. Added on the bigger bedroom and expanded the bath when I started high school. Built the patio and the low wall around it and the firepit over the next few years. Added on the garage when I graduated from college.

There were times when I considered getting my own place, but how could I after everything she'd given up to raise me? And anyway, she'd raised me to be cautious and suspicious of men, so it's not like I was raring to get me a boyfriend. And we just plain enjoyed each other's company, so I never got around to leaving home.

And then two years ago she had a heart attack and died at the grocery, and I've been alone ever since, and this stone cottage that started out so small suddenly seemed way too big. Way too quiet.

Now I sit in Gram's chair beside the fireplace and study the space. The woven basket on the hearth that used to hold my toys but is now full of kindling. The fireplace-bracketing bookcases whose bottom shelves used to be filled with my favorite picture books and chapter books. The corner where I haven't bothered to set up a Christmas tree since Gram's death.

I'm not sure how I'll manage it yet, but a woman and a child have lived happily here before. We could do it again.

I've never thought about having children. Certainly never expected to get pregnant; I've always—always—used protection to try to prevent it. But now that I'm in this situation, it seems... doable. Interesting. Compelling? After all, Lil Bit's already been with me for a couple of months, not causing much trouble. Just kind of hanging out, making me tired, but the doc says I'll probably get my energy back before too long.

My belly doesn't look or feel any different than usual yet. I frame it with my hands.

How could I already be feeling protective? I've only known about Baby for a couple of hours.

My phone buzzes. I haven't told anyone yet, although I did call the center and tell them I'm going to work from home tomorrow and to let me know of any emergencies.

I need...to be alone, to get a handle on this.

My entire life is about to change, forever.

The phone, which I'd already forgotten, buzzes again, and I pick it up from the end table.

Kevin.

Ohhh no. Oh no, no, no.

Gram is up in heaven shaking her head down at me for getting in this situation.

Because what the hell am I going to tell Kevin?

How the hell do you tell a man you're two months pregnant with his baby, when you don't know him well enough to be sure that's safe information to put in his hands?

Ice water creeps slowly through my veins as I hear Gram's voice answering my questions over the years.

Do I have a grandpa, Gram?

Not really, baby, no.

Why not? My friends at school have grandpas.

It wasn't safe for me to stay with your grandpa, Andi. He was mean to me and mean to your mom. We had to get away.

Why did you marry him if he was mean, Gram?

I didn't know at first. He didn't hurt me until after we were married. And it didn't get really bad until I was pregnant with your mama.

I thought it was my dad that was mean. Was my dad my grandpa?

No, baby. Two separate men.

Both mean?

Yes.

Why did my mama marry a mean man too?

I don't know, baby. I tried to talk her out of it. But she said I was worried for nothing, that he was so sweet.

But he was fooling?

He was fooling her, yes. But after they got married, he stopped trying to fool her.

Then did she know he was really mean?

I think so, baby. When she was pregnant, he pushed her down the stairs. And later when she left, he said he'd take her babies from her if she didn't come back.

My teeth are chattering as I stare at the phone.

What in the hell do I do now?

Sweetness can be a show. An all-too-temporary act.

Even if I don't tell him—even if I stop running at the high school or hanging around with him in our free time—he'll see when I start to show. I can only disguise it for so long. And once the baby is born, there'll be no hiding a *child*.

And no matter how nice he seems now, I can't be sure he'll always be that way.

I don't know if we're safe with him. Me or this baby.

———

Kevin

I've been looking forward to seeing Andi all day. It almost killed me last night when she messaged to say she was too tired to get together after her trip. But she was the one who suggested tonight, so I've been imagining it all day. Ironed my best shirt. Researched fancy restaurants. Even bought flowers, which—not a normal friend move. What's wrong with me? I'm going to scare her off if I'm not careful.

She doesn't call me back for more than an hour after I leave my message. Now, as I listen to her ask me if she can come over, I look at the bouquet I'd finally plunked in a water glass on my counter, hoping the limp blossoms would perk back up a little.

"Sure, if you want." I pick up a fallen leaf and toss it in the trash can under my sink. "Or I'd be happy to come get you." I haven't seen her place yet. Haven't been invited.

"No, I'll…come to you. I need to talk to you about something." Her voice… There's something in her voice that bothers me. I can't read it but it's definitely not an I've-missed-you-and-I-can't-wait-to-see-you tone.

"Andi, you okay?"

"Yeah, I'm fine. I'll see you soon."

Twenty minutes later, there's a knock on my door and I open it wide for her. Hold out my hand. Tug her in for a hug that maybe lasts a little too long for friendship.

She pulls away.

My joy at seeing her fades, leaving behind a trickle of fear in my gut. Have I bored her already? We're not even going to make it to a second week as friends?

Dread makes my feet heavy. "Want something to drink?"

"Got any more of that juice? That was really good."

I pour her some and lead the way to the living room. We settle on the couch but I make sure not to crowd her. Gotta stop pushing for too much. I can make it through this…whatever it is. Probably.

I won't beg, won't cry…at least not until after she's gone. "What's up? You sure you're okay?"

"Yeah." She stares down into her glass for a long minute and then looks back up at me. "You know how I've been tired lately? I felt kind of rotten in Asheville. Threw up a few times. So I went to the doctor this afternoon."

She hesitates then, and I panic. Oh god, don't let her have a serious illness. "And?" My voice cracks.

"Kevin, I'm pregnant."

A wave of feeling knocks me back against the cushions. Relief that she's not sick, confusion because we'd used protection, and somewhere under all the shock, a tiny burst of joy.

She raises the glass to her lips, her hands shaking, and then settles it on the end table beside her. Twists back around to face me more fully. "Yeah. So this is a surprise."

My body forgets what to do with oxygen. I study her face, peer into her eyes, waiting for her to say more, but she doesn't. "How—how far along are you?"

"A couple of months."

I wait count back in my head. "That was about when… Is—So it's—Is the baby mine?" Those words. How could a man speak them without a tremor in his voice the first time? This is huge. I've helped create a life. I've *helped*? Create a *life*?

My eyes go to her midsection which, as usual, is hidden under one of her loose work shirts. But I saw her in a swimsuit this weekend and hadn't noticed anything.

This is huge. A *baby*. I'm going to be a *daddy*.

Her shoulders are squared. She's perched on the edge of the couch cushion as if ready to flee. "Yeah. You're the only person I've been with in recent months."

I gaze at her, trying to read messages in her dark eyes, but she seems completely closed off. Inside me I feel something new and vulnerable growing, pulsing, almost like *I'm* pregnant, but she's like a wall, upright and sturdy and impenetrable.

To me this seems like a miracle...but maybe not to Andi? It's her body that has to do all the work, go through all the changes, weather the risks and pain to come...

"Look, I know this is a lot. I'm going to have my hands full with this. I don't expect you to do anything. We can just...step back. Be... You know. Acquaintances."

Oh, hell no. Not if this is my baby, I'm not stepping back. She's not raising my child alone.

I can't tell what she means. "Do you want this baby?" It's a croak.

She holds my gaze. "Yeah. I'm going to have it. But I'm not asking anything of you."

I try to comprehend that. "But—Andi, I'm going to be the baby's *dad*. You *should* ask stuff of me." How could she think otherwise? And how could she think I'd need to be asked? I'm going to be a father.

I'm going to be a *daddy*.

There's no visible emotion on her face. I have no clue what's going on in that busy, brilliant mind of hers because not a trace of it is showing.

What could possibly be as important as us both being there for our baby? Working together to give our child the best life possible.

I reach out my hand to touch her hand. She watches my every move like she's not sure what I'm planning. Like I'm a stranger again. Like she doesn't know I'd never touch her any way that wasn't good. I open my mouth to tell her that, to ask why in the world she'd doubt that, but the words come out as, "Marry me."

Her eyes go wide—well, hell, of course, she's even more shocked than I am—and in an instant she's up off of the couch. "What? Kevin, no!"

She laughs a nervous little laugh but it's too late. I've already registered the horror in her eyes and in her voice as she said it.

No way would anybody want to marry me. Especially not an amazing woman like Andi.

Fucking Vanilla Kev.

Not good enough to be a partner.

How the hell am I going to be a good father?

CHAPTER 18

Andi

GODDAMMIT! I DIDN'T WANT TO hurt him. I was watching for
danger signs…rage, anger, anything that might mean I needed to
get out fast. So I was looking closely enough to see his expression
before he wiped it away.

It wasn't anything scary. It was devastation.

He looked like I'd reached into his chest and ripped out that
big heart of his.

What kind of man blurts out "Marry me" to someone he's
only spent a couple of days with?

"Kevin, I'm sorry. That sounded bad." I reach to touch him
but he shakes his head and I pull back my hand. "I just… I was
stunned. That was completely unexpected."

"Don't worry about it. I don't even know why I said it." His
voice is thick, like he's pushing the words through cotton. He
stares down at his interlaced hands.

"It's a big red flag for somebody in my profession, Kev.
Rushing into relationships really fast. Big red flag."

He nods, stiff, still not looking at me. "I get it. Stupid idea. Forget I said anything."

We sit side by side in silence for, god, what seems like forever. I'm not going to apologize again. I've heard too many stories about guys being manipulative, acting hurt to get women to apologize when really there's nothing to apologize for.

But I don't want to leave him like this, because…I don't think he's being manipulative. I think it was real pain I saw flash across his face. I'm not sure why, exactly, because he's a smart guy. Surely he knows it would be silly for two new friends to all of a sudden get married because of an unexpected pregnancy. Dangerous idea. So we sit here, the living room darkening around us as the sun goes down outside his windows.

Finally he sucks in a deep breath and blows it out. Unlaces his hands and rests them on his knees. Twists just enough to look at me. "So, listen. Have you had dinner? You need to eat something. Let's go get you some food."

What?

But he's right. I can't blow off meals anymore. Doc said I'd probably feel better if I started eating small amounts more often.

So I nod. That would be a good, neutral, safe way for me to gauge where he really is with this. It's going to take me some serious observation time—weeks, maybe months—before I know how much to trust him. "You know what sounds good?"

He says nothing. Just raises his brows, waiting for me to go on.

"You ever get dinner from the hot bar at Ahmed's Market?" His apartment is only a three- or four-block walk from there. "I could do with some air and some exercise."

"Let's go, then." He doesn't touch me as he stands and moves toward the door. Scoops his wallet and keys off the counter and shoves them in his pocket. "Oh."

When I turn to see what he's looking at, my eyes find a somewhat droopy bouquet in a tumbler of water on the kitchen side of the counter.

He rolls his eyes, his embarrassment plain. "I got you some flowers."

Oh my god. He's breaking my freaking heart.

"Never mind." He reaches past me to pull open the door.

We don't talk much on the way to the grocery. The wind has picked up and there's a chill in it. The leaves are in the first stages of turning color.

"You okay? Warm enough?" He looks over but still doesn't touch me.

"I'm fine." I miss our easiness already. A few days ago he would have nudged me with his elbow and teased me, saying something preposterous just so I'd laugh. Now...nothing.

At the market, Mr. Ahmed and his oldest daughter smile at us. "Andi! Good to see you. And who is your friend?"

I introduce them to Kevin who, as it turns out, has beautiful manners. He repeats their names, shakes their hands, and says he's heard good things about the hot bar from me.

"Ah, well, enjoy! Maybe you will join us again soon," they tell him, waving us toward the buffet.

The buffet startles Kevin out of his silence with me. He whistles at the two long tables, one with hot foods, one with cold. Ahmed's always has a combination of traditional southern U.S. foods and foods from his native Pakistan.

I fill a plate with mostly vegetables and melon slices. Kevin piles his with every kind of meat on the bar. We pay and then settle at one of the little tables pushed up against the front windows.

"So you've had Pakistani food before?" I nibble a samosa and watch him dig into some kind of lamb dish.

"Nope. So this is perfect." He closes his eyes as he chews, as if he's memorizing the flavor. "Wonderful."

"Perfect how?"

He blinks at me. "Uh. Well, I…try a few new things every week. See what I like and what I don't." He waves his refilled fork at me. "This is one for the Like column."

"Interesting." I turn my attention to a thick slice of watermelon. "Have you always done that?"

"Um, no. Just the last few months." He seems done with talking then, shoving a big bite of bun kebab into his mouth, then dropping his gaze and busying himself poking at the other foods on his plate.

Why in the world would that topic be off-limits?

Maybe he's still upset about me turning down his proposal.

————

Kevin

I am not going to lay out any more of my insecurities for her to see tonight.

And the last thing I want to think about right now—or, really, ever again—is Cheryl. Cheryl hadn't exactly said, "Don't you have any tastes of your own?" as a taunt, but that's how I hear it every time she comes to mind. Critical. Judgmental. Disappointed.

I'm disappointed in myself. Don't want Andi to join the crowd on that too.

We finish eating in silence, me pretty much cleaning my plate while she nibbles and grazes and has only a little bit of each thing.

When we're done, I thank Mr. Ahmed and his daughter and promise to come back. That promise will be a pleasure to keep. This will be a great place to pick up dinner after long winter days at school. I might start getting my groceries here too, instead of from the Ingles near the highway.

An image flashes through my mind: me and Andi pushing a shopping cart, talking and laughing about our grocery selections, a baby in the child seat in front of us.

I shove the image away fast. Don't want to have to mourn another thing that never came to pass.

We set out for the walk back to my place. I don't have any clue what she's going to want to do when we get there, or whether she'll even want to come inside. So I need to bite the bullet, ignore the potential for humiliation, and just say what I need to say. Find out what I need to know.

Because I intend to be part of this baby's life from now on. And I want life to be as easy as possible for their mama, even if she has no interest in me.

"How you feeling about this surprise?" I ask finally when we're just a couple of blocks from my apartment.

Her hand comes up to her belly. "I'm still kind of in shock, I think. But also"—she shoots me a glance that's sweet and almost shy—"cautiously excited?"

That lucky, lucky baby. I'd give anything to see her look that way when she thinks of me.

One part of the weight pressing on me lightens with the knowledge that at least Andi is happy about the baby. Some of the pressure remains, though, because although I feel that same happiness, my relationship to this baby is more precarious.

Extremely precarious. I need to remember that every single minute.

I clear my throat. "You haven't had much time to think about it yet, huh?"

She huffs a laugh. "Three, four hours?"

"Want help?" Shit. I shouldn't have phrased it as a question.

"What do you mean?"

"I mean...you'll have to do stuff like babyproof your place, right? And you'll need baby furniture and—" I wave my arm, remembering all the baby paraphernalia I've helped my sisters and brother lug around and set up and stuff into trunks and back seats and bedrooms. "I can put stuff together. I can paint a nursery space so you don't have to breathe fumes. And I'll set up a college fund tomorrow.

"And if you want a partner for childbirth classes, somebody to be in the room with you when you're in labor, I can do that too." I can see by her face that she hasn't thought that far ahead. That might be too much too soon, but I don't even wince when I think about it. If she's going through the pain and the work of bringing my baby into this world, I should be there. For both of them.

She's looking sideways at me as we reach my parking lot. "That's...really nice. A really nice offer. I might take you up on some of that."

Phew. Okay. I'll take it. "You got a little bit more energy in you?"

Her brows shoot up and the wariness is back in her eyes. "Why?"

"We have a very important errand to run. Right away. We can be done and back in half an hour. You driving or am I?"

Her lips quirk up. "Well, you're the one who knows where we're going. You drive."

She doesn't need my help but I hand her into my passenger seat anyway. I feel her eyes on me as I drive us downtown. The shops on the square will be closing soon so I park as close as I can and hustle us the half block to Corey's Books.

"What're we doing here?" she asks as I pause inside the door, scanning the topic signs, looking for the right section.

"There." I take her hand and tug her with me and she doesn't resist. She even laughs.

My heart lightens a fraction in my chest. Maybe this will be okay. Maybe everything will turn out okay after all, if I do everything just right.

"Ahh." She nods as we stop in front of the appropriate shelves.

I spot what I'm looking for right away, grab two copies, and head back up front to the checkout counter.

Andi's laughing again two minutes later as we settle back into my car. "How'd you know exactly what book to get? And why two copies?"

"One for each of us. This is important stuff." I say it lightly, but I want her to have no doubt—I'm in this with her and the baby. For good.

Then I shrug. "I wanted this particular one because I've watched my family pass it around, ever since my oldest sister got pregnant the first time." I start the car, signal, and pull back onto the street, not looking at her. "I...may have read parts of it over the years. It tells you what to expect every step of the way. *Everything.* What's going on in your body each month, how the baby's developing, all kinds of issues people sometimes don't think about…"

She flips through the long table of contents as I drive. "Wow, it really does cover everything. This is so thoughtful, Kevin. So useful. I hadn't gotten that far in my mental processing yet." She closes it and hugs it to her chest. "Thank you."

I nod without trying to speak, on account of the lump in my throat. She sounds so touched just to have someone give her a book. Cripes, just to have someone do this one tiny thing for her.

Maybe that's what it will take for her to let me stick around. I'll be *useful*. The most useful person she's ever met.

I find a parking spot next to her car. "What do you need now? How are you feeling?" *Come inside with me. Let me hold you. Talk to me about everything. Let me cuddle you and our baby. Let me hold you while you sleep. Fix you a healthy breakfast when you wake up.*

The parking lot's pole lighting edges her cheekbone with silver. Turns her dark eyes unfathomable.

She doesn't seem as wary this time when I reach to run a knuckle across her cheek, down along her jaw. "No pressure, Andi. Whatever you want. What do you need tonight?"

Her gaze drops to my mouth. I think I see longing there, briefly, before she drags her eyes back up to mine. "I should probably go home. Spend some time getting used to the idea of having a baby. Really wrap my head around it, you know?"

Fair enough. "Okay. You plenty awake to drive?"

She nods. "Yeah." Then, before I can turn to open my door, her arms are around my neck and she's pulling me close. "Thank you," she whispers, her breath warm against the side of my neck.

My arms come around her too and I burrow one hand into

her silky hair where it twists into that loose braid at her nape. It holds her body heat and her scent and for a minute I'm dizzy. "It's just a book." I joke to stop my eyes from tearing up.

"Nah, it's not." She pulls back enough to cup my face and presses her soft lips to mine. "You know it's not."

Then she opens her door and is out and into her own car before my heart resumes its normal rhythm.

CHAPTER 19

Andi

I'VE JUST COME IN FROM the garage, just reset the security alarm, when my phone buzzes with a text from Kevin: You get home okay? I forgot to ask, who knows about the baby? Should I not say anything to anyone?

It's all so new to me that I've been walking around in my own little bubble, not thinking about other people or how or whether to tell them.

I call him as I head to my room.

He picks up right away. "Hey. You home okay?"

"Yeah." I toss my purse on the bed and drop down beside it. Click on the bedside lamp and fall back against the pillows. "I hadn't gotten to the telling-people stage yet. Nobody knows but you."

"Hmm." His voice is low, gruff. I wonder if he's stretched out on his bed too. "Did you know that clerk in the bookshop?"

For an instant I wish we were having this conversation face-to-face, his hand on my waist, our knees touching.

For the first time, that kind of intimacy sounds...enticing.

He's waiting for me to answer his question. Bookshop. Girl. "Um...I don't think so. Did you?"

"No. So probably no danger of her telling anyone."

Good thinking. It's like he's more tuned in to small-town gossip than I am. "You know... I think I don't want to tell anybody else till the first trimester has passed."

"Really?" His surprise morphs immediately to support. "Okay. I won't say anything to my family for a while either, then."

Oh shit. His family. There's someone in this besides just us.

It shores up my snap decision. "Yeah. Doc said anything could happen at this point, but it'll be more of a sure thing in another month or so."

"Makes sense. So...just you and me then, for now?" His voice wraps around me like a hug.

"You and me...and Baby."

"Yeah."

I can hear a tiny smile forming with the word, his bones and facial muscles relaxing into something softer. Warmer. Before I can think it through, I say, "You seem happy about this."

A pause. Then a cautious, "Aren't you?"

"Well..." I hadn't thought about it precisely in those terms, but... "Yeah. I think I am."

"Then so am I."

Another pause. It's hard to know what to say next.

Then, voice low and blurred with a surprising amount of emotion, he says, "This baby's going to be wonderful, Andi. A sweet, beautiful, lucky, lucky baby."

We say good night then, but all through my get-ready-for-bed routine I'm hearing those words, wishing I knew him well enough to feel safe amending his words to "Our baby." I'd love to share this overwhelming *blooming* feeling with him. That's what it's like—my heart's *blooming*.

Maybe hanging out with him, letting him help with stuff, is the fairest, best way I can handle this right now. Stay friends and just...watch out.

Obviously if he's just *acting* sweet like Gram and Mom's husbands did at first, I can't give him anything he can use against me or Lil Bit.

But if Kevin's the man he appears to be, I want him to be able to see and feel and share and remember every minute of his lucky baby's existence.

———————

We settle into a routine: work most of the day, then I go run a couple of half-ass miles with him in late afternoon, then back to work. Sometimes Kevin comes to spend time with the shelter kids after he's finished at school. Then we do dinner together, either out somewhere or at his house.

"We could do this at your place sometimes, if you want. Save you from a late drive home." He's not looking at me as he carves a rotisserie chicken.

"That's okay. I like knowing I can go straight to bed when I get home."

'Cause I'm sure as hell not getting to go to bed here.

Ever since the proposal fiasco, Kevin's been more reserved physically. No flirting and only platonic touches, almost like he slips into trainer role. Back rubs, foot rubs, occasional friendly arm around my shoulders... But nothing to indicate he'd be up for more. Ever since I kissed him on that bookstore night, if I get too close, he steps back fast and says, "Oh, I forgot to tell you…" and then some innocuous thing I know he made up on the spot to defuse the situation.

Looks like I was right about him having no interest in being anything but buddies with plain everyday me. Or maybe he's turned off by pregnant women. Whichever, the result is the same.

And that's a damn shame, because I find myself wanting him every minute of every goddamn day. At the track, when he sees me coming in from the parking lot and smiles, his eyes crinkling, sunlight glinting off the gold fuzz on his perfect legs as he jogs over to greet me. Over dinner, when he teases me and gives me the best cuts of meat and asks me questions about my growing-up years and how I think children learn. At night, side by side on the couch, when his warmth and scent enfold me as we watch movies.

And later, in my bed alone, when he's called to make sure I got home okay and to read me some interesting snippet or other from the pregnancy book he bought us, I lie back against my pillows and wish he were there with me, and I wonder just how bad it would be to let him know where I live.

How dangerous, realistically.

He certainly hasn't shown any desire to spend the night with me.

Kevin

"You seem happy, Uncle Kev."

CeCe and I have just finished playing a new video racing game with her little brothers. The two boys just had to say good night to get ready for bed.

Geez, I love hearing their voices, even when they're trash-talking me and grumbling about having to take baths.

"You mean happy for a guy who keeps getting his butt kicked by a bunch of middle-schoolers?"

But she's serious. "No, I mean really happy. Happier than you did when you first moved. Happier than you did before you moved, even. Happier than…when you were with Cheryl." She almost whispers that last word.

Hmm. "I guess I am. Making new friends, liking work so far… Yeah, I'm good."

I hadn't consciously thought about it, but life does seem pretty good right now. Be a lot better if I didn't occasionally feel like I'm walking on eggshells with Andi, trying not to do anything that would jeopardize my place in her life or the baby's, but… still mostly good.

Although this nothing-physical stuff might kill me.

If I'd thought Andi was ripe and glowing and sweet-smelling and tempting as juicy peaches before, I had no idea. She comes striding toward me from the parking lot and I swear the *air* lights up around her. The grass is greener. The changing leaves are brighter. Her light dazzles me, makes me squint.

And those curves of hers when she's in motion… Could she possibly have gotten any sexier? I can't take my eyes off her, but I'm pretty sure if I did, I'd see that all activity around me had come to a halt, with everyone who's attracted to women just standing, staring, probably with their mouths open, salivating, wanting to sweep her into their arms and taste her just as much as I do.

CeCe breaks into my thoughts. "You know, I saw her the other day."

What? "You did?" How?

"She asked me how you were doing, whether you'd be coming home for Thanksgiving."

Oh. CeCe's talking about Cheryl.

Things in my mind drop from Technicolor back down to black and white. "Huh." I just—don't have anything to say about Cheryl. Or to Cheryl.

"I think she's missing you, Uncle Kev." CeCe's tone is cautious. Tentative.

"Her new boyfriend not keeping her busy enough?" The bitter edge in my voice isn't as pronounced as it would have been a couple of months ago, but I still hear it. A few days after she dumped me, I learned Cheryl had taken up with some guy best known for racing his motorcycle on I-80. Without a helmet. A definitely-not-vanilla guy.

CeCe snorts. "Oh, him. He's in the hospital."

"Wreck?" I should feel sympathy, probably, but…

"O' course. But they broke up before that, anyway."

To my surprise, I don't care enough to ask why. "Well, about Thanksgiving, I'd sure love to see you all, but I have to work some things out here before I know if I can come."

I hear her swift intake of breath. "Uncle Kev! You got a girlfriend?"

I hesitate. Do wishes count? "Um, she's not—No…"

She squeals loud enough that my windows are in danger of shattering. "Wait till I tell Grandma!"

"No, now, CeCe—"

"Love you! Bye!"

Well, heck. Now I'm going to be fielding questions and hints and well-meaning nosiness from Nebraska every day, on top of Steve Jackson's, "So what's up with you and Andi Salazar?" and

Tisha Williams's weekly, "Say hi to my friend for me. She's a fine woman." I always tell Steve, "Just friends, man," and his big laugh trails him all the way down the hall. To Tisha I respond, "Yes, ma'am, she sure is." A fine, fine woman.

At the shelter, I see how she is with other people. She holds herself back just a little, but she's always friendly. Respectful. Calm. Capable. And they talk about her like she can do no wrong. They admire and respect and love her.

And…maybe…I'm falling too?

Which is why I'm doing my best to resist her right now. I think maybe she wants me physically—maybe she'd be up to renegotiating our relationship that way—but maybe not. She's the one who set the boundary and she's got to be the one who lowers it. Even if respecting it kills me. Which it might.

But there's another reason too. When I heard that proposal come out of my mouth the night she told me she was pregnant, I realized three disturbing things at once: one, in some ways it felt exactly right to ask her to marry me, short acquaintance or not; two, on the other hand, I knew it was wildly, stupidly soon for me to be thinking that; and three, that's always been my MO. I've always leapt straight to serious, always fallen easily in love without doing the real work to lay a strong foundation for a relationship. I always just assumed that would fall in place. When or how I thought that would happen, I'm not sure, but I believed it would.

With Andi, things are so much more complicated. So much trickier, with so much more at risk. I'm aware of the sand under my feet…aware that there's no concrete there. Yet.

The idea of doing something that might cause her to pull away scares the hell out of me. Yeah, it would make things more complicated for me as the father of her baby, but also, the idea of a firm and final rejection from *her* might just crush me for good.

So I'm trying to pour some footers for us. Get us on solid ground.

Be what she needs right now, so she can picture me being what she wants for the future.

CHAPTER 20

Kevin

"SO TELL ME WHAT KIND of space you have for Lil Bit." I've started using her nickname for the baby. "What needs to be done to get it ready?"

I've asked before and she always said it was too soon to think about it, that she didn't want to jinx things. But now it's Halloween, she's made it safely through the first trimester, and we're at my apartment, porch light on, answering the door for trick-or-treaters every few minutes, between bites of an amazing salad she made with at least three things I'd never heard of or tasted. A win on all counts.

She still hasn't invited me to her place. I don't even know what part of town she lives in—only that it takes her fifteen or twenty minutes to get home. Maybe now…

She sets down her fork, props an elbow on the table, and drops her chin into her hand. "Hmm. Well…I guess first I need to go through the stuff in that room. I moved into the bigger bedroom a few months after Gram died, but everything I didn't know what to do with is in that smaller room now."

"Need help going through it?" So far I haven't done much beyond getting us those books and setting up a college fund.

"Lemme take a look in there and see. I haven't been in there lately. I'll let you know." She watches me as I take another bite.

Then the doorbell rings and she's up before I am. "I got this one." She glides to the door in that little black dress that makes my heart beat funny, the way the soft fabric wraps around her, clinging to every curve. It's not low-cut—just shows the barest hint of cleavage—but in it she makes my teeth sweat, even though she's barefoot now. Even with that pointy witch's hat perched at a crazy angle on all that beautiful soft wavy hair she left loose for the occasion.

A man can only stand so much.

She compliments all the little ones' costumes, gives out candy by the fistful, and then comes back over to the table, sliding into her seat and giving me a smile that melts me to the chair. "In a few years, that'll be—"

"Lil Bit," I finish weakly, smiling back at her.

Her eyes are misty—okay, mine too—and her voice is a soft, dreamy sigh. "Yeah."

I make myself look down at my salad, chasing a sliver of steak with my fork, careful not to look at her as I ask one of the questions that's been burning in me. "Have you thought about how we'll explain our relationship to people?"

Beside me she goes very still, her hand gripping a hunk of the baguette we're sharing. "Um… I'm…still trying to figure that out."

I wait. I don't know what I hope she'll say. I'm praying it won't be something crushing.

"I mean, yes, I've thought about it…but I'm not sure how

much to say. I don't want to lie to anybody, but I don't want to make our relationship out to be more than it is."

Oh god. My heart lands somewhere under my shoes. I clear my throat. "What do you mean?"

"Romantically, I mean."

"Ahh." Okay, fair. I've been wondering how to describe that too.

"It's nobody's business that we had a hookup before we became friends. And it's not something I'm open to explaining or answering questions about." The bread crumbles in her hand and she sets it down on the table and picks up a napkin to wipe her fingers. Her eyes come up to mine. "How do you feel about it? What do you think we should say?"

This is the first time she's talked about *we*. Like she's thinking in terms of there being an *us*.

I have to push my words out past the lump in my throat. "I'm proud to be this baby's daddy. Proud to be…helping give our baby the best possible start." My throat and my eyes start to burn and I have to tell her the truth. "Andi, my biggest fear is of being shut out of this. I don't want you and Lil Bit to have to do without my help, and I don't want to miss out on being involved. I feel…a lot of worry about that."

When I look up from the fork I've been playing with, I see a sheen in her eyes.

Her voice is husky when she speaks. "This is scary for me too. I really like the way…you've been. I appreciate you helping, and I don't want to cut you out. I just…worry because I've seen so many relationships…go bad. I feel like I have to be extra careful about who I trust, and how much, because now I've got somebody else depending on me for their safety."

It's fear that's keeping her behind that wall. Not a lack of feeling. Fear.

My heart squeezes for her. "I'd never do anything to hurt either one of you, Andi. I promise. No matter what we... It's my job to be here. To help. To protect you from bad stuff, not *be* the bad stuff."

Her gaze roams my face. She looks deep in my eyes for a long minute, then back down at her salad. "I want to believe you mean that, Kev. You've given me no reason not to. My doubt is coming from inside me, and I haven't figured out what to do about that."

Okay, she needs more time to be sure of me. I can give her that. "Then I'll just...be here. Trying to help any way I can. Until you see you can trust me."

She pokes around in the greens with her fork before setting it on the table and looking up at me. Nods just a little, a tiny smile at one corner of her mouth. "It's been good having you around so far."

Sounds like faint praise, but it's still an admission. A positive.

I wouldn't have expected her to be quite so fearful with *me*— I've never been cause for anyone's fear, as far as I know—but maybe it's a mama-bear thing.

I'll keep doing what I'm doing. Sooner or later she'll see she can count on me. I am *not* going to let her down or screw this up.

Andi

It's November. Lil Bit and I have made it safely through the first trimester together.

I pop the pepperjack-topped buns in the oven, give the coleslaw another stir, and turn down the music so I'll be able to hear July's car pull up. God knows I need some advice. And she's the only person besides me who knows both the story of my family *and* the story of how Lil Bit came to be. So I chose an evening I knew Joe would be in class and I invited July over for dinner.

Driveway gravel pops under tires and I go to the door. Make sure it's her, scan the county road to make sure no one has followed, and open the door as she steps onto the porch.

"Hey, you! Long time no see." She grabs me in one of her wonderful bone-crunching hugs before following me inside. "Something smells great."

"I've been wanting barbecue." I reactivate the security system and lead her into the kitchen. "You want your slaw on the sandwich or on the side?"

"Mmm. Pile it right on top there."

I layer pulled pork and coleslaw onto the toasted buns while July pours us fresh lemonade.

It's a little chilly tonight so we eat inside and catch up on our news and restaurant gossip. Most of her employees came to her via the shelter so I know pretty much everybody. Once we've finished our meal, though, I hand her a blanket and we move outside to the lounge chairs on the patio. I touch a match to the kindling I'd arranged in the firepit earlier. We wrap ourselves like burritos and settle back to watch the flames.

I'd fall right to sleep right here if it weren't for the stress of the impending conversation.

"What's up? You got something going on?" July's blond hair is caramel in the firelight.

Deep inhale, then I nod. "Yup. Need your take on something."

"Okay."

That's July, always calm, always accepting. Always ready to help.

I focus on her face. "Turns out you're going to be an aunt. Again." Her little sister had a baby not too long ago.

July's gray eyes widen to comic proportions and I actually laugh.

"No shit?"

"No shit. Apparently, our protection failed back in August."

She does the math, eyes still huge. "What, so you're…almost three months along already?"

"Yup."

"How'd Kevin take it?"

I wince. I knew this part would take some explaining. She knows my history, but July's in a forever relationship with the love of her life, and she had a happy, healthy two-parent family growing up, so… "He seems really happy about it. And he's been great so far. The problem is me."

"How are you a problem?"

"July, I can't read my instincts about him."

She squints. "You mean you don't know how you feel about him?"

"Well, kinda. I mean, that's part of it. I was trying to figure out how I felt about that, and then I found out I'm pregnant."

"Walk me through this slowly. I feel like I need some catching up." She settles back in her seat, hitching her blanket a little higher around her neck.

"That weekend of the pool party at Rose and Angus's was our first weekend really hanging out. As friends."

At her raised brows, I clarify. "Since the hookup." I snuggle deeper into my own blanket. "It was really great. He seems so great… I left for my conference in Asheville thinking if we were still friends in a couple more weeks, I'd maybe start thinking about whether it might be okay to date him after all."

She listens intently, without judgment, and nods her encouragement.

"But I felt lousy in Asheville, so I saw a doctor when I got home, and…" I wave my arm to indicate everything since.

She turns her face to the flames and nods again. "Well. I can see how that would confuse things. How are you feeling about that idea now?"

"So conflicted. One minute I feel like he's great and I'm an idiot for not trusting him totally. The next minute I hear Gram's voice screaming at me that I'm an idiot for even *considering* trusting him totally. And then the minute after that I feel like he's not interested in being more than friends with me anymore anyway, so it's a moot point."

"Have you asked him how he feels? Whether he's interested in more?"

Of course July's mind would seize on the most straightforward approach.

"It's more complicated than that. With a baby in the picture, how do I know it's safe to ask that? I mean, I was *just* starting to get comfortable with us hanging out as friends, with the idea that *maybe* it might turn into a little something more someday in the future. I mean, that's a pretty big shift for me, the idea of being in any kind of relationship with a man. But no sooner had that thought crossed my mind as a distant, far-future possibility than *bam!*—baby. And then he proposed, and then—"

July drops her blanket and waves both arms at me. "Whoa, hold, ho—*what*? He *proposed*?"

"Yeah, just out of the blue! Totally freaked me out. And I reacted pretty harshly and I think I hurt his feelings. But he said no worries, forget he mentioned it, and he's been...pretty great ever since."

July's squinting at me, massaging her forehead. "So...okay... What're you wanting me to weigh in on tonight?"

And here it is. "I really like what I know of him, okay? What I've seen so far of him with kids—of him with everybody—says he's a good guy and would probably be a good dad. But July, I haven't known him that long or that well. He could just be in that first good-behavior period where he's, you know, love-bombing me, and the real Kevin won't make an appearance until later."

She tugs the blanket back around her. "Have you seen any sign of a Real Kevin that's different from the guy you know?"

I shake my head. "Not yet. Which makes it almost worse, because he actually seems happy about this baby. And he's being so sweet, finding ways to help, things he can do to help me get ready... And if he's really that guy, we're all missing out by me holding him at arm's length."

"And you're still doing that now because...?"

"Because for Gram and for my mom both, their husbands got more violent starting with a pregnancy." My hand has crept over my belly without me realizing it until I see July's gaze land there. "It's not just me in danger if I'm wrong about him."

"Ohhh. I get it. You're kinda between a rock and a hard place."

I nod. That about sums it up. "Yup. Don't trust him and risk cheating the three of us of what could be a really amazing experience together...or trust him more than he deserves and risk endangering Lil Bit and me."

July blows out a big puff of air as she turns back to study the flames in the firepit. "Bummer." But her brow crinkles again as she twists to face me more fully. "But you're still spending time with him?"

"Yeah, we have dinner almost every night. And most days I go run at the track."

"So y'all aren't really missing out on the whole experience, right?"

"No, I guess not. I just have this feeling that there could be so much more...if only I were sure of him."

She snorts and turns back to the flames. "Sounds like how Jen felt when she was pregnant."

Jen is July's little sister, the one who recently had a baby. "But she's married."

July glances over at me, then back to the fire. "There's more than one way not to be there for somebody."

I mull that over and am just wondering whether to ask more, when July sits bolt upright and says, "I've got an idea. I'll invite people over. You bring Kevin and we'll help you watch for signs of anything sketchy. We could *even*...give him a test."

"What?" Not sure I like the sound of that. Doesn't sound exactly fair to Kevin.

She waves away my frown. "Nothing weird. Maybe just a little light flirting. Joe'll help. Or even better—you know what they say about not judging a man by how he acts when you tell him yes, but by how he reacts when you tell him no? We can find some way for you to tell him no, and see how he handles it. We'll all be there to help you if he flunks the test."

I frown into the fire, considering it.

It's a terrible, brilliant, excruciating, just-might-work idea.

CHAPTER 21

Kevin

I LIKED THESE PEOPLE THE first time I met them. Must've been out of my mind. I'm not sure they're not trying to kill me tonight.

I'd been excited to see them again when Andi told me July and Joe had invited us over for dinner. She didn't want to ride together though, so I followed the directions she'd sent me to Joe's place just a few blocks from the restaurant. Knocked on the door and Joe let me in, leading me through the empty downstairs space and up to his second-floor apartment.

"Andi texted that she's running a little late. But you know everybody here, so." He waved me down the hall to an open area, sofa to the left, dining table and kitchen to the right.

"Hey, Kevin! Good to see you." July looked up from chopping something at the counter.

"Nice to be here." I moved toward her. "Can I help with anyth—"

Before I could finish the words, Angus stepped back into me

with his hands full of something he'd just pulled down from a high cabinet over the fridge. Caught me hard in the jaw with his elbow, knocking me off-balance. I took a step sideways…and there was Rose, holding a glass of red wine, which sloshed all down the front of me. Nipples to crotch. A crimson tide across my best sweater and the khakis I'd actually ironed, trying to make a good impression.

"Angus, ya big silly!" Rose burst out. "Careful! You'll hurt him!" She gripped my arm. "I'm so sorry! Are you okay? I swear, that man forgets how much bigger and stronger he is than every-body else."

What? I met Angus's eyes over her head. He's only got a couple of inches on me. I'm the second biggest person here, not some frail little kid.

"Sorry, dude. You okay?" His voice was gruff.

"I'm fine. No worries."

July passed me a towel. "That can't be comfortable. And it's gonna stain. We should get some club soda on that. You got anything else to wear?"

"Yeah, in the car, if you don't mind me wearing gym clothes."

I went back out to my car for my gym bag, changed in the bathroom, and doused the stains with the bottle of club soda Joe handed me. Draped my good clothes over the shower door until after dinner.

July commandeered me as soon as I stepped out of the bath-room. "Hey, I want to show you something. It's a drink Andi loves when we go out together, and I've figured out how to make a mocktail version. Thought you should know how to make it for her."

I was cool with that, for the first twenty minutes. But that damn drink had at least forty-five ingredients and a hundred and twelve steps, most of them unnecessary as far as I could tell, and July was the pickiest darn taskmaster I've ever had breathing down my neck. Seriously, is there even such a thing as "cutting a lemon against the grain"? And why would that be such a huge no-no? She made me redo it three times, insisting, "Pay attention, Kevin. This is important!"

I thought surely she had to be joking—I sure wanted to laugh—but she never cracked a smile so I didn't roll my eyes or talk back or offer any response except a meek, "Yes, ma'am."

Joe and Andi were just entering the room as I finally managed to put the garnish on to July's satisfaction.

"You look great. As always." Joe was close beside Andi, his fingers curving around her shoulder.

What? He unhanded her as they got to me, but damn, that contact lasted longer than any she and I have had since our hookup.

He was right, though. She's gorgeous, even in a boxy shirt that hides her shape. She always has that glow and that fire in her eyes that draws me right to its flame.

"Hi." She gave me a smile—no touch—as we stood a little apart from the others.

"Got a surprise for you." I held out the drink with a careful flourish. Don't need any more beverage-clothing mishaps. "July taught me to make your favorite drink as a mocktail."

"Oh." Andi took a big step back, hand on her tummy. "I... don't think I'd better. Grapefruit juice hasn't been agreeing with me lately."

"Bummer," said July, suddenly beside me. "Oh well. I'll drink it." She lifted it from my hand and swept away with it.

I watched her go, wishing I'd at least taken a sip so I'd know what Andi's favorite drink tastes like.

I was just about to ask Andi how her day had been when Rose whistled.

"Whoa, Kevin, nice legs!"

So much for a good impression. Because yep, I was standing there, useless, drinkless, pants-leg-less, the only one in wrinkled gym clothes while the rest of them wore nice slacks and shirts or sweaters.

"Rose, don't embarrass him." Andi shot me a soft, amused smile.

"Hey, I love me a himbo." Rose actually winked.

So here I am, looking sloppy, hoping the red wine on my underwear isn't going to soak through and make itself visible on my thin gym shorts. I'm surrounded by well-dressed near strangers, one of whom elbowed me in the face, another of whom had his hands on my woman—okay, that's untrue and inappropriate of me—while my ruined clothes decorate the bathroom and someone else calls me stupid.

"What's a himbo?" July straightens as she closes the oven, looking from me to Rose.

Rose's expression falters a little. "It's...a big, good-looking guy..."

"Who's not real bright," I finish for her.

"Rose!" July says, just as Rose mutters, "I didn't mean that, exactly..." and Andi nudges me with her elbow, saying, "How did you know that?"

I rub my sore jaw. Shrug. "Got caught in the middle of one too many debates between my mom and my sisters about romance novels." No big deal. It's not like other people haven't assumed

I'm an airhead jock before. I just…really didn't want *these* people to think it.

This night isn't shaping up to be as fun as I'd hoped.

We stand around making conversation for a few minutes, and I try to be unobtrusive about checking my shorts for soakage. Finally Joe says, "Okay, these are about done. Everybody fix your plates."

I'm at the back of the line behind Andi, so I lean forward, try to breathe in her scent without being creepy, and say softly in her ear, "How you doing? You have a good day?"

She turns her head enough to brush my nose with her soft cheek and it's all I can do not to press a kiss there. "I'm good. It was pretty smooth." She blinks up at me, her dark eyes warm. "How about you?"

"I'm good now."

We fill our plates with salad and some kind of heavenly-smelling cheesy potato dish and some spicy beans I can add to my new-to-me list, and then everybody shuffles past Joe, who serves up the juiciest, most mouthwatering-looking pork chops I have ever seen in my life. Between Andi a breath away and that glorious meat, the night is definitely looking up. I watch Rose go by with her loaded plate, and then Angus, and then July, and then he's placing the plumpest cut of all on Andi's plate with a soft smile and a wink.

What is it with these folks and winking?

And then it's my turn and he serves me a wizened little shoe sole of a chop that looks like it might have been left on the grill from last week. "These, uh, smell great," I say, and try not to cry.

Is it possible Joe's got a thing for Andi? And he thinks Andi and I are dating? I mean, I can't blame him, she's amazing, but it would totally suck for July, who's clearly in love with him.

Maybe also for me, because I have no idea how Andi feels about him.

On the other hand, I'm pretty sure Andi would be pissed at anybody who did July wrong.

Joe slides around me, the last big, juicy pork chop on his own plate, to sit at the table with July. And somehow I'm not at all surprised when it turns out there's only seating for five: three on the couch and two at the dining table. Who only has two chairs at a dining table that could seat six?

I try not to hear my mom and grandma's voices expressing horror at this situation. Maybe manners are different in North Carolina. Maybe they've been a group of five for so long they just forgot to allow for another person. Or...maybe they're sending me a pointed message that I'm not really welcome— that they don't think I'm good enough to be hanging around Andi.

I'm not sure I can argue with that.

I try not to think about it as I settle on the floor beside her end of the couch. I stay quiet. Listen to the conversation around me as I eat. I'm actually able to get a few bites of meat from my chop, and the flavor is excellent, as is the rest of the meal.

And after she gives that little sigh I know means she's full, Andi lays her fork across her plate and scratches her fingers through the hair at the back of my head, her voice husky as she says so low only I can hear, "You're being an awful good sport."

Whatever that means.

Then her eyes crinkle with a smile just for me, and the rest of the night doesn't matter at all.

Andi

The group chat, which July creatively named Stress Test, is blowing up by the time I get home.

> **July:** Well what'd y'all think?
> **Joe:** ...
> **Angus:** ...
> **Rose:** That poor sweet man
> **Angus:** Thought he was gonna cry when you handed him that hockey puck, Toothpick
> **Joe:** Bout killed me too
> **July:** I knew it would! You've never served such a bad piece of meat in your life
> **Rose:** [snort]
> **July:** Rose!
> **Joe:** Oh like it didn't kill your Hospitality Queen soul to see him sit on the floor while you were in a chair, July
> **Joe:** And you, Rosie... First you drown him in wine then you treat him like a little baby, then you call him stupid—daaaaaaaaamn! Brutal.
> **July:** She understood the assignment for sure
> **Rose:** I was awful
> **Rose:** Please tell me we can tell him the truth soon so I can apologize
> **Rose:** and maybe buy him some new clothes if those stains don't come out
> **Angus:** Now y'all have done it—Rosie's crying
> **Andi:** Are you freaks sitting there side by side talking to each other by TEXT

July: ...

Joe: ...

Angus: ...

Rose: ...

Rose: well not like all FOUR of us. I'm with Angus and July is with Joe

Angus: I can't believe he didn't go down when I hit him. Clipped him a lot harder than I intended

July: Dude's got excellent balance

Rose: Sturdy—almost as sturdy as Angus

Andi: He did good, right? No red flags?

Joe: ...

Angus: ...

Rose: ...

July: ...

Andi: I thought he did good. He was really sweet to me, I thought

Rose: I thought so too Andi

July: Me too

Joe: I didn't see any red flags

Angus: Me either. He did good, Andi

Andi: ...

Andi: ...

July: Andi, you there?

Joe: You okay?

Rose: You're crying too, aren't you

Andi: shut up—just hormones

Angus: congratulations btw

Joe: yeah

July: love you, girl

And then I *am* crying. For that big, sweet man. And for me. And for our baby.

The phone rings a second later. It's July and Joe. They've got me on speaker.

July goes first. "How you doing, really?"

"Good." I dab my nose with a tissue from my nightstand, hoping they won't hear me sniffling.

"Does this ease your mind any?"

Pretty much, but I have to make sure their instincts match mine. "Joe, you didn't see anything concerning?"

"Naw, Andi, there is nothing about that guy that in any way reminds me of my dad." His voice is gentle. "He didn't get tense or red-faced or grim... Didn't get nasty—or seem like he *wanted* to get nasty—with anybody. Didn't seem to blame any of our assholery on you."

I feel again Kevin putting his arms around me and burying his face in the curve of my neck in a long, sweet, totally unexpected good-night hug just before opening my car door for me. "He didn't seem to want to take anything out on me, either."

"His expression gets soft whenever he looks at you." July again.

I draw in a long breath. "I think maybe it's time for me to trust him a little further."

"Time to date him?" July's voice sounds almost hopeful.

"Not that—not just yet. But I think maybe I'll let him know where I live. See how he handles that information." Not going to leap too far too fast. I don't remember my own father, but he destroyed my family. The damage he did took me and Gram years of therapy to work through. Nobody wants that for their kid. I know better, so I have to do better.

"Oh, he hasn't even been to your house?"

"Nope." Baby steps. I am my Gram's cautious granddaughter. Cautious and sensible…most of the time.

CHAPTER 22

Kevin

ANDI'S GOT THE CUTEST HOUSE in the world. It's like a magical little witch's cottage.

I shouldn't have hugged her the other night. I can't stop thinking about how she felt in my arms, her arms coming around me to hold me tight too. If she's a witch, she's welcome to lure me right into her oven. She can do it sight unseen, even, using just words. Like last night, on our good-night call, when out of the blue she said all casual-like, her voice low and husky and inviting, "Hey, wanna come up to my place tomorrow afternoon? You can see what I have in mind for the baby's room."

We'd just been talking about the month-four chapter in our baby book, and a couple of kids I've been working with at the shelter, and a student I'm concerned about at school. Andi's every bit as interested in it all as I am. She's a wonderful listener. Asks great questions that help me see answers more easily.

I could swear I'm not boring her any more than she bores me, which is never. Not once. Not in any way.

So I jump at the invitation. All casual-like too, of course. Riiight.

She doesn't even really live in town. She's a few miles up in the hills along a twisty, woodsy roller coaster of a road. Her mailbox doesn't have a name, only a number, and it's made of stone to match the cottage. No baseball-bat-wielding hooligans are going to damage that sturdy little sucker.

I pull into the gravel driveway and turn off the ignition, looking my fill. She must park in the garage; her car's nowhere in sight. The modest front yard is probably shady in summer, but now the leaves blow in gold and orange eddies beneath bare branches. The house is low, built of river rock, and looks like it's been here forever. Only three windows across the front, one to the left of the blue front door and two to the right, all of them multipane with blue trim, none of them big.

I wonder if it's dark and mysterious in there. Whether I'll have to stoop to avoid bunches of dried herbs hanging from low ceiling beams.

Thick clouds were gathering on my drive up here and the first raindrop spatters my windshield as the front door opens. Andi crosses her arms, leaning against the doorframe, and smiles at me. Warms me up from twenty feet away. I am out of the car and up that walk before the next drop hits.

This feels momentous to me. Andi hadn't *said*, "Hey, I finally trust you enough to let you in," but that's how this feels.

I reach for her as I step over the threshold and the rain starts in earnest behind me. Andi laughs and pulls me inside far enough that she can shut the door, and then my arms are around her. I mean to only allow myself one brief hug, but then she's holding me too and I can't make myself let go. Can't not bury my nose in her soft fragrant hair, and then in the warm spicy curve of her neck...

But something starts beeping behind me and Andi says, "Dammit! Hold that thought!" and grips my hoodie with one hand while with the other she punches in a code on a wall security panel. She comes back into my arms, snuggling against me, and I allow myself the absolute joy of holding her just to be holding her again. I know I should let go, step back, but I can't.

And she burrows into my arms, her own tight around me, her nose in my collarbone, and gives a little sigh. "God, I love your hugs."

And how can I help but fall for this woman? This kind, affectionate, brilliant, warm, beautiful woman who makes me feel so good with every word and touch and smile. How could I not love her?

I can't not fall.

But I can't let myself get in too deep too fast. That's exactly the mistake I've made over and over in my past. Andi is too important to me to take the chance of messing it up like that.

Even without a baby in the picture, I wouldn't be able to stand messing up with her.

So I take hold of her arms and lean back. Smile down into her eyes and say, "Give me the tour."

We're in a little entry area, a bench and coat hooks to the left beside a door that must lead into the garage. The living area is one mostly open space, with the kitchen part a few steps from where we're standing and a dining table beside that, before a rain-flecked sliding door to what looks like a patio at the back of the house. To our right is a love seat and two chairs in front of a stone fireplace flanked by built-in bookshelves. Contrary to what I expected, the space isn't dark and the ceiling's not low. Not a cathedral ceiling, for sure, but it does taper up to a peak. The colors are light and mellow, there's the scent of something delicious wafting from the kitchen, and the whole effect is as warm and welcoming as Andi herself.

It feels like home.

Unlike my apartment, which only feels like that when she's there with me.

Speaking of home... "Hey, there's something I want to ask you," I say as she leads me across the living area to the far corner of the room where three doors open from a tiny hallway.

"Yeah? What's that?" She doesn't let me answer though. She points to the doorway on the left. "My room." She nudges the middle door with her elbow. "Bathroom." Then she turns me to the right-hand doorway. "This will be Lil Bit's room. Used to be mine."

It's small, but there's plenty of space for a crib and changing table and dresser and maybe a rocker. And when Lil Bit gets older, to swap out the baby furniture for a twin bed and desk. Maybe one of those lofted twin-desk combos, to make room for a friend to sleep over.

I can imagine building shelves in here for my kid. Building Lego castles in the middle of this floor. Putting together bright, massive puzzles at the dining room table.

Standing hand in hand with Andi in the quiet of the night, watching our child sleep...

She's beside me now, leaning in, bumping me with her shoulder, her hip soft against mine. "What was your question?"

"Oh. Uh." I clear my throat and shove the dream images from my mind before I tear up like I'm the one with pregnancy hormones. "My mom wants me to bring you to Lincoln for Thanksgiving." I hold my breath, hoping this won't freak her out. I couldn't think of a better way to bring it up.

"Your... Why...? What does your mom even know of me?" She searches my face. Anxious, I think.

"Listen, it's no big deal. Whatever you want to do. No pressure, okay?" I take both her hands and squeeze them to reassure her. "My niece got it in her head that I've got a girlfriend. I tried to straighten her out. Anyway, she ran and told my whole family, and they all halfway think so too now."

"Halfway?" Her dark eyes are boring deep, deep into my brain.

"I told my mom—everybody who mentioned it, really—that that's not the case, that I don't want to jump too fast into another relationship. I think Mom even kind of approves."

She frowns. Wiggles her jaw side to side. "So...what does she think I am to you, exactly?"

I shrug and go with the truth, without even knowing how she'll feel about it. "My best friend here. I told her you're my best friend."

Andi

My best friend.

My first thought is, *But you're a man!*

My second thought is, *Wow, Andi, really?*

And then it sinks in deep, like a firm, heavy press to my gut and my heart. I am his best friend, at least here.

I've been weighted down with indecision and worry, all jumbled up with the wonder and pleasure of pregnancy, and he's been experiencing our relationship in a totally different way. His own unique and valid way. As a close friendship.

And…he's absolutely right. All these hours we've spent together, running or talking or making food or eating or reading the books he bought us, asking each other questions about favorite childhood games, best teacher ever, saddest song lyric… all those hours were not just passing time. Not just Exceptionally Cautious Andi Trying to Belatedly Vet This Person With Whom She's Created a Baby. We've been *building* something.

Kevin's not just somebody I want desperately to sleep with again, or somebody with whom I have to balance attraction with fear and suspicion. He's somebody I would call for help if my car broke down and I was stranded by the side of the road. Somebody I look forward to seeing, whether we've planned a dinner date or errands or just a quick run. Somebody whose stories and thoughts I like and want to hear more of.

Kevin's become one of my close friends too.

I'm not sure how to reconcile that with my fears. How is it that I trust him implicitly in so many ways…but can't seem to manage it at all in others?

He stirs beside me, like he's been deep in thought too, and waves his arm at the room. "How do you want the nursery to be?"

I force my brain to switch gears. "Well, obviously I have to figure out what to do with that stuff." Five boxes stacked in the far corner, some with Gram's things I couldn't make myself part with, others with stuff of mine she'd saved from when I was growing up. "There might even be something in there I could use in here, but…I don't know."

"Don't try to move it, okay? I can carry it to the garage for you, or wherever else you want it."

There he goes being thoughtful again. "Okay." I move to stand near the boxes. "I'd like some kind of rocker or comfy chair here, for nursing."

His face softens instantly, so that it's all I can do not to cry.

I clear my throat. "Crib on that wall nearest the bathroom. Changing table just inside the door. And maybe a little bookshelf under each window."

He nods. "Sounds perfect."

"I was looking at furniture online… Haven't decided on any yet, but if you like, I'll show them to you later." I do love the way he listens to and looks at me, the slightest thinking furrow on his brow.

His smile when my words sink in. "I'd like that."

I have to blink away to keep from walking right back into his arms, welcome or not. "So, um, I don't much care for blue or pink. I like the idea of a nice sunny yellow. Not too bright."

"Nice. You remember I'm doing the painting, right? Don't want you breathing fumes or climbing ladders."

I laugh. "Dude, I'm the one who used to do all the manual labor around here. Haul paving stones, demo walls, paint, hammer… you name it. If you want to baby me, knock yourself out."

His grin is sheepish. Cute, even, with that damn dimple winking at me. "I know you're plenty capable. And strong. I just want to…do something to help. Take care of you and the baby."

"I appreciate that." Not sure what to make of the peculiar sensations it causes in my gut, warm and cold twisting through me though.

"Can I do the painting today? Won't take but a minute for me to move those boxes. Do we need to run out for paint and supplies?"

"Nope. Already got it."

He starts to frown, maybe even to gripe at me, and somehow it's not at all alarming. Huh.

I hold up one hand. "Calm down, big boy. The home store people loaded it into my trunk for me and it's all still there."

His brow clears and as I head past him to the door, he wraps his arms around me and pulls me in for another one of those delicious-yet-not-nearly-enough hugs.

"Smart lady," he murmurs into my hair. "Smart, pretty lady." And then, as I knew he would, he lets go and steps back.

I sigh. "I'm cooking. You want to eat first or work first?"

"Let me get a good start on the painting before I take a break." He pulls his hoodie over his head, flashing me a mouthwatering glimpse of his midsection before his T-shirt settles back down around his waistband, and then pauses in the act of hanging it on the doorknob. "Or wait, do you need to eat now? We can do it whenever you need to."

The man just will not *not* be nice. "Nope, I nibbled while I was prepping the ingredients." I take his sweatshirt and resist the urge to bury my face in it to inhale his scent.

It takes him all of three minutes to carry the storage boxes to the garage and the painting stuff to the nursery, and then he sets to work in there. I crank up a playlist I've made of songs he's mentioned he likes. "Nice!" he calls from the other room.

I put the finishing touches on the soup and whip up a batch of cheese sticks using the top secret recipe Gram and I developed when I was a freshman in high school. Then I make batter for the brownies he liked so much when I took them to July's, and I get those in the oven.

"You're trying to kill me, aren't you?" Kevin hollers from the nursery when the chocolate scent starts to waft from the oven.

"Maybe. But not till your work is done." I grin the rest of the way through the laundry load I'm folding, remembering him calling my brownie-eating friends *buzzards*.

This is an amazing way to spend a day, with the sound of rain outside, us safe and warm and snug inside with good music and a good meal to come. Having somebody to share and appreciate these things with.

Sorry, Gram, but I can almost imagine myself getting used to this.

The brownies are cooling and I've put away the laundry and baked the cheese sticks a second time—that's the secret to getting them crispy enough—when Kevin finally steps out of the little bedroom, a big wad of blue painter's tape in his hands.

"All done. Come see." He's speckled with white and yellow and smiling from ear to ear.

The fumes aren't bad at all because I'd bought water-based paint. Semigloss, for ease of cleaning. He scoops up the drop cloth and waves me in first, stepping in behind me.

It's lovely. He's done a lovely job, from the gleaming white ceiling and woodwork to the sunny walls. What a fresh, cheery place for Lil Bit to come home to. My eyes have welled up so that it's hard to see. "Kev...let me get a paper towel. There's a couple of smudges... Wait... Are those...*Peeps*?" The horizontal window trim boards, upper and lower, have yellow blotches on them.

I move in to look more closely. Behind me, Kevin makes a sound of exasperation.

"Peeps? Dang, Andi..." But then he leans over my shoulder to see too and starts laughing. "Well, okay. I can see why you might think so."

He has somehow, with one of those clunky paintbrushes, painted little blobby ducklings on the trim.

Little blobby ducklings for the baby I've worried he might hurt.

"They're wonderful," I say on a sob—fuck me, these hormones are going to be the death of me—and fling myself into his arms.

CHAPTER 23

Kevin

THERE ARE WORSE THINGS THAT can happen to a man than have this lovely woman fling herself at him.

I wrap my arms around her and smile into her hair, breathing her in, savoring the feel of her warm full curves against me, fighting the weird urge to both laugh and sob right along with her. What is this feeling? She's just... She's...*appreciating* me. I feel *appreciated*.

I've made her happy.

Me.

Vanilla Kev.

Before I can puzzle that out, she's letting go. Stepping back, leaving my arms empty. Wiping away tears and saying, "How did you make the little eyes? And the beaks?"

"Sharpie. There was one in your trunk with the paint stuff." *I stole office supplies from your trunk* is kind of an embarrassing admission, but she just nods.

"They're adorable, Kevin. Thank you. I love them." She takes my hand and tugs me to the door. "Wash up. Dinner's ready when you are."

And criminy, dinner is spectacular. Autumn Soup, she calls it, hearty and amazing-smelling, with beef and corn and tomatoes and red wine and I forget what else she listed. It disappears from my bowl too fast for me to inventory. And the crispy cheese sticks she serves on the side? I've never had anything so addictive. I think I probably wolf down half of what she baked. And then more of those brownies we'd all nearly come to blows over at the pool party.

"You have made me a happy, happy man," I tell her, finally coming up for air and patting my full belly. "Two new items to go at the top of my Likes list."

She laughs. "Just two?"

"Your brownies were already on there."

She pushes aside her soup bowl and leans her elbows on the table, chin in her hands. "I tried to think of what you might like. I'm glad I guessed right. Tell me more about this list."

Well, hell. I had to go and bring it up, didn't I? I sigh out a breath. "It's...something I started in January."

Andi just watches me, eyes bright. Expectant.

I push on. "After Cheryl and I broke up." I wipe my fingers on my napkin and take my time placing it on the table. "She'd said something that got to me. And I started thinking maybe I needed to...start a list. Not for her. For myself."

Andi doesn't move, but her voice is as soft as a touch. "What'd she say?"

I shrug, not quite meeting her eye. "She said, 'Don't you have any likes or dislikes or personality of your *own*, Kevin?'"

Andi's expression, when I get the guts to look at her, is

thunderous. "I don't think I like that woman," is all she says, through gritted teeth.

That's...surprisingly comforting. "Well. I hadn't...exactly ever insisted on...having things my way in the relationship. She probably...really didn't know what I liked and didn't like."

"And what, she didn't care enough to pay attention? That stinks, Kevin. I'm sorry she said that to you." She shoves away from the table, picks up our bowls—that only moments ago had contained food Andi *had* known me well enough to figure I'd like—and carries them to the kitchen. Huh. Okay. She's got a point.

I follow with the other dishes, still eager to change the subject. "You going to show me the furniture you were looking at, after we clean this up?"

"Yeah! I was torn between a couple of different styles. Wanna hear your thoughts on it?"

Don't know whether she's consciously stating her belief that I do have my own valid opinions, but her words warm me.

We do the dishes, put away leftovers—after I grab two more cheese sticks and another brownie, god help me—and wipe up all our crumbs and smears. Andi goes around closing her blinds and switching on lights and then we settle back at the table with her laptop.

One of her favorite baby bedroom sets has all straight edges. One has curves. "And I also have to decide what color to go with. White? Natural wood? Some other color? Now that I've seen how cute the room looks the way you painted it, I'm wondering—"

And before she can finish her thought, all the lights go out and the music cuts off. We're in darkness except for the laptop screen and a faint glow from the security panel by the door.

Andi reaches for her phone. "I didn't hear it storming, did you?" Outside there's only an intermittent smattering of rain now, no wind or thunder.

I shake my head. "Maybe somebody hit a pole."

"Sometimes it comes right back on. I'll wait a few minutes and then call the shelter. See if they've still got power in town."

We talk more about baby furniture and then she calls work.

I can tell from her side of the conversation that their power's still on.

"Okay, great. Holler if y'all need to." She ends the call and looks at me, her face eerie in the glow from the laptop screen. "They're fine."

"I don't want to leave you up here with no power. Okay if I stick around for a little while? Or you could come spend the night at my place." Her eyes widen, brighten, and I hear a second too late how that sounds. "You can have my room. I'll take the couch."

She drops her gaze to her hands. "That's okay. Gram and I spent plenty of nights without power. I've got candles, and I can use the fireplace if it gets cold. You should probably head out, though. Shelter staff is saying the roads are terrible."

"Is there flooding or something?"

She shrugs. "Don't know. Want me to call back and ask?"

"No, that's fine."

Her mood has shifted somehow and I think she wants me gone now.

I can't leave her though. "Let me stick around for a while, okay? I'll be quiet, stay out of your way."

She shakes her head. "No, really there's no need. I'll be fine."

"What if I sit out in my car for a while, in case you need help with something?"

Huh. First time I've ever seen her roll her eyes. "*Kevin. No. Get out of here. Go be grateful for your ability to watch TV or something.*"

I try a few more arguments, but then it's pretty obvious I'm starting to piss her off. I've stalled as long as I can. So I scoop my hoodie off the back of the little love seat and head reluctantly to the door, Andi trailing behind me, probably fighting the urge to give me a good hard shove.

She leans in the doorway watching as I reach the two wet steps down to the sidewalk. It's a lot colder out here than it was earlier, and I go to pull my hoodie over my head, twisting at the same time to say, "Or hey, I could—" and then my feet shoot out from under me and I land hard on the edge of the first step and then bounce/slide/spin right on down onto the sidewalk on my ass, my head landing in the wet grass. Which is not so much wet as...crackly?

"Oh my god, Kevin, are you okay?" Andi starts out toward me.

"*No!*" I've never spoken so sharply to anyone in my life. "Stop! It's not safe—It's solid ice out here." At least a quarter inch on the sidewalk, my worm's eye view tells me.

"Are you okay, though?" She does stop, thank heavens, and shivers in the cold night air, rubbing her arms. "You can't drive in this, Kev. Can you get up?"

I do, slowly, after maneuvering my feet into the grass. I feel about twenty years older, and I'm going to have some great bruises, but I manage to hobble back to the porch, my pride in tatters.

Andi holds out a hand to me. Nods at the thick coating of ice on every visible surface. "That must be why staff said the roads are bad. The temperature must've dropped by at least twenty degrees."

Now I feel silly for not paying more attention to the weather. Yeah, I'd seen the heavy clouds when I drove up. Heard the rain off and on over the music while I was painting. And I know how fast weather can turn nasty in Nebraska, but shoot, this is North Carolina!

Andi slides her arm around me and we step back into the house, me doing my best not to limp. She leads me through the dark room to the love seat. "I'm going to get you a couple of ice packs. You can shower with whatever warm water's left before bed."

Oh, hell.

I got a glimpse of that bed—that little double bed—when she gave me the tour. No room for impenetrable pillow walls there. And any virtue I have is already teetering on the edge of a cliff with this woman that close.

I call after her as she locks up and heads to the refrigerator. "Does this love seat fold out into a bed?"

"No." She's back in a flash with her hands full. Two ice packs, which she wraps in plastic bags and then in kitchen towels before handing them to me.

No graceful way to do this, but it's dark anyway. I raise up, put one pack on the seat, and gingerly lower my butt onto it, tucking the other pack between my lower back and the love seat cushion, barely keeping from groaning. "Do you have a sleeping bag? Or does one of these chairs recline?"

"Nope." She's moving around at the fireplace now, fiddling with a lever for the flue, then striking a match and touching it to the paper and kindling. Smart lady had a fire already laid. It crackles to life now, the flames gilding Andi's beautiful profile.

I could gaze at her all night in firelight, if she'd hold still. But she's up moving around, using her phone flashlight to collect candles, lighting them and placing them on the end tables and the dining table and in the bathroom.

Because what this situation and my virtue needed was an even more romantic setting.

She's back in a minute with her arms full of pillows. "Here, help me tuck these around you to make you as comfortable as you can be till we go to bed. At least till you're done with the ice, okay?"

I take gentle hold of her wrist and she freezes. "You keep saying that, Andi, but I can't spend the night with you here." My voice cracks on the last words. Does the woman think I'm made of stone?

She gazes back at me, her eyes dark and fathomless in the flickering light of the fire. "Now you're just being insulting. I'm not going to force you to do anything you don't want to do. I don't know whether it's just me or pregnant women in general you're not attracted to, but I get it. No need to rub it in."

Oh my lord in heaven. Is she daft?

And is that—Does she look *wounded*?

I give her wrist a tug and she lands on my lap, pillows and all. My ice-bagged butt isn't pleased, but every other part of me is. And I've got more important concerns than my butt right now. I wrap my arms around her and tip back my head to see her face. "Is that what you think?"

She narrows her eyes. "You've made it pretty clear. I mean, sometimes I wish you felt different, but I'm not gonna seduce somebody who's uninterested. I'm the one who said no first anyway, so it's ridiculous of me to want more now."

"Andi." I cup her cheek.

She's pressing her lips together, avoiding my gaze.

"Andi, look at me, please?"

She raises her chin and looks me in the eye, and I pour every ounce of truth in me into my words. "Andi, I have wanted you every second of every day since the first minute I laid eyes on you." *Starting when you were up onstage in that impossibly sexy red fringe.* "You make my mouth water and my eyes sweat and all my other parts twitch. Yeah, I was disappointed when you didn't want to get together that way again after our hookup. I respect that though. And it thrills me to think you might change your mind at some point. But my current problem is, I want you *too* much. Too fast. I'm trying not to mess up with you the way I've always done in relationships. I'm trying to give us a good foundation."

Her expression softens but she stays quiet, so I keep talking. "I know I scared you with my dumbass out-of-the-blue proposal. I'm sorry. That was ridiculous and I know it. But I really do care about you and I really don't want to screw this up. I'm trying so hard to go slow. I've gotta be careful, because where my"—I wince—"dick goes, my heart goes."

"Oh. Whoa. I misread that." She tilts her head, searching my face, laughing a little sheepishly. "I could take good care of it. Of them. I'll take good care of both of them."

I bark out a laugh, but god help me, her words have me melting and twitching all over again.

"But...you're right. I'm trying to figure out my feelings too. Trying not to make a mistake. So if you're not comfortable having sex right now, that's okay." She tips her head and rolls her eyes again. "I mean, I can't promise not to think about it. A lot. But I won't push. You're safe with me. Best friends don't take advantage of each other."

She wraps one arm around my shoulders and hugs me, then climbs off my lap, fussing and tucking the pillows in around me. "So was your freak-out because of your extensive knowledge of romance tropes? What's this one called...forced proximity?"

I sigh. "Worse. Only one bed."

She laughs and the sound warms me up more than the cozy, crackling fire. "You know I'm telling July and Rose about this, right?"

This time I make my sigh extra theatrical, hoping she'll laugh again. "I would expect nothing else."

And when my efforts are rewarded with not just a laugh but also a fragrant hug, even my sore, frosty, ice-bagged butt is happy.

CHAPTER 24

Andi

THE BEDROOM IS MUCH COLDER than the living room, and after we blow out the candles, it's pitch-black. All my nonvision senses are tuned into him, though. The bulk of his body, pressing down half of the mattress I usually have to myself. The sound of his quiet sigh as he gets comfortable on the other side of the bed. The warm brush of his knee against mine when we roll to face each other as if we could see. The scent of my soap and my toothpaste on his skin and his breath.

He showered, but he did it quickly, insisting on leaving some warm water for me.

Having him here now, inches away, and not being able to touch him is killing me.

I hear a slide of skin over the cotton sheet and reach out with my own hand to meet his, here under these covers I've layered on the bed. His little sigh this time sounds like contentment.

"Thanks for getting me to stay." His voice is soft and rough.

"My pleasure." Kinda. Also kinda my torture.

No, really this *is* nice.

He tugs my hand up and presses warm lips to my fingers, and now I'm the one fighting a little sigh.

"I've been wondering what pregnancy's like for you." His words whisper over my knuckles.

If he's just acting, he deserves an award for "most convincing sweetness."

The darkness and intimacy call for hushed voices. Mine comes out almost a whisper too. "At first, before I knew...I guess there were little twinges of difference, but I didn't pay a lot of attention to them. Just thought, 'Oh, I'm tired' or 'That food didn't agree with me.'"

His hand is warm under my thumb. He doesn't pull it away.

"And then in Asheville when I couldn't ignore the twinges anymore, I got scared, thinking I might be seriously sick."

He squeezes my fingers.

"And then, in the doctor's office, when I got the test results..." I shake my head, remembering. "I was stunned, and relieved it wasn't a serious illness...and confused, and amazed. And kind of in denial. All at the same time."

"And now?"

"Now..." I think about how to explain it. "Now it's like...I've got company. I'm not alone anymore. But it's somebody I'm comfortable with. Somebody I don't have to explain things to, because they're living it with me. A constant little companion I look out for. It's...kinda nice." It surprises me to think it, much less say it out loud.

He kisses my knuckles one by one and then holds my hand against his heart over the worn T-shirt I've loaned him. The strong, slow thump of it is so comforting and lovely I have to fight the urge to press my other palm there too.

"Do you want them to tell you whether they think it's a boy or a girl?"

"I've thought about that. Not sure I want them to say. Would you want them to?"

He's silent for a long minute. "I can see pros and cons both ways. And I guess sometimes they're wrong, anyway." Pause. "Would you raise a boy differently than a girl?"

His question surprises me. *I've* thought about it, but I wouldn't have expected *him* to.

"Purposely? I don't think so. I mean, kids'll choose their own interests, right? And there's a lot of things I want my child to know and to be able to do, whatever their gender." I stop, holding my breath, not sure how he'll react.

I hear a soft rustling sound I think is him nodding. "Yeah. I think I'd want to instill pretty much the same stuff too."

"Such as?" Yes, this is a test question, but I'm genuinely eager to hear his thoughts.

"How to be kind. Responsible. Stand up for what's right. Work hard. Stuff like that."

Now I'm the one nodding. I could have made that list. "Yes! And...a love of reading."

I hear a smile in his voice when he says, "Yeah. I've always pictured reading to my kids."

I remember him doing math with the little boy on the patio at the shelter. The image morphs into him holding a toddler and a picture book on his lap, and I'm smiling too.

My heart is getting mushier and mushier. "Do you read to your nephews and nieces?"

"As much as they let me, yeah." His soft laughter so close in the dark makes this bed seem like our special, secret hideaway. "After a while they always drag me out into the middle of the floor to wrestle. They've always liked kicking my butt one way or another."

Damn it. I'm trying to stay objective here and evaluate the risks he poses, not swoon and sigh and melt into a useless sentimental puddle.

We're silent in our thoughts for a long moment and then, from out of the darkness, I hear him say so softly I have to lean in, "Do you ever feel scared to be having a baby?"

His words press every bruise from my past and my present. Every fear I've ever had.

"Yeah." I let the cracked syllable hang there in the air. "Every day." A silence falls between us then.

Finally I hear his other hand slide over the blankets toward me.

"Do you think"—his voice is scratchy—"you could sleep with my arms around you?"

I inch to the center of the bed. He does the same, and I settle into the comfort of his solid embrace with something that feels like relief. Or homecoming.

I wake up slowly. The light peeking in around the edges of the blinds tells me I've slept in. I'm toasty warm and comfy...except for my nose. My nose is oddly cold. So is the air I suck into it.

And then I remember, and suddenly I'm acutely aware of the hard forearm banded beneath my breasts. The firm biceps under my cheek. The delicious warm ridges and planes pressed all along the back side of me.

"Good morning." His husky whisper stirs my hair where it spreads wild over the pillow and his arm. He doesn't move away, and I'm sure not going to.

"Good morning." I keep my voice as soft as his. "You sore? Bruised?"

"Pretty sure I feel great."

Yeah he does. But I'm his damn best friend, so no commenting on that. No turning over to wrap my arms around him. No shifting to rub against him in any way that might call his attention to...all the things I feel like doing with him. Gotta just lie here and pretend I don't notice and appreciate his morning wood and the way he's holding me and the tantalizing nearness of his hand to my breast. If I shift just a little...but no. *Dammit.* Best friend. Best friend.

I have never been a saint, but I have never deserved the title more than at this moment.

"How 'bout you...? You sleep okay?" He does move now, but only enough to gather my wild hair in a bunch and smooth it over my shoulder. To take a handful and sift through it, rubbing it lazily between his fingertips. "So soft." His words seem more for himself than for me.

"Mmm." I keep still and revel in his heat and his touch, my eyes half-closed, drifting back toward the sleep of the impossibly comfortable. He presses his lips to the top of my head.

It's quite a while before we stir again, but eventually my bladder demands a pit stop.

"You getting up?" His sleep-rough voice raises goose bumps—the good kind—on my arms.

"Just for a sec. Be right back." I duck into the bathroom, brush my teeth while I'm in there, and then I crawl back into bed.

He opens his arms and welcomes me in, warming my feet between his own. "Tell me what little Andi was like," he murmurs into the side of my head.

I take my time settling back against him. Getting comfortable again. "Little Andi was…quiet. Serious." Anxious. Scared of loud noises and the dark. "Read a lot. Followed Gram around like her shadow."

"You were really close, huh?"

"Yeah. I thought she was the smartest person in the world." I notice different things now in my memories, now that I'm going to be a mother. "I used to ask questions *all the time*. She never got impatient. Never blew me off. If she didn't know an answer, she'd help me find it, or we'd try to figure it out together."

"She sounds great." He tightens his arms almost imperceptibly around me. "I'm glad you had somebody like that."

"Me too." The alternatives are unthinkable. "How about you…? What're your folks like?"

"They're…" He pauses as if he's not sure what to say next. "Good people. I think they've loosened up some over the years. The grandkids probably had something to do with that."

"Do you have pictures of your family?" Maybe I can pick up a vibe from them. Loving? Gentle? Tense? Powder kegs about to explode?

He twists to reach his phone on the nightstand, then pages through different screens till he finds what he's looking for. He presses it into my hands. "Here. That's my folks on their fortieth anniversary."

They're good-looking people. Both tall and blond like Kevin, and dressed in fancy-dinner-out clothing. They're surrounded by people but looking at each other, grinning, as if one has just reminded the other of an old joke. They're holding hands.

The only vibe I get from this picture is love. Well, and... comfort.

"They look lovely."

He reaches around me and swipes to the next photo. "This is me with my brother and sisters. Pete, Pam and Cathy." Swipe. "These are Pete's kids. This one's CeCe. She's a hoot." He points to a tall, thin girl wearing jeans and a GBR sweatshirt and an adorable smirk.

"GBR?"

"Nebraska thing. Go Big Red." Swipe. "This was her when she was newborn."

The photo knocks the air right out of my lungs. It's a baby, all right, looking pretty much like every other new baby—red and wrinkled and cranky—but it's the man holding her I can't take my eyes off of. Kevin, his jaw covered with blondish-brown stubble, looking as if he's been up all night, an expression of pure awe on his face as he gazes down at the tiny creature he's cradling so gently in his big, powerful hands.

"Ohhh!" I can't help it. I turn in his arms and press a kiss to his cheek before I settle back to look at the picture some more. It's every bit as holy as any Madonna-and-child image I've ever seen.

"Yeah, that was a pretty special moment." The huskiness is back in his voice. He tightens his arms around me in a brief, sweet hug.

Then he flips through more pictures, telling me way more names than I can remember...CeCe's younger brothers, his sisters' husbands and kids, including one that just started college this year. "She came out to the family on her birthday in June, right before I moved. Said all she wanted for her birthday was honesty and to know her family still loved her."

"Wow, gutsy." I squeeze his hand.

He nods against my temple. "I'm so proud of her. I mean, I think most of us already knew or suspected, but still... Conservative area, and a family that mostly doesn't talk about stuff like that? But Mom and Dad came through just fine. Dad reached over and hugged her and kissed her head. Mom handed her a big slice of cake and said, 'If anybody gives you any trouble, you send them to me.' And that was it."

Fucking hormones. I need two tissues from the nightstand to handle this story. "Your family sounds great, Kevin."

He holds me, seeming unfazed by all the mucus. "They really are. So keep that in mind as you decide whether to accept the Thanksgiving invitation, okay?"

The power comes back on a few minutes later. We climb out of bed. Kevin heads to the bathroom and I step into my fuzzy slippers and robe and out the French doors to the patio. The air is warmer than last night by a long shot. I stand by the low wall and enjoy the view of a hillside full of trees glistening in the sunlight as the ice melts and drips off of them.

Kevin whistles as he comes up behind me and looks over my shoulder at the dazzling vista. "Geez, Andi, this is something!" His hands settle on my flannel-clad shoulders and he looks his fill before he turns me to him and hugs me the way he did when he arrived yesterday. Melts my bones.

I ache for more but...smarter to wait.

We make a big breakfast together, teasing and laughing and feeding each other bites of omelet and ham and honeydew melon.

Afterward, we clean up our mess and determine that the roads are just wet now and it's safe for him to drive home.

I get another long, warm, lovely goodbye hug at the front door.

"I've gotta confess," he says as he finally lets go and steps out onto the porch, "I'm not sure this no-sex stuff is doing any good to keep me from falling for you."

And before I can formulate a response or drag him back inside to the bedroom, he's in his car, windshield wipers brushing away the fragments of ice still there, his tires crunching on the gravel as he backs out to the road and heads into town.

CHAPTER 25

Andi

"SALAZAR, I CAN'T BELIEVE YOU don't know which way a toilet paper roll is supposed to go."

I pause with plates and flatware in my hands. "Mahoney, I can't believe you think there's only one way. Or that you even care. What do you want to drink?"

It's a Tuesday evening and we have just spent an hour examining every inch of the cottage, making note of every electrical outlet, every long cord or breakable item, every corner or pointy, sharp thing, to get some idea of what needs to be done to baby-proof this place. Now Kevin's standing in the bathroom doorway, drying his hands on a guest towel and looking at me with an expression I can't completely place.

"Don't change the subject. This is upsetting to me, coming on the heels of you not liking marshmallows in your cocoa. And not being able to see constellations when I'm *right there* pointing them out to you." He ducks back into the bathroom and comes out without the towel. "Got any milk? If not, water's good. Wait,

I take that back. Water is absolutely *not* as good as milk, and don't even try to tell me it is. Every decent household—every household with sensible people in it—should be well stocked with milk at all times. If they can afford it. And aren't lactose intolerant." He joins me at the table and reaches into a paper bag to unload some of the goodies we've brought from Ahmed's hot bar for dinner. "And I'm not talking about that watery blue skim stuff. No self-respecting milk drinker wants to be able to see through their beverage. Give me the thick, creamy stuff or nothing."

I peel back the lid of the foil container of samosa chaat I've been craving all day. It smells heavenly. "What in the world has gotten into you?"

"These are important issues we should be on the same page about." He hops up from the table, goes into the kitchen, and comes back with three serving spoons. Dips one into the chicken karahi, holding it over my plate and raising his eyebrows to ask if I want some.

"Just a little, please." I put a piece of paratha on each of our plates. "Is it possible you're trying to pick a fight?"

He's got his face back in the bag, but I hear him grumble, "I certainly have grounds for doing so. As I have just illustrated."

"On account of…milk? And marshmallows? And my inability to distinguish one faint dot from another in a giant dark sky full of the damn things?" I go to the refrigerator and bring back the milk carton and two glasses. Pour for both of us. Probably won't hurt Baby and me to get a little more calcium. "Mahoney… is it possible that you *like* arguing with me?"

He pulls his head out of the bag and looks at me, brown eyes wide. "Um…"

"Ha! I'm onto something, aren't I? What's this about?"

"Well...I hadn't really thought about it until you asked. But... yeah, maybe you *are* onto something." He takes the milk carton from me, his fingers brushing lightly over the back of my hand, making me shiver, and returns it to the fridge.

"You miss having people to argue with, is that it? All your favorite people to gripe at are back in Nebraska?" *Because I can* totally *drag you to the bedroom and have it out with you good. Make you forget all about other states.* My energy levels are coming back to normal and every touch, every smile of his, lights me up like a Christmas tree.

"Noooo..." He settles into his seat next to me, not looking at me, focusing instead on opening his napkin.

"Then what?"

"I...maybe...have never really argued with anybody?" There are those big brown eyes again. He looks every bit as surprised to hear it as I am.

"*What?*"

"Don't peace-shame me, Salazar. Look, I think it's maybe been part of my MO, okay? Get along. Go along. Make everybody happy."

I lay my hand on his ropy forearm, resisting the urge to trace whatever tendon or muscle that is under my fingertips. "But arguing can be *fun.*"

"So I'm learning." He turns his arm, squeezes my hand and gives me a bemused half smile.

"Belatedly." I squeeze back.

"Belatedly." He scoops up a big bite of food and pauses with his fork halfway to his mouth. "Weird thing to add to my Likes list, though."

That makes me smile. "Yeah. You are a unique guy, that's

for sure." Uniquely sweet. Uniquely sexy. Uniquely thoughtful. A unique gentle giant…so far.

He takes his bite and stares at me, unblinking, the whole time he chews it. When finally he swallows, he says, "You are the first person to think so in my entire life."

Kevin

"How's your girlfriend?" is the first thing CeCe says when I answer her call.

"My *friend* is just fine." Spectacularly fine. Bare-faced, bare-foot, her thick braid coming loose and her boxy jacket nowhere to be found. She's beautiful, standing in my kitchen in some kind of loose wraparound dress, slicing mushrooms and peppers for stir-fry, sunset from the window gilding her hair and the curves of her shoulders and breasts and bottom so that my free hand forms itself into the same shapes just from looking at her across the room. My whole body feels her pull.

At my words, Andi glances up with a little smile and a tiny, almost too-fast-to-see wink.

"I want to see a picture," CeCe says. "You can tell a lot by a picture. Take a selfie with her. I want to see how she looks at you."

CeCe's bossy and perceptive and I miss her dearly. But what does it say about me as a full-grown man that my barely teenage niece feels the need to protect me?

"You're not the boss of me," I say belatedly, and Andi snorts from over near the stove.

"CeCe, stop badgering your uncle. Hand me the phone. Let *me* badger him." My mom's voice in the background and then directly in my ear. "How are you doing, honey? How's school going?"

"Hi, Mom. Great. Everything's good." True. Things are going really well. "How's everybody there?"

"Fine, fine. Listen, honey, I'd like to send a card to your friend to invite her myself. Maybe that will help her feel more comfortable coming with you. Do you have her address handy?"

I have some reservations about this but no good reason to say no. "Okay, but don't push."

"I promise."

Andi glances over again, eyebrows raised when I rattle off her address.

I get off the call as soon as I can and face her. "Is that okay? My mom wants to send you an invitation to Thanksgiving." I cross to her and my hands go straight to her hips before my brain can stop them. "And CeCe wants me to send her a picture of us. Says she'll be able to tell a lot by the way you look at me."

I'm bracing for resistance but Andi says, "Let's do it." She sets aside her knife, plucks the phone from my hand, makes a terrifying face at me, and snaps our photo.

"Geez, Andi." I've wrestled the phone away from her, not trying very hard because the wrestling is so fun, especially when I get tantalizing glimpses down the front of her dress and feel her all soft and squirmy up against me. But the picture is truly hideous. "How'd you even get your pretty face to *do* that? You look like a gargoyle."

She laughs and peers over my arm. "Yep. My work here is done. Send it."

I do and then we both watch the phone screen. Three dots appear next to CeCe's name in the chat box. Then they disappear.

Appear, disappear, over and over for a full two minutes before finally a reply comes through.

> **CeCe:** jesus uncle kev
> **CeCe:** not to scare you, but do you have any holy
>   water?

Andi bursts out laughing. "I love that girl, sight unseen."

I type back see? she likes me to CeCe, toss the phone on the counter, and wrap my arms around Andi. Can't help it. She's right here, back in her gorgeous human persona, so warm and lovely I physically can't *not* touch her.

I mean yeah, if she was *just* pretty, I could keep my hands off of her. But she's so *fun*. So easy to be around. I might as well face the facts: my resistance plan has failed. I'm hers, mind, body, heart, and probably soul.

I nudge her chin up with my thumbs and gaze into her eyes. She gazes back.

Here I go, breaking my own rule, but I can't *not* do it. I tilt my head down slowly, slowly, and taste her. Just lightly at first, but what the hell was I thinking? That's not going to be enough. As her arms come up around my neck, I press her against the counter and take the kiss deeper. Slide one hand into her hair, the other into her dress to cover her breast, the growl I've been holding back breaking free at the firm, full, heavy weight of her, at her nipple tightening against my palm, even with the cloth of her bra separating our skin.

She presses her breast deeper into my hand. Receives my growl into her sweet mouth, her lips curving up under mine, her hum of pleasure vibrating between us. Then she takes a handful of my hair, tugging my head back so we can see each other. "You know what you said the other day? About holding back from sex to try to keep yourself from falling too fast?"

"Yeahhh…" My voice sounds like sandpaper.

"It's okay if you fall for me a little. I'm falling for you too." Her eyes are intent. Serious. "So…here we are."

Here we sure as hell are. There's my growl again, and I am reaching behind her, cupping her big beautiful ass, lifting her to sit on the countertop and then stepping between her legs, letting her heat me, sliding my hands up her thick strong thighs, teasing her skin with barely controlled fingers as my teeth graze the side of her neck.

So be it. I'm not fighting this anymore. "Salazar." I take her earlobe between my teeth and nip at it.

"Mmm?" She's clutching my shoulders, her eyes closed.

My fingers find the flimsy lace high up on her hips—she's going to be the death of me—and tug downward. She helps, shifting from side to side so I can pull those pretty panties off. Seems a shame to drop them on the floor, so I shove them in my back pocket.

"I'm going to kiss you here now." I push her skirt back up and stroke my fingers through the wetness between her legs. "You got anything you want to say to that?"

"Mmm, please? Thank you?"

"Glad to see you're not being difficult about this, at least."

She laughs, her breath catching as I tilt her back and tuck her legs up over my shoulders.

She stops laughing when my mouth finds her. Her hand comes to the back of my head as I nibble and stroke and explore, finding all the places and touches that make her sigh and moan, letting her little pleasure sounds be my guide, her soft skin and her taste and her scent my world.

CHAPTER 26

Andi

KEVIN'S A MAN ON A mission. Apparently he's been storing up. Banking his lust like I've banked mine.

Because holy moly, when he finally peels my melted, boneless, multi-satisfied self off that kitchen counter, he leads me by the wrist—carefully, on account of my wobbly knees—into his bedroom and pulls off the rest of my clothes.

"Hello, I've missed you," he murmurs to my collarbones, kissing and tasting me there. "Hello, I've missed you," he whispers, kissing and tasting my shoulders. The top curves of my breasts. The undersides of my breasts. My nipples and ribs, my hips and knees and ankles and toes...all get the attention of his warm lips and tongue, the thrilling brush of golden stubble as he nuzzles me.

Then he reaches into the bedside drawer, pulls out the condom box and raises his eyebrows to me as if asking, "Okay?"

I manage a nod, every follicle and goose bump and engorged bit of me attuned to him as he stands and strips, baring that gorgeous body of his to my hungry eyes and waiting hands. I hear a high tiny sigh in the back of my throat as he rolls on a condom and climbs onto the bed, hovering over me, holding my gaze, his eyes serious. "I am starving for you, Andi. I've been starving for you forever." He brushes my cheek with the side of his hand. "If I get too…enthusiastic, tell me right away, okay?"

I nod and reach for him, my hands clutching his hips and his glorious firm ass as he surges into me, and then I don't have another coherent thought for a long time.

Hours or days later, we're crosswise on the bed, spent and tangled, his nose in my armpit, my hair covering most of his face. I feel *perfect*, every part of me satisfied to the point of stupor.

He opens his eyes. Sweeps one hand over my forehead, smoothing my rumpled hair back. "You're sure pretty." His thumb strokes my cheekbone once, twice, and then his mouth is on mine, warm, soft, gentle. Seeking…something.

I'm not sure what he wants but I try to answer anyway, pulling him close, wrapping myself around him.

"Andi Salazar, you," he says between kisses, "are the sexiest, prettiest, kindest, smartest, most fascinating person I have ever met."

I've never had a lover whisper such things. Never had any of them say anything during sex that wasn't explicitly *about* sex. It takes this to a whole new level of intimacy.

I wind my arms around his neck and press closer, deepening the kiss, tracing patterns on his skull with my fingertips. I could lie here with him like this all night, never get out of this bed, except… that twinge that means Baby's ravenous. I pull back regretfully and kiss the end of Kevin's nose, loving the way his eyelashes brush my cheek. "Hey, sweet, cuddly man. We need food. Electrolytes."

He groans. "You take the bathroom first. I ought to be able to move again by the time you're done."

Five minutes later we're in the kitchen, resuming our stir-fry preparations. He pulls the marinated meat from the fridge and sets about making rice while I finish cutting the vegetables. "You think any more about coming with me next week?" His eyes are on the cooktop controls but I feel his focus on me.

The truth is, I'm torn. Gram and I didn't celebrate it. And it was always just the two of us. We never had a giant crowd of relatives like so many families. But also…it's a holiday. I've never been far from the shelter on a holiday, in case they need me.

"Hmm. How does your family generally celebrate?" I move the cutting board full of veggies closer to him so he can do the honors at the stove.

"We all go to Mom and Dad's. Everybody contributes to the meal, even the kids. We always have more food than we could possibly eat. Whoever spends the least time cooking does the cleanup. Afterwards, football on TV and board games in the dining room." He glances at me as I wash my hands. "Pretty normal."

I turn off the tap and pick up the towel. "Not for me. Gram was from Mexico. Had a lot of indigenous blood in her."

"Ohhh. Shoot. I didn't even think of that." He reaches out and takes my hand after I set the towel aside. "Does that make you want to stay away, then?"

His gaze is so soft and so sincere it takes me a minute to realize he's waiting for an answer.

"I'm not sure how I feel about it. I mean, I definitely wouldn't celebrate it as a historical event, but I would like to meet your family." True. But how the hell would I present my nearly-four-months-pregnant self to my child's grandparents and aunts and uncles when Kevin and I are supposed to be just friends?

I've been mulling that over for days, trying to decide whether to bring it up to Kevin. I'm almost sure it's safe to take another step toward a relationship—sure he's the wonderful guy he seems—but some tiny part of me still screams, *Stop! Wait to be sure!* whenever I think about raising the topic. He's been nothing but patient and supportive and loving, and his family sounds equally lovely, and after today...

Still, I've got this fear that stops me.

We always tell shelter and crisis line clients not to ignore their instincts. If something feels wrong, pay attention to that. It can save your life.

But I don't know whether this fear of mine is a real instinct or leftover childhood trauma. I thought I'd worked through everything a long time ago, but...I've never tried to have a real relationship with a guy before.

And I've never had a baby growing inside me to protect.

"Okay. Well, think about it and let me know." He runs his fingers through my hair, kisses my forehead, and goes back to the stove.

I spend the night with him. I'm tired but still I lie awake in his arms, watching him sleep. Relaxed like this, he looks like a Boy Scout. He's been a Boy Scout when he's awake, too; he's never not been wonderful to me. How could I have worries about this man?

How could I not?

The next morning I race home to shower and change clothes and get to work in time to find a new note from my favorite stalker: SEND THEM HOME BITCH OR ELSE. TICK TOCK. Creepy motherfucker.

I toss it in the file, call the police, inform the staff that we got another one and to be alert, and then dig into my paperwork, but all morning I'm restless.

By lunchtime I feel like I have to get out, so I go to July's for takeout.

Rose is there, in a booth with Miz Ames. I will never understand that relationship. If Scarlett O'Hara had lived to be in her eighties, shrunken and dried out but still with her damn sixteen-inch waist and snooty attitude, she'd be just like Miz Ames— toxic southern belle. Most people avoid her like the plague, but not Rose.

Rose spots me and tries to wave me over but I hold up a "just a sec" finger and head to the counter to give my order to Sonya. She too is casting glances at Rose and Miz Ames.

"What are they talking about today?" I ask.

She shakes her head. "Who knows. I'm always afraid to stand there any longer than I absolutely have to."

To be fair, Sonya is afraid of pretty much everything.

But I think of the threatening message I got today and, to be fairer, maybe Sonya's right.

"Has Sabina been in lately, by any chance?" I ask as Sonya turns toward the kitchen with my order.

"Not since last week. I imagine she's swamped. She said she was booked solid through the holiday weekend."

And there's my answer to whether the B and B might be able to help with holiday shelter overflow. Damn.

————

Kevin

"Have you told anybody at work you're pregnant yet?"

We've just finished running. I'm leaving the high school with her today to get in some volunteer hours at the shelter.

She shakes her head, her pretty face flushed from our run, a few loose strands of wavy hair glinting in the afternoon sun. "No but I'll probably say something to them soon."

A car goes by on the road beyond the parking lot. I hear raucous laughter just before several rapid loud bangs. Andi jumps and sucks in a sharp breath, color draining from her face. Obnoxious little jerks must've tossed firecrackers out the window as they drove past.

I reach to steady her. "You okay?"

She barely meets my eyes before looking away, frowning. "I fucking *hate* firecrackers. Scares me to death every time."

I don't think I've heard her use language like that before. She must be really upset.

"Wanna ride to the shelter together?" I run my hand up her arm, give her a squeeze.

She straightens, squaring her shoulders. "No, we should take both cars."

So we drive separately. She still seems a little off when we get there.

Which is why it's probably a mistake for me to ask again about her coming to Lincoln with me, but heck, it's Friday and Thanksgiving is next week.

Her answer is an impatient headshake as we cross the parking lot to the building. "No, I'm sorry, I don't know yet. Still trying to work out a plan for shelter overflow, since the local hotels will be full too."

"Well, what'd you do about it last year?" I'm shocked to hear an echo of her impatience in my own voice. I've never heard it there before.

But I've never been in the situation of having to convince the soon-to-be mother of my child to come meet my family, either. Mom's driving me crazy asking about it and Andi's been stalling me for a couple of weeks now. In bed she's a human flame, warm and exciting and giving and lovely, but elsewhere it seems like she's been pulling back. Cooling toward me. And I don't know why, and I don't know what to do about it.

I wouldn't have made love to her if I'd known it would have this effect.

We wave into the camera and Pattie at the front desk buzzes us in. Andi strides toward her office, gesturing for me to follow.

And of course I do, because that's what I always do. Like a damn puppy.

I follow her in and close the door softly behind us. "Andi, I really want you to come. I really want you to meet my family. And you seem like you could use a break. You're so tense."

She stops in front of her desk and spins to face me. "I *told* you, I don't know yet."

She's never snapped at me before and *I've* never snapped at *anybody*, but I do now. "Well, can you make up your mind today, please? Because my family wants to know and I've got this airline ticket I should cancel if you're not going."

"I didn't *ask* you to buy me a ticket, Kevin."

"I know. I wanted to. I want you to meet my family, and I didn't want to tire you out or spend the whole weekend driving. Please, just give me an answer one way or another."

She throws up her hands. "Okay then: no."

No words come to me. I stand there ten feet away and just look at her, knowing I provoked this, knowing what's coming next, seeing it as clear as I would see a train barreling down on me.

She glances away. "It's probably best if we spend a little time apart anyway."

There it is. I'm on my back on the tracks, the train chugging and churning over—through—my paralyzed body.

My mind is just as numb. All my attempts to be helpful, to be there for her and our baby... All the times I've walked on eggshells to keep from scaring her off... All the effort I've put into showing her she can trust me—that I'm not like the monsters who put her clients in this place... All for nothing, really.

I'd started to believe that maybe she actually really liked Vanilla Kev, or at least liked what I'm becoming with her help.

But no, we've got these few precious months to build our relationship before our baby's born...and instead of working on it, she wants time away from me.

Something unfamiliar is rising up in me. Little prickles. Sparks, moving through my veins, setting parts of me on fire. Is this anger?

I want to yell. No, I want to *bellow*. Let out my rage and frustration.

Maybe if we were outside away from people I would, just this once. Just howl to the stars this darn woman can't even see properly.

But we're in a building full of people who have been traumatized, and I am not going to be the cause of more pain or fear for them.

And yet...

I am *tired*. Tired of waiting for the trust I haven't done anything to lose. And I am not going to wait one goddamn minute longer.

"Andi, how evil do you think I am?" I face her, my feet planted, my voice low but clear enough I'm sure she can hear every word.

She's turned to face me too. Her eyes are wary. She looks like she's bracing herself. "What are you talking about?"

"Were you ever going to trust me, or were you just going to keep stringing me along, hoping for some day that was never gonna come?"

She doesn't blink. Doesn't look away. Just gives a tiny head-shake with a you're-not-making-sense shrug.

And it *pisses. Me. Off.*

So this is what being pissed off feels like.

It doesn't bring out the best in me. "I'm sorry; maybe I should have been clearer. Why do you keep holding me responsible for something I've never done?" My voice is cracking with misery and frustration. It's pathetic and I'm embarrassed, even as the words exit my mouth. "Something I would Never. Ever. Do?"

CHAPTER 27

Andi

ONCE WHEN I WAS LITTLE, some kids and I were sliding across the gym floor in our socks, trying to see who could get closest to the wall. I got a running start, slid, and slid, and…slammed into that damn wall so hard the wind was knocked out of me. Falling on my butt didn't bother me, but not being able to suck in my next breath was terrifying.

I feel like that now. Life is going on like normal all around me, with nobody noticing I'm in serious danger.

I'm gripping the back of one of the office chairs hard, just to stay upright. "How long have you felt like this?"

Kevin glances at my white knuckles, then back up to my face. "Andi, sit down before you fall down." His voice isn't so desperate now, but he's definitely not my gentle lover at this moment.

Maybe this is where he loses his mask. Maybe this is where I learn my hesitation was warranted.

He moves around the other chair and drops into it. Doesn't

take his eyes off me, but…doesn't make any kind of aggressive or threatening move. His hands aren't even clenched.

After a second I perch on the edge of the seat across from him. "How long?" I'm stalling, trying to gauge risk.

He actually rolls those damn brown eyes.

It's like he's aged twenty years. Become sad and weary, a different person, and I can't begin to predict what this stranger will do or say.

"I've been mad for about five minutes, I guess. I've been worried ever since you told me you were pregnant."

The whole damn time. He's been worrying about something the whole time too. "Why didn't you say something?"

He barks out a laugh so harsh it has to hurt his throat. "What could I have said that wouldn't have spooked you?"

Fair.

I nod. I still don't know whether there's danger here, but it's time for me to come clean. "The idea of starting a relationship has always been unthinkable for me. More so now that I'm pregnant."

"Why?" His voice is taut but I think that's vulnerability in his eyes.

"Gram drilled it into me that I'd be better off staying single. Because of family stuff. And then I started working here right out of college, and I…don't get to see many happy endings here." I fish my phone out of my pocket and pull up my photos. Find one of Gram with my mom and my sister, Lola, and pass it over to him. Our fingers don't brush when he takes it.

His eyebrows go up and he whistles. "This is your Gram?"

"Yeah, with my mom."

"They're almost as pretty as you are."

Okay, so, even when terribly upset, he's sweet. No name-calling, no nasty accusations... He's giving me space. Asking reasonable questions and actually listening to my answers.

What was I thinking, wasting all this time not trusting him?

It actually feels *good* to be talking with him about this. Brings relief, lightness. There's nothing remotely threatening in his voice or his manner or his posture...

So now my job is to heal any pain my mistrust has caused him.

"This little girl you?"

I shake my head. "My older sister. I wasn't born yet."

He hands over the phone, looks back up at me, and I know my truth telling has only just begun. "So when you found out you were having our baby, you didn't think that might be a good time to share your fears? Since I was about to become a daddy?"

I can see how it looks like that from his perspective, but he still doesn't get it. And he won't, until I tell him the whole story. I sigh. "I was just starting to consider the possibility of more with you when I found out I was pregnant. And the risk ramped way up."

"Yeah? Why's that?" He sounds detached but I know he's not. Not really. My Kevin—the one who touches my belly with reverence and makes sure I have whatever I need and that he does everything possible to make things good for me—is anything but detached.

He's going to hate this. But I have to tell him, if we're to have any chance of my fears and my caution making sense to him. "The risk seemed huge to me because of my family history. Remember I mentioned that my grandpa and my father were not good guys?"

He nods.

"Well, they both started being *worse* guys when their wives were pregnant. It's often that way in abusive relationships—the violence often ramps up around pregnancy."

He's clenching his jaw again. He looks past me and mutters, "I'm going to need some addresses. I've got some asses to kick."

"You can't, Kev." I push up from my chair and walk to the filing cabinet behind my desk. I feel his eyes on me as I find the folder I'm looking for, and the specific clipping from the Charlotte newspaper. I bring it back to where he's sitting and hold it out to him. "Gram's ex probably died years ago. But my...father is dead too."

Kev looks like he doesn't want to take it. Like he's sorry he asked. Like he knows this is going to change things, somehow. But he takes it from my hand and begins to read.

There's a picture of my mom and Lola at the top. I settle back in my seat and watch Kevin's eyes move over that and then on to the text of the article I know by heart. The article that tells how Anthony Zoeller pushed his way into his estranged wife's house and shot her to death, after shooting their older daughter, aged four, as she tried to escape to the neighbor's. How he then turned the gun on himself.

And how two hours later a crime scene tech found the baby everyone had thought was missing. She was still strapped in her baby carrier, under the kitchen sink behind the trash can. The tech found her when the little girl managed to spit out her pacifier and let out a hungry wail.

Police speculated that the baby was only alive because of her mother's quick, desperate thinking—that otherwise baby Andrea too would have been killed by the monster who wiped out the rest of her family. Of his family.

The article ends with a statement that the baby would be sent to live with out-of-town family.

Kevin's hand drops and the clipping flutters to the floor. He curls forward, pressing his fingers into his eyes.

I watch warily as his lips begin to move. Takes me a minute to realize he's praying. The Hail Mary, I think, but I'm not sure. Gram didn't raise me to pray. Pretty sure she'd decided there was no god a Salazar woman could place her faith in.

Kevin moves. Uncurls from that chair and comes to me, kneeling on the floor in front of me and sliding his arms between me and the back of my chair, gathering me in, his broad shoulders sheltering me, his head in my lap.

"Andi, I'm so sorry," he whispers, his voice broken.

We stay like that for a while, just holding each other, me curled over him, until he speaks again, voice still soft but firmer now. "You were a miracle baby. You're a miracle. And this baby is *our* miracle. And I won't let anybody hurt either one of you."

I start to cry when he presses a kiss to my belly.

Kevin

I am barely holding it together. Everything inside me is raging, quaking with fury and despair and sadness for Andi and her mom and that precious little girl who was her sister. I want to burn down the whole world. Bring her monster dad back to life so I can kill him again, over and over, once for every time he hurt or scared Andi's mom and sister. And then I'll kill him a hundred more times for stealing them from Andi and her Gram.

No wonder I've been picking up such mixed signals. No

wonder Andi was afraid to trust me. I'm the father of that vulnerable little person growing inside her. No freaking wonder.

She's the strongest person I've ever known.

She sits quietly, letting me hold her, pretending not to notice
that I am silently falling to pieces. She just runs her fingers through
my hair and lets me hold on.

But when I promise to protect her—a foolish, foolish promise no one can be sure they can keep—a single tear drips onto
my cheek. And then another, and another. And then I'm rising,
scooping her up in my arms, and resettling with her on my lap,
and now we're really holding each other.

"How can I help you feel safe around me?" I whisper, kissing
the little saltwater trails on her face.

Her eyes are full of more than tears as she gazes back at me
and gives a little I-don't-know shrug. I feel like I would do *anything* for her when she looks at me like that. Leap tall buildings,
stop bullets...

"What about... What about a safe word? If I ever start to
freak you out, you can say a safe word and I'll stop whatever
I'm doing and ask you what you need. And you can tell me to
stop talking, or leave you alone for a while, or...whatever you
need."

She wipes tears off my face and manages a soft, sweet, broken
smile. "Perfect."

Her cheek is velvet under my thumb. "Choose a word then.
Pick one we wouldn't use in everyday life."

She shakes her head with a little laugh. "I don't know...lemur.
Our safe word is 'lemur.'"

"Good one. At least until Lil Bit gets old enough for us to
take her to a zoo."

"Then we'll call it 'the L-word.'" She takes hold of my shoulders and pushes herself to standing. Moves to the other chair and sits down there, distracting me from another L-word I want to say to her.

She crosses her legs, folds her hands in her lap, and looks me over. There's new warmth in her gaze. She's looked at me this way before, kind of, but there's something softer, more comfortable, in it now. Trust. I think it's finally trust. "Had you thought about what you'd say to your family if I did go home with you? How you'd explain your pregnant best friend? In a way you'd have to awkwardly revise later?"

Pretty sure I'm blushing. "I was hoping we could figure that out together."

She nods. "I wanted to believe you're the good guy you've always been to me, Kev." She shakes her head. "It was a war zone in my head. 'Trust this sweet man' versus 'No! Danger! Danger!' I just...couldn't make up my mind. My Gram was smart, and from what I've heard, my mom was too. And yet two terrible guys managed to fool those two smart, beautiful women into falling in love with them. It's not like those guys would have shown who they really were on their first few dates. How could I be sure I wasn't being fooled too?"

The time I'd spent worrying over her mixed signals suddenly doesn't seem like much, now that I know the context. I can't even imagine how a child could grow up able to deal with that history, much less have to suddenly face becoming a mom in a whole new untried relationship.

I shift in my chair. "Yeah, I can understand that." Pause. "Anything else you need to tell me, though?"

She actually laughs. A real laugh that makes me smile too.

"How about—I'm starving? What do you want to do for dinner tonight?"

Some inside still-worried part of me relaxes. She *doesn't* want time away from me.

I feel like celebrating what seems like a leap forward for us. "Tonight...I think we need a break from cooking. Wanna go out to the roadhouse?"

She tips her head, then nods. "Yeah. I think their barbecue chicken might be just what I need. But I have a couple more hours of work to do here."

It's almost five already. No way should she put off eating for hours if she's already hungry. "How about I go get carryout? I'll see if any of the kids need homework help after we eat."

"Sounds good. I'll walk you out. I accidentally left my phone in my car."

Out in the lobby, Andi stops at the desk and tells Pattie I'll be coming back in a bit with food.

Pattie looks us over, clearly trying to decide what we were doing in Andi's office all that time, but she just says, "Okay. Y'all got any Thanksgiving plans?"

Andi pauses at the door. "Kevin's going home to Nebraska. I'll be here in case of emergency."

Darn. Still a "no" on the trip. Okay, then. Time for me to show I'm a big boy and not a controlling, whiny, demanding asshole.

"You should go with him." Pattie gives Andi a stern look. "Maybe if you disappear for a few days, your stalker will finally give up and leave us alone."

Well, that stings. "Dang, Pattie, that's harsh. I'm not a stalker."

Pattie looks at me oddly and frowns. "What?"

"I mean, calling me a stalker is a little rude." Criminy, is that me standing up for myself?

Her eyebrows shoot up and her gaze moves to Andi, who has me by the wrist and is urging me toward the door. And Pattie says, "Oh, honey, no, I'm not talking about you. I mean the asshole who's been sending the anonymous threats."

My brain stutters, freezes, and then bursts into flame. Andi, who I *just* asked if she has any more secrets, seems to have neglected to mention that someone has been sending her threats.

"Salazar..." The word comes out a growl as I swing around to look at her.

She gives my wrist a hard tug and we're through the door, and just as I'm about to start yelling, she says, "Mahoney, there's a lemur you need to see in the parking lot."

CHAPTER 28

Andi

THE MAN IS AS GOOD as his word. No sooner does he hear me say "lemur" than he cuts off whatever he was about to bellow. He swallows, shakes his head, takes a deep breath, and says, "What do you need?"

I scan the street and parking lot and then lead the way to his car. "I just wanted to tell you about it out here, okay? Not in the lobby where anyone could hear."

He sighs. "This is why you always look at your surroundings so carefully, isn't it?"

"Yes and no. I've been doing that for years. We all have. There's no shortage of guys who hate everyone and everything to do with the shelter."

An old high school "friend," when he'd learned where I work, had said, "You like to put guys in jail, huh?"

I was so shocked and pissed that I snapped, "Only the ones who beat up people they're supposed to love." Later I wondered what his family life had been like, for him to have had that reaction.

Kevin's waiting for me to say more.

"This guy's recent. He sends vaguely threatening notes in which he calls me 'bitch' and demands that I 'send them home or else.' That's one reason I run at the high school now instead of on the street. I'm careful about not giving out my address and about making sure no one's following me, so I'm pretty sure he doesn't know where I live. I've never actually seen anyone around here either."

"Do the police know about this?"

"Yeah. They tried to pull fingerprints off the paper but didn't have any luck. Now I just tell them whenever I get a new one and we all try to be extra vigilant."

"Well, have they investigated all the assholes who put your clients here?"

I shake my head. "No, for a couple of reasons. One is that we protect the identities of our clients. We never give out that information without a court order. But also, we don't know that it *is* from somebody connected to one of our clients. It could be from somebody whose partner or family left them and Threat Guy mistakenly *thinks* they came here."

Kevin's frown is ferocious, his cheeks are pink, and his hands are clenched, and somehow I have zero fear that he will direct his anger and frustration toward me.

I should have tried trusting him sooner.

"Isn't there *any*thing they can do?" Pretty sure he's gritting his teeth.

"Just wait it out. Gather more information if we can. Keep on being careful. And you know, the problem might take care of itself if whoever he thinks we're sheltering decides to go home to him. Lord knows that happens all the time." *I'd rather they not, though.*

"Gahhhh! This makes me want to break things." He throws up his hands and slumps against his car.

"Welcome to my world." I stand on tiptoe to press a kiss to his mouth, and his arms come around me like he's never going to let go.

And I'm tempted to stay right here for a long, long time. But. "Go on, Kev. You know all my secrets now. Fetch us some dinner and figure out whether you've got more questions for me, and we'll talk about whatever you want when you get back." I pull away so he can open his car door.

He heaves a sigh and climbs in. "Okay, but you go inside first. I'll watch till you're safely in the door."

He does, too. Gives me a nod as I wave from the doorway, then he drives away.

Pattie looks up at me, wincing a little, as I pass her desk. "I'm sorry I said that. I didn't know he didn't know."

I wave it off, stopping at my office threshold. "No problem. It's probably good he does know now, so he'll be careful too. Oh shoot, I forgot to get my phone out of the car."

I swivel around and walk right back outside, fishing in my pocket for my keys.

Just as I expected, the phone's in my cup holder. I grab it and am back on the sidewalk on my way inside when there's sudden movement to my left—a man, coming from between two parked cars I just passed.

I duck away but he lunges, grabs my sweatshirt, and yanks me back toward him.

"Hello, bitch," he singsongs, his voice oily and venomous.

He's got the advantage of evil on his side.

But I've got the love of a determined grandma plus thirty years of self-defense and martial arts classes.

I let momentum carry me back and I stomp with all my weight on his instep. Shove off and spin right to clock him in the side of his head with my elbow, my other hand swinging around to grab his hair and ear and slam his face down into the knee I raise with the fury of thousands of years of women fending off men's attacks.

Then everything turns to jerky slow motion, fragments and fleeting impressions. Blood spatters. The asshole staggers backward, I hear something like an angry bull bearing down on us, there's a flash from near the guy's hand, and a sound like an explosion. A ping, a soft thump. Bodies colliding, rolling and skidding past me. A pungent smell. A clatter of something metal and dense hitting the sidewalk.

And Kevin's urgent voice. "Andi, you okay? Get the gun!"

Kevin

No sooner do I turn the corner than I realize there is no way I'm leaving town if Andi's staying here with a freaking stalker on the loose. I tell my phone to call her so I can let her know I'll be canceling both plane tickets, but the phone rings and rings until it goes to voicemail.

Oh, hell. Andi's phone is still in her car. She'd gone back inside without it. And if she realizes that, she'll probably go right back out for it.

And I can't call to tell her to wait, that I'll get it for her when I come back.

I can't stand the thought of her going out alone, now that I know what I know. I turn the corner and circle the block. I'll get her keys, fetch her phone myself, and *then* go pick up our dinner.

But as I turn onto the shelter street again, I see Andi already on the sidewalk, heading back to the front door, and a guy leap out from the parked cars to grab at her—and he's got a fucking gun...

And I slam my gearshift into park and am out of my car running, my sneakers making hardly any sound compared to the blood rushing and pounding in my ears. I'm five steps away when she stomps his foot. Three steps away when she spins and catches him hard with her elbow—Jesus, my woman is kicking this shithead's ass!—going into my dive as she slams his head down into her knee, and that's when things get weird.

I don't think the guy pointed the gun at either of us—he's too busy trying to hold his broken face together—but it goes off with a flash and a *boom!* just as I hit him. It bounces toward the building while the asshole and I skid and bounce up the sidewalk away from Andi. I land on top of him, pressing his jaw into the cement with my forearm as I twist to look back at Andi to make sure she's all right. "Andi, you okay? Get the gun!"

She's already scrabbling for it, grim and determined, but she pauses, looking at me instead of grabbing it. She puts her foot on it, pulls her phone out of her pocket and dials. "Yes, I need an ambulance and police, right away, at the Women's Crisis Shelter. This is Andi Salazar. There's been a shooting on the sidewalk out front."

The guy under me struggles feebly.

"Hold still!" I push his jaw down harder and he stops.

Then Andi's words register and I turn back to her, frantic, my eyes scanning her up and down again, looking for any sign of injury. "Are you okay? Andi? Are you hurt?"

"I'm fine, Kev. I wasn't hit." She's moving fast, yanking her sweatshirt over her head, leaving her in just her running bra, and for one ridiculous second I think she's proving she's okay in a way she knows I'll especially enjoy.

But then she picks up the gun with the sweatshirt sleeve, tucks it in the back waistband of her sweatpants, and hustles over to me. I hear sirens as she kneels beside me, wads up the sweatshirt into a tight ball, and presses it hard against my inner thigh.

And it hurts like a motherfucker.

And for the first time I notice the puddle of blood under me.

"Lie down on him, babe," she says softly, looking in my eyes. "Get your heart low to the ground."

And I get it now. A bullet got *me*. And Andi's afraid I'm going to bleed out.

Come to think of it, I'm not feeling so great. I lie across the asshole, wishing I was wearing a belt we could tie him with instead of my running clothes. Glad help is on the way, in case I pass out.

Andi elevates my leg, resting it on her thigh, applying pressure with near-inhuman strength, and murmurs something. She's singing to me—"Cover Me Up," a Jason Isbell song we've argued about—her voice sweet and rough at the same time.

Sirens scream closer and the asshole squirms again. Andi leans over him. Says conversationally, "Hold still, Asshole. Unless you want me to kill you with your own gun. No, you know what? I think I'd like that. Why don't you try that again and give me an excuse?"

The guy freezes. Doesn't move a muscle, even when first responders surround us and the medics slide me off of him onto a collapsible gurney. Andi waits for officers to restrain the guy and then runs to the ambulance the medics have loaded me into. "I'll be there as soon as I can, Kev, okay? I'll follow y'all the second the police are done with me." She reaches out and I reach out and our fingertips brush and as the medic starts to close the doors I say, "I love you, Andi."

But the stubborn, cautious woman doesn't say it back. She just says, "Tell me again in a few hours."

CHAPTER 29

Andi

FOCUS. FOCUS. FOCUS. BUT AS I watch the ambulance drive away, lights and sirens spinning on, it's all I can do not to run after it. To pound on the back door and demand they let me ride with him.

I love you, Andi. What the fuck is wrong with me that I didn't say it back? All that blood, all that goddamn blood... What if he dies and that's the last thing he ever said to me and I didn't say it back?

But I couldn't. It had sounded like he was saying goodbye. Letting go. And I won't have any part of that.

"Andi. Ms. Salazar."

I jerk around at the sound of a quiet voice behind me. Officer Jimmy Moran, a young guy July used to babysit for in high school. Three other officers are with the asshole, cuffing him.

"Whatever you do, don't let that guy go, Jimmy. I don't know who he is or what kind of story he's got, but he attacked me. He had a gun. And when Kevin tackled him, it went off."

"That's what I need to talk to you about. I see a gun…" He leans to look around me, which is unusual; lately everyone's eyes go straight to my chest. To be fair, the girls were always impressive, but pregnancy has made them spectacular, like goddamn monuments to fertility. But he gestures to my back, which is mostly bare on account of me standing here in a running bra.

And oh, shit, I have a gun in my pants.

"Don't touch!"

Jimmy's eyes widen at my command, like he thinks I think he's going to molest me.

"No, I mean, the gun. I put it there so that asshole couldn't get it back, but I tried to not mess up any prints on it. Is there a way you can take it from me without messing them up?" I can't give him my sweatshirt because it's with Kevin. Soaked with Kevin's precious blood.

My thigh muscles start to shake. "Take it from me, Jimmy, please. I need to sit down. No, I need to get to the hospital to be with Kevin. Can y'all question me there?"

But they don't let me go immediately. They do carefully take the gun and put it in an evidence bag, and Officer Jimmy leads me to the curb, holding my arm as I lower myself onto it and put my head between my knees. Suddenly I feel the cold and I'm shaking harder, my teeth chattering. Pattie comes outside with two of the big soft sweatshirts we keep in stock and helps me put them both on. She hugs me before an officer leads her away asking what she saw and heard from inside the shelter.

I tell my story to Jimmy and another officer. Answer their questions. Tell them about the folder of threats in my office. Ask Pattie to fetch it for them when she's done answering questions.

Someone moves Kevin's car from the street where he'd left it running, door wide open, and brings me his keys. Someone else brings me cocoa. I wrap both hands around the warm cup, answer more questions from the officers, and then a couple of detectives arrive and want to hear it all over again.

"That guy's saying you and Mr. Mahoney attacked him," one of them says casually, and rage shoulders aside my shakiness and worry and straightens my spine.

I look the detective straight in the eye. "That's total bullshit."

He tips his head, eyebrows raised. "He does look like someone attacked him. Pretty sure he's got a broken nose. Talking about suing the shelter."

"If he didn't want to get beat down, he shouldn't have jumped out from between parked cars and grabbed me."

"That when Mr. Mahoney kicked his ass?"

"No, *I* kicked his ass. Kevin came running up and tackled him after I broke the guy's nose." I swallow down a surge of guilt and fear for Kevin. "I didn't know the guy had a gun until it went off."

The detective's eyebrows are up at his hairline now. "*You* did that to his face?"

"Yeah. I mean, I'm sure Kevin would have been happy to, but he had to get to us first."

It's another half an hour or more before they're finished with me. Pattie's done with her shift and has come to stand beside me. Our part-time HR person has shown up, too. Pattie's doing, I'm pretty sure.

"We're trying to keep everyone inside and away from the front windows to minimize trauma," Pattie's saying in one of my ears as HR Jean says, "I've started the worker's comp process for you. I'll have stuff for you to sign but right now you should go get yourself checked out," in my other ear.

"Okay, thanks, both of you." I take my purse from Pattie, who asks if I'd like her to drive me to the hospital.

"No, I'm good, but thanks. Thank everybody for me for all their extra help, okay? We're going to need to talk to the therapists about helping people process this… I don't know where I'm going to be tomorrow. It depends on how Kevin's doing…" My throat seizes up and Pattie squeezes my arm and gives me another hug.

"Don't worry about us. You call me if you need anything. And tell that sweet man to get well quickly."

I duck my head in a nod—the best I can do for goodbye at the moment—and head to my car at a run. Drive to the hospital with one hand on my belly. "You okay in there, sweetie? We have to find your daddy." I try not to think about all that blood. About how pale Kevin looked when they loaded him into the ambulance. How I didn't say it back when he'd told me he loved me. I have to clench the wheel to stop my hands from shaking.

Marnie at the ER and I go way back, from years of me doing hospital advocacy with our clients.

"He said you'd come looking for him," she tells me when I ask where I can find Kevin. "They took him up to surgery. He was insisting that we make sure you get checked out before you go find him. You got time, anyway; he probably won't be out of surgery and into recovery for another hour or two."

Recovery. They expect him to be in recovery within the next couple of hours.

Relief makes me weak and I'm happy to sit and let them check me over.

This wasn't how I'd intended to announce to the world that

I'm pregnant. But it's good to hear them give me and Lil Bit a clean bill of health after they inspect me from head to toe. And better still to know that Kevin knows Lil Bit's on the way, so that he'll have all the more reason to fight to get well.

Because I know he will. Fight to be around for me and our baby. I saw that picture of him holding his newborn niece, awe and joy and wonder on his beautiful, tired face.

Finally they release me and I go straight to the family surgical waiting area. It's empty, basically tidy but depressing as hell, with dark furniture and blue-gray walls probably meant to be soothing. I take a seat near the door so I'll see anyone who goes by.

God, this day. It's been a million hours long, full of every overwhelming emotion in the world, and I am ready for it to be over...but only if Kevin's going to be okay at the end of it.

Just a little while ago, I was in a chair like this in my office and he was on his knees, strong arms tight around me, tousled head in my lap, telling me he wouldn't let anybody hurt me or Lil Bit. He'd kissed my belly right here where my hand is now.

And he'd kept his promise.

I didn't even know that guy had a gun. If Kevin hadn't tackled him...

Somewhere in the recesses of my memory, the sound of that *boom!* meets its matches, and all the dread I've felt through the years whenever I hear similar sounds rushes to fill me now. Makes air feel too scarce, makes my heart beat too fast.

Please, Gram, look after Kev. Let him be okay.

When I was down in the ER, I scrubbed his blood off my hands and arms, feeling sick and guilty and scared as fuck. But now I see there's blood on my sweats, too. Dried smears on both my thighs. *Fuck.* I can't stop shaking.

Voices in the hallway. I look up, ready to leap if it's a doctor or nurse from the OR, but it's my friends, trickling into the room in ones and twos and threes over the next several minutes, all with Band-Aids on their arms, talking over each other to ask about Kevin and say how glad they are that I'm okay. July and Rose settle on either side of me, Joe and Angus on the other sides of them.

"I don't know anything yet. What's...?" I gesture to the Band-Aids.

"We gave blood." July wraps a strong arm around me and squeezes. "Tisha's down there now with a bunch of the high school folks and some of the restaurant staff. The Blue Shoes are in Charlotte tonight or they'd be here too."

My eyes fill up so fast I almost can't see July's right-hand women from the restaurant, Donna and Tina, coming in with Sonya between them. Former shelter residents, all, and all amazing women. Sonya's pale but looks oddly energized, her eyes traveling from her inner elbow to Donna's face. "I did it!" Sounds like she can't believe it herself.

Donna nods. "You did good." They wave at me and take seats across the room.

"How'd y'all even know?" Silly question. Word travels fast in this town, and if July hadn't heard about the shooting right away, Rose would have.

"Pattie called us. They're organizing the shelter folks to donate blood too. Sounds like they've got a lot of volunteers— Kevin's a popular guy." July opens the paper bag she's carrying, unwraps something and hands it to me. My favorite sandwich from the restaurant. Correction—*two* of my favorite sandwiches. And a banana.

Rose pops up from her seat. "I'm going to go get you something to drink."

She's gone before I can protest. Angus moves over to take her place.

"How you holding up?" His voice is low and gruff, his eyes shrewd and warm. He works with people suffering from trauma. He's probably cataloging all kinds of mental health indicators I've never even heard of, just by looking at me.

"I'm okay. Just...really anxious for some good news."

He nods. Glances toward the door and then back at me. "Heard you beat down somebody else who deserved it."

"I did. And he *definitely* did."

"Good job." He makes a fist, gently bumps my hand where I'm clutching my sandwich, crumbling Tina's good bread.

"I didn't know he had a gun, Angus. And I didn't even know Kevin was there until the gun went off."

He nods again, slower this time. "Think you'd have done anything different if you'd known?"

He has the most amazing turquoise eyes. They're full of patience now as I stare at him. Finally I shake my head. "I don't know what I would have done."

"Really no way *to* know. And then no way to know what that guy would have done next. No need or reason to give yourself a hard time about it, okay? The other guy set it in motion, and then you and Kevin did your very best in a very bad and very unpredictable situation."

He's right. I know he's right. It's just really hard not to wonder, not to feel terrible, when Kevin's in the other room having freaking *surgery* because some asshole attacked *me*.

For a second I'm back on that sidewalk again, reaching to

pick up that gun and then realizing that Kevin is bleeding. That he's been shot.

Because instead of being the kind of man I'd feared he might be, a guy like my father who would sacrifice us to his ego and his rage and his need for control, Kevin is the kind of man who would sacrifice himself for me and Lil Bit. Without hesitation or a second thought.

Angus squeezes my arm and I'm back in the waiting room again.

Everyone makes small talk as we wait for news. I nibble on the sandwiches, more because I know I should rather than from actual hunger, and drink a ginger ale Rose brought me with a cup of ice from the nurses' station.

Finally a woman I don't know comes to the door.

She glances around at all of us waiting. "Ms. Salazar?"

I'm on my feet before I know I'm moving. "Call me Andi."

"I'm Dr. Travels." Her scrubs still look crisp. She's not tall but she's got a presence about her. A barely contained energy. Smooth dark skin and bright mischievous eyes. "Kevin told us to give you his updates. He said you're his 'person.'" Her eyes crinkle and I almost smile back. "He came through surgery just fine; the wound was a graze, deep enough to nick the artery, but we think it must have hit him after it ricocheted off some other surface, maybe the sidewalk. That's good; it probably would have done more damage otherwise. We repaired the artery, got the wound cleaned and stitched, and he's in recovery now. We're preparing a room for him; he needs to stay still for a day or so. You should be able to see him in about an hour. A nurse will come get you when it's time. Do you have any questions for me?"

Usually I'm calm in emergencies, including hospital-type

emergencies. Tonight I've got nothing. "My mind is blank, Doc. But he's okay... He's really going to be okay?"

"He'll have to take it easy for a while, but I expect him to make a full recovery."

Rose and July each have an arm around my back.

I nod my thanks, unable to speak without bawling like a baby.

"I'll see you in the morning, then, if you're here for rounds. The nursing staff will keep me updated tonight." She touches my arm, crinkles those eyes at me again, and leaves the room.

July and Rose steer me to my seat. I tip my head back against the wall, listen to the sounds of happy conversation rising around me, and let silent tears of relief slide down my temples and into my ears.

CHAPTER 30

Andi

WHEN THEY FINALLY BRING ME into Kevin's room he's mostly still and quiet, pale and statue-like, his wounded leg propped up and his hospital gown stretched tight across his wide shoulders. After the nurses finish hooking up all the things that need to be hooked up, they show me the call button and tell me to let them know if he seems restless or tries to get up. They reassure me they'll be in frequently to check on him, and then they leave us alone.

There's a recliner beside his bed. I tug it around backwards so I can face him and hold his hand, my own feet up. I watch his face and the monitors. Breathe with the rise and fall of his chest. Celebrate the warmth of his fingers in mine and the thump of his heartbeat when I press my hand there.

It's not long before his eyelids begin to flutter.

"I'm here, babe." I raise his knuckles to my lips for a long moment.

His slow eyes-still-closed smile has me sitting up straighter. Leaning closer.

"You called me 'babe,'" he murmurs, voice soft and rough and dreamy.

"Yes I did." I blink away a tear so he won't catch me crying. "How you feeling?"

His eyes open a fraction. "Glad...to be here. Glad you're here. They check you over?"

"Mm-hmm. I'm fine. Better now that you're awake and talking."

He squeezes my hand. "You are so dang cool, Salazar." His eyes drift closed on another smile.

That surprises a laugh from me. "What?"

"When I was shot. You were so calm. Practical." He swipes his thumb across my palm. "So comforting. Ha!" His laugh is cut short by a grimace. "Okay, no laughing just yet. But dang, woman, when you leaned over and called that guy 'Asshole'... and begged him to give you reason to shoot him..." He gives me a ridiculously soulful look. "Probably would've made my dick hard if I'd had enough blood left in my body."

I don't know whether to laugh or cry. "Are you still doped up, Mahoney?"

"Maybe I am. Maybe I am." He closes his eyes, gives my hand another faint squeeze, his voice drifting a bit. "Maybe I'm just high on my partner."

He falls quiet then, his breathing slowing into sleep rhythms, and I cradle his words to my heart like treasure. *High on my partner.*

Yeah. Partner.

Never had a partner before.

Didn't realize it could feel so good.

The next time he stirs, he asks me to find his phone and cancel the plane tickets. "And help me figure out how to tell my folks about…this…without scaring them."

But when I pull his phone from the bag of personal possessions the nurses had hung in the little wardrobe near the bathroom, it's blinking with messages, and when Kevin gives me his passcode, we find several texts from his family.

> Kevin, the vice principal from your school called and
> let us know what happened. We're on our way.
> Hang in there, honey.
> We love you.

Turns out they'd checked flight times and found it would be just as quick to drive through the night. Kevin's parents, his brother, and his niece CeCe had left Lincoln already. His sisters, grandparents, and the rest are going to rent a big van and leave in the morning.

We cancel his airline tickets and then I use Kevin's phone to text his family to tell them he's doing well and resting after surgery. I give them my own cell number too, and his mom immediately texts me. She and I have a whole little conversation while Kevin slides in and out of sleep.

In the wee hours, we both wake up when a nurse comes to check his vitals. Kevin thanks her, his eyes clearer and his voice stronger than they were earlier. He watches her leave and then turns his head back my way. "What are we going to tell my folks about Lil Bit?"

Not something I'm prepared to deal with yet. I thought I'd have more time to think about it.

I survey my sweats-clad body. Since puberty I've had a big,

exaggerated hourglass shape. In loose clothing like this my figure's not obvious, which is the whole point except when I'm onstage. I doubt anyone would know I'm pregnant. My only-slightly-rounder-than-usual tummy is well hidden.

I think I catch a hint of worry in Kev's brown eyes when I look back up at him. "Do we really need to talk to them about it so soon? Maybe they won't be able to tell."

"Is there a reason you don't want them to know yet?" His tone is guarded.

I shake my head. "It's more about me than about them. I'm— We—I'd like a little time to enjoy—Well, we feel different to me now. You and me. I'd like a little special time for us to have this new stage to ourselves. So much has changed in the last twelve hours. I'm kinda spinning from it."

His eyes soften as we link hands. "Okay. Sure. It does feel different now."

Kevin

I hear them coming from down the hall. I've been arguing— seriously *arguing*, for cripes sake—*Me!*—with the nurse, who doesn't want me to have real food yet. Andi's here quietly smirking in her comfy chair...but she's got to be hungry by now too.

I wave the tiny bowl of jiggly blue stuff the aide had dropped off with toast and broth as my lunch. "I'm not saying I won't *eat* the Jell-O. I'm just saying I need some meat, or some potatoes, or something I can *chew*, too." To Andi I say, "Brace yourself. Incoming..."

And then they're on us like a Great Plains tornado. Mom

and Dad, Pete and CeCe, all talking at once. "Oh, honey!" and "You're awake!" and "We finally made it!" and "What are the doctors saying?" all at the same time.

Andi's eyes go round and she struggles to extricate herself from the recliner and the flimsy hospital blanket someone had brought her in the night. She makes it to her feet and everyone turns to her and…I think we all see the dried blood on her sweats at the same time.

I reach for her hand. "That's mine, right? That's not yours or…?"

Andi looks from me to my mom, who is pressing her fingertips to her lips, as distressed as I've ever seen her. "Hello, everybody. Kevin, I think I, uh…should go take a shower and get cleaned up and let your family have some time with you so they can see everything's all right." She leans down and kisses my cheek, then says to the rest of them, "I'll meet y'all properly later. I'm so glad you got here okay," and scoots out the door, leaving an actual silence in the room.

It only lasts a second, but still. With my family, that's a first.

"Was that Andi?" my mom asks.

CeCe snorts. "She's a lot prettier than that picture. Was that photoshopped?"

My dad's frowning after Andi. "But she's okay? She wasn't injured?"

"No, Dad, she's good, but you should see the other guy. Andi was so cool…" I spend a few minutes telling them the story, and then an exhausting hour answering ten questions at a time, and then Andi's back, scrubbed and so fresh I want to taste her. She's wearing jeans and a bulky sweater I don't recognize, her wet hair pulled back in her usual braid.

I tug her over to perch on the side of my bed and formally introduce her to everyone.

My family is in proper awe of her after hearing what happened, but Andi's not having it. "I think y'all are mistaking who saved who here. Kevin is the one who *tackled* the guy with the *gun*." And before they can argue, she says, "Have y'all made sleeping arrangements yet?"

My mom and dad glance at each other. "I have another couple of places to try," Mom says evasively.

"They're full, aren't they?" Andi actually looks happy about that, for some unfathomable reason. "Don't worry. There's no need for you to get rooms." She turns to me. "I showered at July's apartment. Joe's turning over his whole building to your family while they're here."

To Mom she says, "There's a nice little apartment with kitchen and full bath and bedroom and couch upstairs, and a big empty space with another bathroom downstairs." And to me, "July and Joe are stocking the kitchen as we speak, and Rose and Angus have already inflated a bunch of those thick air mattresses and put fresh bedding on them downstairs. Between that and your apartment—and Rose and Angus's guest room, if we need it—I think everybody's set."

I glance at Mom to see how she's taking this evidence that she's finally met her organizational match. To my surprise, she looks relieved enough to cry. She closes her eyes and for the first time I notice the lines of fatigue and worry and stress on her face. "It's okay, Mom. Everything's okay." She's close enough that I can reach her hand, so I take it.

She squeezes mine and a tiny tear streaks down her cheek. "I know. I can feel it. I'm so, so...glad."

CeCe steps in and wraps her arms around Mom and everything is really…moist…for a few minutes.

Andi's charming my dad and Pete when a nurse comes in and says the doctor has given the okay for me to have a real dinner. Andi turns to me, grinning. "How about I go get you something?" and CeCe says, "I'll go with you!" and they're gone before I can answer.

Pete and Dad say something about getting something to drink from the cafeteria. Mom sinks back in the recliner. I'm not sure which of us is more exhausted. She holds my hand and we both close our eyes and doze off.

Sometime later I wake up to the smell of heaven and the rustle of paper bags.

"Mmm!" my dad says, sniffing the air.

"What you got there, Cec?" Pete reaches for one of the grocery bags.

I know what it is.

Andi meets my hopeful eye and nods.

"Woman, you are the absolute *best*." The words fly out of my mouth before I can grab them back. My family turns to stare at me.

CeCe leaps into the rare silence. "Uncle *Kevin* likes Pakistani food now."

Mom's eyebrows shoot up. "*Really.*"

Oh *come* on. I may have been a little less adventurous before my move, but I wasn't really picky.

Andi steps over beside me with a foil pan. "Mr. Ahmed wouldn't let me pay. He'd heard what happened and said to tell you to eat and build your strength back up. I got all your favorites."

Yep, that's the heaven I was smelling. She hands me a fork and I dig in, trying to remember my manners enough to not choke to death in my hospital bed.

Mom watches with a look I interpret as amazement. I ignore it.

"Honey, come fix yourself a plate," Dad says to her. "We've got a feast here. Fried chicken, shrimp and grits, macaroni and cheese..." He elbows Pete aside and waves my mom up to join them.

CeCe hangs back, watching. "And *guess* what *else*," she says dramatically, as if no one else had spoken since her last announcement. "Andi's never seen him wear his Nebraska hoodie!"

Aw, geez. Here we go.

"No, I've seen him wear the gray one. He just doesn't like red," Andi says, and I wince, knowing all hell's going to break loose. But before Pete and Dad can start hollering, she says, "We stopped by the apartment. I brought you the gray one and the black Cornhusker T-shirt and some sweats." She sends me another tiny wink because somehow she knows that just like that, she's gotten me back out of trouble.

"We changed the sheets and tidied up your apartment, Uncle Kev. And picked up the key to that other building from your friend Joe." CeCe's given up on Mom fixing her own plate and has handed her one with a little bit of everything on it, including Ahmed's incredible pimento-cheese hush puppies.

I register what she said. *Your friend Joe.* Not "Andi's friend." Mine.

Andi must have read my mind. "Everybody was here last night," she says softly, beside me. "Joe and July, Angus and Rose, the restaurant crew, the high school folks, people from the shelter..."

"And they all gave blood for you!" CeCe is just a never-ending spout of information. "Andi got all misty-eyed when she mentioned it." She shoots a now-what-you-gonna-do glance and a grin at Andi, who just laughs.

"Kevin failed to tell me what a brat you are, kid."

"Yep, she's already got you pegged," Pete says, and tugs CeCe back to the food. "Let's see if you can get that mouth busy chewing instead of trying to cause trouble."

CHAPTER 31

Andi

IT'S CERTAINLY *INTERESTING* TO WATCH Kevin with his family.

A lot of love flowing in all directions, that's for sure. But as I hang back, trying not to intrude, I begin to understand why Kevin wasn't entirely devastated by leaving them to strike out in a new direction. They kind of resemble human steamrollers. They ask him questions and then answer themselves before he can speak. Talk over each other in a way that makes my head spin trying to sort out the various threads of conversation.

They're loving and enthusiastic...and they take him for granted. He's not invisible, exactly; it's more like he's a piece of comfortable, dependable furniture. Or no, maybe a beloved pet. An old golden retriever—sweet and loyal but not about to make waves or talk back. They talk around him, seeming to assume he'll be happy to go along with whatever they say.

And for the most part, he just...does.

Kevin's doctors say they want to keep him one more night but that he can get up and take a short walk as long as he's not dizzy. A nurse shoos us out of the room and removes his catheter, saying he can start going into the bathroom if he feels up to it, and he seems thrilled. No sooner do they let us back in than he's climbing gingerly to his feet, shuffling carefully down the hall, one hand on his IV pole, flanked by his brother and CeCe.

His mom has seemed to gain energy and strength right along with him. We watch Kevin leave the room and then she turns to me. "Andi, thank you for taking care of him."

"He took care of me too, but you're welcome."

She brushes at a smudge on her jeans. "He seems...a little different than he used to."

"Oh?" I see Kevin's dad listening, but he doesn't say anything.

"I'm not sure what it is. Maybe it's because of the shooting? Or maybe...I don't know. He just seems...livelier."

Kevin's dad snorts. "That boy used to be laid-back to the point of being catatonic."

Kev's mom—Amy, I'm supposed to call them Amy and Trey—shoots him a look I can't interpret. "Well. He does seem a little...brighter-eyed now? More interested in all kinds of things."

I think back to the first night I met him. "I think he's been like that as long as I've known him. Must be something about North Carolina. Maybe it's his job." *Or maybe he's just visible to people here and he's responding to that.* No, not fair. Look how they all dropped everything and came as soon as they found out he was hurt.

Amy looks directly at me. "Might be you. You're a little different than other women he's dated."

"How so?" This I really am interested in hearing. I'd especially like to hear her describe that jerk Cheryl.

Amy frowns a little. "At first I wasn't sure how. But I'm beginning to see that he did have kind of a type. Before. Kind of—" She
waves her hand. "Kind of small and obsessively tidy and uptight.
All of you have been pretty in your own ways, but...I'm not sure
the others were as comfortable in their own skin as you seem."

I mean, it *sounds* like it could be a crack about my size and
my lack of makeup and my big bulky sweater, which is actually
July's, as are these jeans, but her tone sounds completely sincere.
Nonjudgmental. I'm not detecting anything barbed or fat-phobic.

I want to hear more of what she's thinking, but Kevin and his
entourage are back. He looks tired and he's limping, but there's
a light of victory in his eyes. He pauses by my chair, bends over,
and drops a kiss on my lips. "Hi." As if I've just come in.

I can't not smile back at him. "Hi."

He moves to the bed, somehow managing to sit and twist and
swing his legs onto it without shrieking in pain or flashing any of
us. He does look like he needs a nap, though.

Truth be told, so do we all, except for CeCe, who is up and
around a lot, never straying far from Kevin's side (now that she's
vetted me thoroughly on our trip to Ahmed's), darting glances at
him, asking questions...basically, I think, just reassuring herself
that her beloved Uncle Kev is really okay.

I totally get that. It's not easy sitting across the room from him
when some still-scared part of me is wanting to confirm and recon-
firm that he's still warm, his heart still beating, his eyes still aware.

Dr. Travels has said that he seems to be doing very well but
she'd rather not discharge him in the evening. If all goes well
overnight, he'll be discharged first thing in the morning.

Pete and Kevin's folks had been discussing who should sleep
where, with Amy and Trey staying at Kevin's—"I get the couch!"

CeCe chimes, surprising me, as I'd figured she'd want to be with her brothers and cousins and parents—while everyone else stays at Joe's building. But suddenly Amy repeats Dr. Travels's words and her head comes up, her stricken gaze finding Kevin.

"We forgot about Kevin! Where will Kevin stay?" Her eyes move from him to me and back.

He's right here, awake and fully adult.

I move to his side. "I hadn't had a chance to ask you yet, but Joe and July delivered an air mattress to the cottage for me. I'm hoping, since my place is all one level, you'll agree to stay with me. It'll be quiet, and you like the view, and…I'll be able to help out. Pattie brought my laptop to me at July's, so I can work from home the next few days."

His expression is full of too many things for me to read. Relief, I think, and embarrassment…and tiredness. "That would be great. Thanks." He picks up my hand and kisses it.

"Well," his mom says after a little silence. "I guess that is better than you having to climb to a second-floor apartment or lower yourself to an air mattress in a big room full of a bunch of other people."

"Some of whom snore," CeCe says, shooting a mischievous look at her dad.

I'm not sure how many more people, exactly, are coming. Kevin's two brothers-in-law are staying in Lincoln to work and take care of the pets, but CeCe rattles off a list of other names too fast for me to count. Including, I think, her cousin who just started college.

Maybe I'm more out of practice than usual at this peopling thing, because the idea exhausts me. Yeah, I work with people every day…but then I've always gone home to my little stone refuge in the hills. Even when Gram was alive, that always felt peaceful and mostly quiet. Kevin never seems like an intrusion. He's a welcome addition to my world. And his family seems lovely, just...lively. And loud. The nurses had to come shush them once, and since then they speak in stage whispers whenever a conversation gets animated.

I like them, and I know Kevin loves them, but when I look at the fatigue on his face, I want to push them all out of the room so he can take a nap. With me.

Kevin

Andi looks shell-shocked. She's so beautiful I'm not sure anyone else notices her exhaustion, but I do. I tug her down so I can kiss her cheek. "You should go home. Get some rest. Have you taken your vitamins today?" She's on a prenatal vitamin with folate and iron and...I don't know what all. Sometimes the iron doesn't agree with her. "How's your tummy feeling?"

She widens her eyes at me, but no one is listening. They're squabbling about...where the grandparents should sleep, I think.

"I'm fine. I'd like to stick around."

And she does, and so does everyone else, and sometimes I nap and sometimes I pretend to nap. I'm not sure why everything seems different to me now. My family hasn't changed, but I feel different with them. More aware of...myself, maybe? I don't think it's just because I was shot.

I think it's because I've changed since I've been here. If this were a sci-fi movie, I'd be a creature that started out as a soft blob and is gradually taking on a distinct shape of its own.

I never have thoughts like these. Maybe I'm still drugged up.

It's late when the others arrive. Just like before, I hear them coming.

Andi has just texted my address and Joe's address to the others, and now she's drawing a little town map on a napkin for Pete and Dad, showing them where those two places are in relation to the hospital and the town square. Telling them that if they need good food, July will fix them up.

Four...three...two...one... "Kevin!" my grandmas say, together, from the doorway, and then they pour into the room with my sisters and grandpas and the older kids, all talking at once. Pete's wife is out in the van with the younger kids, some of whom are sleeping. That's one of many, many things they tell me.

Again Andi's pretty eyes widen. She eases to the back of the room and then around to close the door to try to contain the noise. My mom is shushing people as best she can, even as she doles out hugs.

They flock around the bed and I feel like a frog in a specimen jar. One by one they touch my arm or kiss my cheek or give me gentle fist bumps. CeCe's little brothers clamor to hear the story of How Uncle Kev Got Shot, and everyone else leans forward to listen too, including the ones who've heard it before. So I tell the story, making sure to describe Andi's role very clearly, and soon they are darting her glances full of awe and admiration.

I've never seen her blush like this. Even beet red, she's *so* dang pretty I forget where I am in the story, my words trailing off as I look at her.

And there's another of those surprising silences, and then my mom's mom speaks up. "Well, it's late, and everybody's tired, and I think we should all get some rest. What hotel are we staying at?"

My mom and dad start telling them about what Andi's friends—*our* friends—have worked out, and Pete shows them Andi's little map and sends them Joe's address, and then it happens.

My other grandma says, "But who will stay with Kevin?"

I'm just about to say I think I might sleep better knowing everyone else is getting a good night's sleep elsewhere when Andi says, "I will. That chair's really comfy. I used it last night."

And my grandma says, "Bless you, honey, you are so sweet. But you and that baby need a real night's sleep on a real mattress."

And the small unusual silences from before have *nothing* on the one that settles over the room now.

"Baby?" my mom says in a tiny voice, her eyes going to Andi's well-hidden belly.

"*Baby?*" my sisters say in a simultaneous not-quite-a-shriek.

Dad and Pete stand there with their mouths open.

And CeCe says, "Aw, Uncle Kev, you're going to be a *great* dad."

"Well," one grandma says to the other, "I guess we've really stepped in it now."

"Don't tell me the rest of you didn't know," my other grandma says. "*Look* at her! She's glowing up the whole room. And her hair is so shiny! And she doesn't look like the type to go for implants, so *those*—"

And oh my god, she's waving at Andi's breasts, which are, admittedly, even more spectacular than usual lately, even in that bulky sweater.

Aaaaaaand…Andi's blushing furiously again. And my nephews are giggling, and Pete is elbowing them.

"All right, everybody. Thank you all for coming. You can see

I'm okay, but we're all tired, so why don't you all head out? Andi and I will figure out a way for me to see everybody again before you leave..."

Damn if that's not my voice, taking charge like a boss. Everyone turns to stare at me.

"Oh, honey," Mom says. "We're planning to stay a while."

Andi moves to my side and we reach for each other's hands.

"Oh, good. That'll be nice. Thanks." That stranger inside me speaks up again. "Well, I'll be discharged first thing in the morning, and then Andi and I will be busy trying to get me settled at her house. How about everybody take it easy in the morning, maybe explore town a little, and later we'll make a plan to get together?"

Everyone looks around at each other like, *Who is this guy, and what has he done with Kevin?*

"The town square is really nice." Andi waves at the map in Pete's hand. "The kids could run off a little steam there in the morning, and there are nice little shops and restaurants and the library. Our friend July would love to meet you. Her place is on one corner of the square. Best food in town."

More looks exchanged. Eyebrows raised. "I guess we're being dismissed," Dad says, an odd note in his voice. Not anger. Maybe...amusement?

More fist bumps and cheek kisses, a hug from CeCe, and then they actually begin to shuffle toward the door. Pete's the last through it. He turns at the threshold. "Call me if you need the van to get you to Andi's."

"Will do. Thanks, Pete."

Andi and I watch them leave. Listen to them move down the hall at a volume that is very quiet, for them. Pretty sure I hear a few more "a *baby*?"s.

"Well." Andi resumes her place in the recliner, facing me within hand-holding distance, and then we're touching without me knowing who reached first.

"Well."

"So much for nobody being able to tell. How did she *know*?"

"I'm not sure. Maybe you should raise that sweater up and let me take a look. See if I can figure it out."

To my delight, she actually does flash me. Day made, because...damn.

"Might as well. Feels like everybody else in the world has seen me in a sports bra in the past couple of days. You. Every police officer and medic in town. Half the shelter. My stalker." She sounds glum.

I tear my mind off her breasts and squeeze her fingers. "You okay, really? D'you find out anything about him?"

She shakes her head. "Not much. I talked to police and the shelter a couple of times while your family was here and you were resting. His name is Carl McCarthy. Apparently his wife and two little girls left him and he thinks that the shelter and I have them." She sighs. "And that the best way to handle that would be to arm himself and catch me alone."

A shudder runs through me hard enough to jar my leg. I can't even stand to think about that. "They're holding him, aren't they?"

"Yeah." She shivers and hugs my hand to her. "So I guess we no longer have to worry about how or when to break the news about the baby to your family, huh?"

I'm all for this subject change. "Guess not. They'll still have a million questions, though. Or my mom and sisters will, anyway. The others will just sit back and enjoy the interrogation."

"But you bought us a little time to think about what to say." Her smile is faint but it reaches her eyes. "Well done."

"Yes I did." And it worked this time, because they were so shocked at me taking charge. But they are relentless and next time I won't have the element of surprise.

CHAPTER 32

Andi

THE NEXT MORNING I GET to see a whole new side to Kevin. A whole new *very cranky* side. Makes sense; I think I'd heard that day two or three after surgery is usually the most painful.

"What day is this?" he grumbles when a nurse comes in to do an early-morning vitals check. The sky is starting to lighten behind the blinds.

"Sunday." She's brisk. Cheerful.

He grimaces, raises his arm, sniffs himself, and grimaces more fiercely. "I am disgusting. Can I take a shower?"

The nurse raises her brows. "I don't know. Let me check. I'll be back in a few minutes."

He watches her go. "I'm supposed to teach tomorrow. I didn't even think of that. I've got to get hold of the school." His voice is brusque. "I can't believe I didn't already do that."

"When you were bleeding on the sidewalk?" I can tell he needs a little teasing. "Or when you were in surgery, or all doped up in recovery? Or when half the residents of Nebraska came swooping in?"

"Yeah, I guess that was…a lot." He manages a half smile and a shake of the head.

The nurse comes back to say that he can take a shower very carefully, trying not to get his wound wet, on two conditions: someone has to be in there with him, and he has to sit on the shower stool to do it.

That sets him off again. "I am a full-grown man. A big, strong full-grown man. Who has managed to shower by himself for—"

I interrupt so the nurse won't have to. "You are a big, strong full-grown man *with a bullet wound and a surgical incision.* Honestly, I'm a little insulted that you don't want me in there soaping you up."

He opens his mouth to argue, then he looks at me and changes course. "Okay, let's do this."

The nurse lets down the side of his hospital bed and we flank him as he slowly maneuvers himself to his feet. She sees us to the bathroom door and then, as she pulls it closed, says, "No sexual activity just yet. Be very careful in here, okay? If you fall, you might not be able to be discharged this morning."

Kevin growls and limps over to the shower, reaching up to untie his hospital gown.

I tug the tie at his waist and then move around him to turn on the shower. When the water's warm, I position the seat partly under the spray.

He drops the gown, glaring at it. I think he'd kick it if he could do it without hurting himself. He steps into the shower and I watch the water run down over his head and his big, beautiful body.

"Mmm. Bullet wound or not, you are a fine, fine man, babe."
I say it partly to raise his spirits and partly because it is so abundantly true.

His growl has a completely different tone to it this time. "If you're gonna help me, you should at least take off your sweater and jeans so they don't get wet." He grips the grab bar with one hand and my arm with his other and lowers himself to the seat.

I eye him. "That is an excellent idea *if* you remember we're all business in here. You want to go home, right? So no messing around, endangering that."

"Gah! I *hate* this! Being so weak, not being able to walk right, not being able to take care of myself, not being able to..." He does look miserable, at least until I pull my sweater over my head and step out of July's jeans.

We mostly do keep it to all business, with only a few stolen kisses and nibbles and caresses. Maybe a nuzzle or two. It's actually relaxing. I suds him up in lazy circles, massage his scalp through his hair. Enjoy the feel of him relaxing back against me. His eyes drift shut and he says, "I can't wait till we can do this right, with me doing my share...but I guess this isn't so bad."

Afterward, I hand him a towel and make him promise to stay seated while I grab the clean clothes I'd brought from his apartment. Not the sweats yet, because they'll need to examine him during morning rounds and change the dressing one more time before they discharge him.

And everything does go smoothly with all that, even though it seems to take forever. At least they bring him a normal breakfast this morning.

He makes me eat some of it. "You and Lil Bit need fuel. I can eat more at the cottage."

It's three more hours before we can finally head home. Kevin had balked at first when the hospital staff insisted they had to wheel him down to the curb where I was waiting with the car, passenger seat partly reclined and pushed back as far as it would go. But he gave in to speed things up and because, I think, some part of him recognized that he really wouldn't be able to safely walk that far so soon.

He calls Steve Jackson and Tisha from the car. Between the two of them, they had texted me four times yesterday to make sure he was okay. Now I can tell from Kevin's side of the conversation that Tisha has already made arrangements for a sub and that she's saying Kevin should just focus on getting well and they'll talk next weekend about what to do after Thanksgiving.

My phone buzzes as we're pulling into my garage. A text from Pattie: Some guys came by yesterday and cleaned up the street after police took down the caution tape. Spoke mostly Spanish. Said their kids are in Kevin's class. Said to tell him they're all praying for him.

Now I'm the one not feeling like a grown-up, sitting here in my garage, bawling like a baby, because other people love my big, sweet man too.

Oh shit.

Well, I'll just have to think about this admission later. Thank god I only made it to myself.

Kevin takes the phone from my hand and reads the message himself. "This is…a really nice town." His throat sounds clogged.

I squeeze his hand. "Yeah."

It takes a few minutes for him to maneuver himself out of the car.

I hover and mostly try not to get in his way. "Think we should've gotten crutches?"

He grunts as he finally makes it to his feet. "I don't think so. Or, well, maybe later. Not today."

They'd told him to be very careful not to overdo things for the next week or two—no lifting of any kind, nothing too physical, a little walking but not too much, spend a lot of time with his leg elevated.

I unlock the door. "Where do you want to settle?"

He glances across the room to the love seat and then admits, "This morning was way more tiring than I expected. I think maybe the bedroom right now. Little nap..."

I move to his bad side, sliding my arm around his waist and lifting his arm around my shoulders, and we shuffle to my room. The borrowed air mattress leans against the far wall, already covered in sheets. My bed is turned down, ready for Kevin to slide in, and I know that if I go peek in the fridge, I'll find it stocked with easy-to-serve foods.

Bless our friends.

Instead of giving in to teariness again, I help Kevin untie his shoes. He tugs off his hoodie and T-shirt and lowers himself to the mattress.

"Lordy, this feels good." It comes out on a long sigh as he settles in and closes his eyes. He reaches out a hand toward me. "Why don't you undress and come keep me warm?"

Tempting, except for the possibility that fooling around could kill him. "We're not supposed to do that for a while."

He sighs again. "I know, I know. I just want to cuddle. How about I lie here on my back just like this and you climb in and snuggle up real gentle-like." He opens one eye and looks at me.

"You don't even have to take off your clothes if you don't want to. But I'd be a happy, happy man if you did."

It's an irresistible idea, after all we've been through. "Let me take a quick shower and I'll join you."

I managed to control myself around all that smooth muscle while he was naked in the shower. I can maybe manage it again with him in sweats.

Kevin

I must've dozed off while she was showering, but I sure as heck wake up when she slides into bed and curls up next to me, smelling of toothpaste and her sweet shower stuff, one hand on my chest and her warm curves pressing against me.

"Mmm. Nice." Her eyes are closed, her smile dreamy. She's wrapped in her worn flannel robe, the soft fabric doing nothing to hide the lush, glorious shape of her.

I give her the best hug I can while flat on my back. Her hair is still damp when I slide my hand up her arm to tangle in it.

I meant what I said in the ambulance. The words are so clear in my mind that I watch for a reaction, in case I'd said them out loud.

But her eyes stay closed and her breathing is already slowing, this woman who has not left my side for more than an hour since my surgery. This woman who inspires enough love from her friends that it spills over onto me and onto my big, loud family none of them has met. This woman who slept in a recliner to be near me the past two nights, and who is more than a match for my force-of-nature mom and my smart-ass niece and my sometimes-overbearing brother. This woman whose body is sheltering and growing our little miracle as we lie here.

And who was the intended target of the bullet that almost took me out.

My fist clenches in her hair, so strong is my desire to hold her tight and keep her safe.

She doesn't even stir, and eventually I drift back into sleep beside her, grateful for every moment of this life I am miraculously still part of.

A beeping sound rouses us. Andi yawns, kisses my pec, and rolls away to reach for her phone. "I set an alarm for one. I told your mom we'd call them by two."

I take hold of her robe and tug her back, then groan when I see I've exposed her magnificent cleavage, all the way to her navel. If I could roll over without screaming, I'd bury my face right there.

Somebody needs to convince my dick to chill out for a few more days.

"The plan is, we stay right here and they stay wherever they are, and we'll see them tomorrow." I sound as cranky as Steve Jackson with a hangover. I'm starving in multiple ways and my leg aches like crazy.

Andi cuddles close again, studying my face, gently trapping my hand when I try to slide it into her robe. "Really? I can tell them that, if you need today to sleep without people waking you up every couple of hours."

I sigh. Don't know why I'm not more eager to spend time with my family, when I've missed them so much since I moved here. Wait, oh yeah, I do.

"We need to figure out what to tell them about the baby." I trace her cheekbone with my knuckle. "Because when we see them, Mom will make exactly five minutes of polite small talk and then she'll dive right into the interrogation."

Andi's eyes crinkle when she smiles at me. "So...we aren't going to tell them we hooked up in an alcove in a bar an hour after we first laid eyes on each other?"

"Hey! We didn't—I mean, sure, I *wanted* to...but I am a gentleman. A classy, responsible gentleman. I took you back to my place for privacy and a real bed. *After* making a stop for condoms."

She frowns. "Yeah, I wonder what went wrong with those." She shakes off that distraction right away, though. "What *do* you want to say, then? How are they likely to take it if we tell them some version of the truth?"

I lace my fingers through hers. "I'm not gonna tell them Lil Bit's the result of a hookup, if that's what you mean." Not that it was ever really a hookup to me. "It's gonna bother them—Mom, especially—that we're having a baby without being married. Or at least engaged."

She shrugs. "Well, you proposed. You tried. Tell them that."

"No." I shake my head. "If they find out I proposed and you said no, it'll open up a whole new can of worms. Maybe make them mad at you. They get...protective. I don't want them blaming this on you. Or thinking that you somehow disrespected me by turning me down."

"Kevin, it *is* on me. It's not fair to let them be upset with you. Let them be mad at me. I don't have to have a relationship with them like you do."

I stare at her, not sure I heard right. "Andi, you're going to be the mom of their newest grandbaby. You're family now, whether we're married or not."

Her dark eyes widen. Her mouth opens, then closes. All kinds of expressions cross her face. Alarm? Realization? Alarm again?

"Something bother you about that idea?" Two minutes ago I was ready to blow them off for the day, just spend it in bed here with Andi even though we can't have sex, but now I've got those weird prickles I'd felt in her office right before I demanded to know why she still didn't trust me. Anger. And protectiveness toward my family.

She looks back at me. "No, I'm just... I mean, I'd already thought about *Lil Bit* being family to them. Just...not me." She shakes her head as if to clear it. "I... It's a huge change. I've never had much family. I'm not sure I know how to *do* family."

Those heat prickles die down. She's not disrespecting my family; she's unsure of her *own* role. "Does that scare you?" I squeeze her hand.

"I'm not... I mean, I'm not sure. I'll need to think about it, I guess. Get used to the idea." She studies me, her dark eyes liquid.

We lie there looking at each other as the idea settles in her mind.

"It's still better if they're upset with me than with you," she says softly, finally.

Nope. "Wouldn't be fair. I knew as soon as I proposed that it wasn't a good idea. I pulled back too. I'm not letting you take the fall for that."

She raises her graceful brows. "I don't suppose you'd consider telling them it's none of their business...?"

Gut punch. How had that not even occurred to me? Other

people can say things like that to people they love. I know they do. Why does the thought of it make my insides squirm?

I guess my silence stretches too long, because Andi sighs. "Okay, well, I'm sure we'll figure something out."

CHAPTER 33

Andi

IT'S A GOOD-HUMORED, LIVELY, *LOVING* invasion, but an invasion nonetheless. My cottage has never seen so much action or heard so much noise. I have this sense of it vibrating, of tiny fissures forming between the old stones until eventually it'll burst apart, all its bits rattling down the mountain, bouncing and ricocheting off bare tree trunks.

I haven't felt this level of overwhelm since I went up to the residence part of the shelter last year after all the kids had just chowed down on Halloween candy.

Kevin's mom and I decided ahead of time that we'd both watch him closely for signs of exhaustion or pain, and then adjust the visitation accordingly. He mostly seems okay so far. Before they got here, I pushed his chair—and the little table he's using to elevate his leg—up against the wall on his bad side, to minimize bumps and collisions from little bodies. Good thing, too, because they all want to be near him.

He's probably also feeling good because July and Joe stocked the fridge to bursting, as we discovered after our nap. He rubbed his hands together, took his meds and had a feast of peppery pasta and salad and a perfectly grilled pork chop even bigger and juicier than the ones Joe had fixed the night my friends tested Kevin. "Oh, lordy," Kev whispered when he saw it. I thought for a minute he might cry actual tears of joy.

So now he's well fed and the pain relievers have kicked in and he is surrounded by people who adore him.

He seems to have a hard time telling the kids, *No, I can't hold you on my lap,* so one or the other of the adults is always having to remind them or tug them away. He has the little ones sit on the hearth and the floor so he can read to them from the bagful of picture books one of his sisters brought. The grandmas take turns beaming at him from Gram's old chair and doing god knows what in the kitchen with Kev's mom. Amy. His dad and grandpas and Pete and CeCe and her college cousin are in and out from the back patio. The other adults are playing cards with the kids or putting together a massive puzzle on a card table I'd set up with some folding chairs.

I alternate checking on Kev with sneaking out to the garage to make calls or work on my laptop in the peace and quiet of my car. I've given up on locating overflow motel rooms for the weekend; instead we work out a plan to let people bunk in the conference room if necessary. Rose promises to find funds for sleeping bags if it comes to that.

Pattie and the therapists and the shelter staff all ask about Kevin. "We've arranged for extra group therapy and individual sessions for anybody who needs it," Pattie tells me. "But I think they'll all feel a lot better when they see for themselves that Kevin's going to be okay."

I use that as an excuse to go inside to see how he's doing. When I tell him what Pattie had said, he borrows my phone and takes some silly selfies, including ones of himself holding up a notepad with "See you soon!" and "Do your math homework!" written in Sharpie.

"Here, they should see that you're okay too," he says, beckoning me over beside him for a few shots.

"*There it is!*" someone shrieks from the patio door. CeCe, pointing and waving her hand at me. "*That face!*"

"I'm sure I don't know what you mean," I say, erasing all traces of gargoyle from my expression.

"It haunts my dreams." CeCe collapses against the doorframe, covering her eyes.

I sure hope she's involved in youth theater somewhere.

Kevin laughs. "You mean this pretty woman? Gimme a smooch…" he says, and tugs me down for a kiss.

Amid the little kids' "Ewwww!"s and giggles, I make my way back to the garage and send the pictures to Pattie. She promises to print them and post them all around the shelter—"Even the scary one."

My next call is to July.

"Excellent timing," she says. "I just went on break."

"Thank y'all so much for everything. Tell Joe that pork chop almost made Kevin weep."

She laughs. "So, I hear they're staying till Friday morning."

"I didn't know that. How do *you* know that?"

"They came in for lunch. Kevin's mom asked for me so they could thank us. She said they wanted to have Thanksgiving dinner with y'all and then if Kevin still seems fine, they'll head home."

It is so annoying sometimes how July learns news before the people most affected by it.

Does this mean my house is going to be…like this…for four more days? Jesus. I need to do some adjusting. And figure out how the hell to cook for that many people.

July's laughing again. "Stop your grumbling. I can hear your brain spinning from here. I invited everybody here for dinner Thursday since we're closed. We're also having my family and any of the staff who want to come. I told your folks it'll be a special meal using recipes from that *Sioux Chef* cookbook I bought when Joe and I went up to Minneapolis to try Chef Sherman's place. Dee-licious."

She's always been able to read me, even when I'm silent. "I may have dropped word to Kevin's mom that you're not keen on celebrating Thanksgiving." I hear a clink of silverware on a dish. "She was actually pretty cool about it. Just said, 'Well, that's okay. We'll just have a meal to celebrate that they're both okay and that we're all able to be together.' So that was when I said y'all should plan to come here where we've got plenty of space."

"July, that's—" I'm at a loss for words. It's perfect. It's too much.

Fucking pregnancy hormones. I try not to let her hear me sniffle but she's laughing again.

"Andi, don't worry about it. This is no big deal. I serve crowds bigger than that three times a day, every day. It'll be good to get to know them better. Make sure they're as nice as they seem."

Her *if they're going to be your family now* goes unspoken.

They really do seem wonderfully nice. The kids are high-spirited but polite and well-behaved. The others are fun and funny and helpful and appreciative. And the grandmas take turns saying things that remind me of Gram.

Fucking pregnancy hormones.

All in all, things go really well until evening when they start packing up to go back to Joe's building and Kevin's apartment. Kev's mom uses the cover of that chaos to corner us by the fireplace where I'm sitting on the hearth near Kevin's elevated foot.

"I've been meaning to ask," Amy says in a low voice. "Should we be preparing for a wedding? Do you know where you'll have it? Can we throw you a shower?"

Shit. For a while there I'd thought Kevin was wrong—that they might not butt in. When I turn to him, I can see by his deer-in-headlights expression that he's been hoping the same.

Kevin

Should've known we wouldn't get off that easy.

Mom's wording is a lot smoother than "You're not going to have that baby out of *wedlock*, are you?" but her meaning is clear. And she's obviously been thinking about it ever since she learned Andi's pregnant.

Andi could probably handle this better than I can, but she's waiting for me to speak up. *Dammit.* "No, nothing in the works," I say finally, carefully. "We're...not that far along."

"But you're having a *baby*!" As if no one has ever done that outside of marriage.

"Yes, we are. We didn't expect to be, but we are. So we're still figuring things out."

"But...are you saying you aren't serious about each other?" Yep, her cool is slipping.

I glance at Andi. Her pretty face is solemn, her gaze on me.

"I didn't say that, Mom. But we don't want to rush."

"But there's a baby on the way! Why would you do that if you aren't sure what you want? There are ways to prevent pregnancy!" Mom is actually turning red. I've never seen that before. And I don't think I've ever been the cause of her—or anyone—getting this upset. I start to sweat, my mind racing with absolutely useless, nonsensical thoughts. Like how peaceful the garage must be right now. And how scary and awful everything seemed when I was four and my baby sister was sick. And how much I want to drag Andi back to her bedroom, shut the door behind us, and just hold on till these feelings go away.

Shit.

Andi speaks then, her voice quiet. Calm. Firm. Just what I should be able to be.

"We're adults. Of course we know about birth control. But sometimes those methods fail."

That's a gut punch. I don't want to think about "fail" in relation to Lil Bit. Whatever else happens between Andi and me, I'm not going to ever be sorry about this baby. And I will *not* fail as a dad.

Andi's hand moves to her tummy. Protectively, I think. She looks a little sick at the idea of Lil Bit as a mistake too.

Mom opens her mouth, pauses, closes it, and looks around, as if unsure what to do or say next. And here comes Dad, two minutes too late.

"You ready, hon? Everyone else is already in the cars." He touches her elbow. "Kevin, sleep well. We'll see you tomorrow, Son. Andi, thanks for putting up with us."

Mom's voice is faint as she tells us good night. Dad hustles her out the door. Andi trails behind them and locks up. Sets the security system. Habit, I guess.

She's had lots of reason to build habits like that. Lots of reason to fear lots of things.

And yet when it comes time to make a stand, she's always there. Always rock solid. Always doing what's needed, with as little fuss and drama as possible, whether it's running a crisis shelter, kicking an attacker's ass, keeping her boyfriend from bleeding out on the street or standing up to his pushy mom. Andi always steps up.

And I'm always too late. Getting in the damn way. Or not showing up at all.

She looks as exhausted as I suddenly feel. She's not meeting my eye, instead glancing around the room. Except for the card table with its partially worked jigsaw puzzle and two decks of cards, everything is in its proper place, the dishwasher humming softly in the kitchen. My family does not leave messes at other people's houses.

Except for that last conversation. And this won't be the end of it. Mom will worry it nonstop and she'll talk about it with Dad. What he'll do or say is a question mark...until and unless he thinks Mom needs help. Then he'll swoop in like a hawk, and god help us.

Dad knows how to speak up.

"You ready for bed?" Andi's voice is subdued. "You can have the bathroom first. I think I'll drag the air mattress out here to sleep on so I don't accidentally hurt you in the night."

"Andi." I may be useless with my family, but I know how to hold Andi. And when she needs to be held.

She waits as I lower my foot to the floor. Push myself up out of the chair. *Ouch, ouch, ouch.*

I open my arms, and after a moment's hesitation, she glides

into them, wrapping hers around me, pressing all those soft, warm curves up against me, making me feel stronger and more balanced again, the way she always does.

"I want you with me, if you think you could sleep okay in there." I squeeze her to me. Kiss her hair. Rub her back and her arms, inhaling her sweet scent.

She hesitates. Then, "Okay. We can try. But the second I jolt you or bump you or hurt you, I'm outta there."

A little while later we're in bed, Andi cuddled to my side, her head on my shoulder and her hand curled on my chest. I bury my face in her hair. "Don't let Mom get in your head, okay? They're leaving Friday morning. We just have to hold on till then and we'll be free."

"You don't think that conversation tonight was the last, then?" Her tone is wistful.

I laugh. "Not a chance. She thinks child welfare is at stake."

We lie there in silence. Somehow I've said the wrong thing. I try to make out the words swirling unspoken in the air around us.

Andi speaks before I decipher them. "What would it take to end that conversation?"

I shrug, uncomfortable. "I mean, I don't know… Pete would probably come right out and say something like, 'Ma, I'm not gonna talk about that with you.' My sisters… Their husbands would step in for them. You know. Make clear that they're a decision-making unit on their own, or something."

More silence.

Finally, softly, Andi says, "But you don't want to do that?"

The air hangs heavy between us, the answer obvious and damning. The idea terrifies me.

I *want* to be a decision-making unit with Andi. I do. I just don't want to have to upset anybody by saying so out loud. I want people—Mom—to just *get* it, without being told.

Andi closes her eyes. I guess looking at me is too painful. "How did it work when you were with Cheryl?"

Man, I don't want to think about this stuff. She's not calling me unmanly—Andi would never say something like that—but that's how I feel. I sigh. "Andi, I don't know. I've never been in this situation before. Cheryl and Mom always seemed to agree about stuff, and I...just went along."

Why *did* I always just go along? I can think of some times when I wasn't thrilled about whatever the plan was. Places I didn't want to go, things I didn't think were a good idea. But speaking up...would've made waves. And I purely hate making waves.

"So...your mom probably thinks I'm a bitch now."

That jolts me. "What? No! Why would you say that?" I twist to see her face. *Ow, ow.*

"Because I *didn't* agree with her. And I spoke up. Firmly."

Because you wouldn't, Kevin. You just sat there like a weak fool. I don't know if those are her thoughts or mine I'm hearing. Possibly both.

"You weren't being a bitch. You just said what needed to be said." What *I* should have said.

Aw, god, what if she's right. What if some kind of rift opens now between my mom and my lover because I didn't do my part-ner job and speak up?

I've worried before that Andi would get tired of Vanilla Kev. So far, by some miracle, she hasn't.

But Silent Kev, Weak Kev...*those* assholes might break us.

Because she deserves better. And our baby deserves better. I know it, and so does she.

CHAPTER 34

Andi

BY WEDNESDAY I HAVE TO get out of the house. I've been working from home; Kev and I had agreed we'd go to the shelter together our first time back, after he's had a few more days to heal physically. We'll drive over together and take it slow, from the parking lot to the street to the sidewalk to the lobby. Talk ourselves and each other through it each step of the way.

We've got an appointment next week to see a trauma counselor in Asheville. We want to see someone till we're sure we're handling everything okay, and we agree it shouldn't be anybody from Galway where almost everyone knows one or the other of us. And it would be questionable ethics-wise for the shelter therapists to work with either the center director or a volunteer, even if they didn't already have their hands full.

I've been checking in a few times a day by phone and they reassure me everything's going fine, so I have no good reason to break my promise to Kev by going to the shelter without him. But his family filled the cottage to overflowing from late morning till after supper Monday and yesterday both, and they're coming back today, and I've been dreading it since they left last night.

Mrs. Mahoney—Amy, dammit—and I have been doing an awkward, odd little dance around each other, extra polite, extra solicitous, while everybody else pretends nothing is wrong.

I can't stand one more second of it. Or of Kevin ignoring it.

I mean, it's not like she's an ogre. She's done her absolute best to be a good guest and to make sure the rest of her family is too. Every day she mentions how wonderful my friends have been. She's not said anything that wasn't kind to or about me or anyone else—nothing passive-aggressive, nothing I can object to at all, really. It's just...she's a mom, an observant, caring mom who has a lot of experience seeing to her family and trying to give them whatever she thinks is best. And she's got her mind set that marriage is best in this situation.

If it were just me, I could handle this. She wouldn't seem like much of a problem at all.

I'm afraid the real problem is Kevin. I feel squirmy and disloyal and awful even considering it, but there it is.

It's like he has no boundaries, no sense of where his family's wishes end and his own adult decisions begin. He's not dependent on them and not immature, so I don't really understand what the issue is.

It plagues me all the way into town Wednesday morning.

Have I ever noticed him having this problem, this boundarylessness, before? He's a leader to the high school kids, and to the shelter kids. My friends like him a lot, and from the sounds of it, so do his fellow teachers and Tisha. With everyone else he seems easygoing, sure, but not a pushover. So why does this family thing seem like such a red flag?

I head toward the square, figuring I'll see if July will let me work upstairs in her apartment today. That reminds me of how Kevin keeps changing his mind, every time he tries another of her foods, about which one is his favorite—and then it hits me.

Those little "arguments." Those silly, little mostly joking pronouncements he makes about his preferences when he's trying to goad me into a disagreement over some goofy, doesn't-matter thing... Those *aren't* just him playing around. They're practice. *I...maybe...have never really argued with anybody*, he'd said.

He was trying to learn to stand firm in the face of opposition. To voice his opinion and stand by it.

The very thing he's struggling with now.

Because he wants to be his own person. He wants to stand up. He just doesn't seem to know how.

I don't know what caused him to have such a hard time with it—his family shows no sign of being bullies or abusive—but he's genuinely struggling. The stricken, almost-nauseous look on his face during that fraught conversation with his mom... His silence, then and later when I'd asked about the possibility of him telling them to back off... His desire to comfort me and keep me happy afterward, even as he didn't want to make his mom unhappy by opposing her... He's not sure how to balance love with assertiveness.

And he needs to figure it out. Quickly.

Because if he and Lil Bit and I are going to have a chance as a real, happy family unit, he needs to learn this. I can't be the only one recognizing and protecting our boundaries.

I park on the street and walk the block to July's on the square. Breakfast rush is tapering off when I push through the door. Sonya's at the booth the staff uses for breaks, a fistful of bright-colored markers in one hand, her lip caught between her teeth as she pretties up the Today's Lunch and Dinner Specials board.

July's sister, Jen, has just slid out of the booth, baby in her arms. We smile at each other as she says to Sonya, "Thanks for the lead. I'll go to the B and B now, see if Sabina needs help today." With a wave, she's gone.

"Nice." I nod to the cornucopia Sonya's drawn, bright fruits and veggies and flowers spilling out of it.

"Thanks, Andi. How you doing? How's Kevin? Can you sit with me?" Her smile is bright and quick, her voice sweet and breathy.

Every time I see her, I want to kill the monstrous ex who brought her to town, abused her one too many times, and then dumped her here like she was trash. Asshole changed his mind and tried to come back and force her to leave with him, but July—thank god—stopped him. *That* story has become part of town lore.

But to the sweet, soft young woman across from me, it's all too real, and I worry she'll never fully get over what life dealt her.

"I'm fine, Sonya, thanks. Kevin's okay too. Sore, but healing. His whole family's at my place with him now." I'd made him text me the minute they pulled up, because as much as I needed to get away, I didn't want him alone for long. "Thank you for donating blood."

Sonya shakes her head, gazing at me, her big blue eyes welling with tears. "I am so glad y'all are okay."

I no sooner say, "Me too," than people begin to gather around the booth, asking questions and wishing us well, everybody finding a way to work in a story about some sweet thing they'd heard

Kevin had done for the high school kids. Some of them drop in a sly comment with a glance at my stomach.

I've known this was coming ever since the day of the attack. I hope it wasn't someone at the ER breaking a HIPAA privacy rule, but between them and the shelter folks and first responders who all learned I was pregnant that day, I'll probably never know who told.

Turns out it's not as bad as I feared. I get a few veiled "I didn't even think you *liked* men" comments and questions, but most people seem to be genuinely glad we're okay.

Still, it's a relief when they drift away, waving goodbyes and telling me to tell Kevin to get well soon. I turn back to Sonya. "July swamped back there?"

"Nah, Donna took over when things started to slow down so July could take a tray up and eat with Joe. She said he's got stuff spread all over the dining room table up there, working on some big project for one of his classes. Said she was afraid he'd forget to eat if she didn't remind him."

Oh, they'll eat, all right. Among other things. Those two in the same space are like matches and kindling.

Guess that's a big No to me working up there today. I have to stifle a smile so Sonya doesn't ask what I'm thinking.

She's not even looking at me, though. "Gah! No! Not there, not there, not there... Gahh." Her frown is so fierce I turn to see what she's staring at, but it's just some guy, sliding into a booth over in the far corner. A perfectly ordinary-looking white guy. Medium height, medium build, receding brown hair, drab clothes...

"What's up? That somebody you know?" I don't recognize him.

"No, not really," she mutters, jamming the cap back on the

marker she'd been using. "He's just some jerk who *always* ends up sitting in my section, even though we *hate* each other's guts."

"He give you trouble?" If so, July should hear about it.

Sonya sighs. "No. I just...don't like him."

Verrry interesting. I've never known her to get irritated or be less than sweet to anyone. But before I can find out more, she changes the subject. "Andi, can I ask you something?"

"Sure." I might regret saying that—Sonya's a little wacky sometimes—but I can always refuse to answer. Because *I* am damn good with boundaries.

"How—How did you and July get so brave? Have you *always* been like that, or did you have to learn it? And if you had to learn it, can you tell me how?" Her brow furrows, marring her normally porcelain-smooth skin. I can feel her concentration from across the table.

"I...don't know if I'd call us brave, exactly..." This is tricky. This is obviously important to her, and I don't want to say the wrong thing and cause harm. "I think it's more just...doing what needs to be done at the moment."

She works her jaw, still frowning, still studying me. "But don't you ever, like, *freeze*? Or just not know *what* needs to be done?"

Not so far, no, thank god. But. "I'm going to tell you something in confidence, okay? Please don't talk about it with anybody."

She nods so fast I'm pretty sure she thinks I'm about to share some great secret to life.

"When that guy attacked me on that sidewalk, I didn't know he had a gun."

Sonya's eyes widen but she stays silent.

"I don't know what I would have done if I had known." I shrug, my shoulders stiff and heavy with dread as I relive the attack. "I might have frozen if I'd known. Because that would have tilted the power balance, right? I thought I had a fighting chance against him when I didn't know he was armed. But...I'm pregnant now, and between that and the unfair advantage a gun gave him...I just don't know."

Sonya's blue eyes are fixed on me but I'm pretty sure she's seeing something in her past.

"So...we do the best we can manage in the moment, I guess. Sometimes we have regrets later...but sometimes we get lucky. I think the best we can do is just try to learn from everything." I pluck a menu off the table behind me and pray Kevin and Lil Bit and I never have to face such a situation again.

Kevin

It's looking like I might make it through this week, but I'm not sure I deserve to.

July had told us all to show up around noon. Of course everyone insisted she let them bring something, so my family spent the morning using the kitchens at my place and Joe's, and Andi was bustling around the one here at the cottage. I propped my leg up on one of the dining chairs and made her bring me stuff to chop and dice and mince. She was practically dancing around, singing and humming, and I know it was because we had the place to ourselves again. She never made a single complaint about my family this week, but I know the lack of private space has taken a toll on her.

Just before we walk out the door to the garage—where Andi already has our dinner contributions stashed in her trunk, because my useless ass isn't allowed to carry anything—she pauses, turns, and wraps her arms around my waist. "Thank you for diving at that guy to save me and Lil Bit."

I'm only too happy to let my arms come around her. To kiss her temple and nuzzle her hair. "Anytime, Andi." And I mean it.

She leans back to look in my eyes. "You know I have faith in you, right?"

What? "I…"

She raises an elegant finger. Traces my eyebrow so gently I can barely feel it. "I see you, struggling with things that are hard for you. I have faith in you."

This is the closest she's come to mentioning the tension with my mom. And my failure to deal with it. I'm not exactly sure what she's saying, but she's saying it with love. And I feel a little like crying.

She stands on tiptoe, presses a kiss to my mouth, squeezes my ass, and then goes into the garage, leaving the door open for my bemused self to follow.

The square is quiet, with everything closed for the holiday, so we're able to get a close parking space. Decent hobbling distance.

My family is already at the restaurant, along with people July introduces as her parents, her brother, Brendan, and their sister, Jen, who's there with her husband and baby. Rose and Angus are standing near the kitchen doorway talking to Joe.

July has arranged tables and chairs in a long curve, leading from a booth on one side almost to the other side of the room, leaving space for people to cut through to get to the kitchen and bathrooms. The big dessert case is full of every kind of sweet in the world and the countertop above it is loaded with side dishes.

"Here, Uncle Kev! This space is for you!" CeCe waves me to the booth. "You can sit sideways and see everything and keep your leg propped up on the bench."

I settle in, feeling useless as usual lately when I see Andi grab CeCe to go out to the car with her to get the rest of the food we brought. As if she's equipped with radar, Mom glances up from where she's fiddling with a covered dish, sees me alone, and heads my way.

Thank god Joe beats her over here. He hands me a glass of tea and then makes pleasant small talk with her until my younger sister, Cathy, calls her over to settle a disagreement she's having with my older sister, Pam.

I have the distinct feeling that Cathy did that because she knew I needed rescuing.

Despite all the wonderful smells of all the wonderful foods here, my appetite disappears. Here I am, a grown man who can't walk worth a damn or carry anything heavier than a toothbrush or make love to his woman, and I need to be rescued right and left from conversation with my own mother.

CeCe's little brothers slide into the booth across from me, and I try to take part in their conversation. Seems like everyone is in high spirits, getting along with folks they just met and folks they already love, looking forward to a delicious meal in cheery company. Laughter and conversation rise and fall around the room. Finally July calls for everyone to come fix their plates and a long, happy line forms. I stay put, figuring I'm less likely to be bumped if I let the traffic clear out a little.

So of course Andi brings me an enormous plate of food.

Brings it right to me with silverware and a smile, like I'm a little child.

Goddammit.

And she's paid close enough attention these past few months to know exactly what I would have put on my own plate. Just like a mom knows her kid.

I watch glumly as she gets back in line for her own food, glowing and sparkling and charming people the way she always does.

She's amazing. She's been amazing every second of every day since I've known her, and probably every second of every day of her life leading up to that point.

What the fuck is she doing with a guy like me?

Finally she's back, sliding in across from me in the spot my nephews vacated, CeCe beside her. July clinks a spoon on her glass to get everyone's attention and then welcomes us all and invites people to take turns giving toasts, offering grace, saying something they're grateful for...

Then she sits and Joe wraps an arm around her and whispers in her ear. She gives him the purest, warmest smile I've ever seen, and I see her parents watching them, smiling and giving each other a small, silent fist bump. They know their daughter got lucky with her choice of a man.

I can't help but wonder what Andi's Gram would think of me.

I can't help but think she'd be disappointed. And she'd be right.

July's mom goes next, giving thanks for this chance to be here with her husband and kids and beloved new grandbaby. One of my grandmas toasts July and Joe and "all of Kevin and Andi's wonderful friends" who have made them so welcome and made this occasion so special. Then my mom opens her mouth and starts to rise, and I see my sister Cathy turn to look at me, stricken, as if to say, "I'm sorry, I can't help this time, big brother."

And in a flash I remember that terrible time when Cathy was a tiny, premature, and very, very sick newborn, and my folks, who already had three kids including a spoiled-rotten four-year-old named Kevin, everybody's baby and darling up to that moment. One terrible day of stress and strain in a long string of them, and that little boy broke. I threw a tantrum. Yelled, "Somebody. Pay. Attention. To *me*!" And my beloved, exhausted, sleep-starved, and scared-out-of-her-mind-for-her-fragile-new-baby mom burst into tears. And my big, calm, gentle dad bellowed, "Kevin, go to your room! You're making things worse!" And my big sister and brother dragged me out of the room, shushing me the whole way. Because speaking up, and showing displeasure, can get you banished.

And that's the last time I ever remember demanding anything for myself or doing anything I knew would upset my family.

Somehow, sickly little baby Cathy got stronger and grew up into a compassionate young woman who wants to save me from normal grown-up challenges.

But I've grown up too. I'm not a spoiled little kid who doesn't understand what's going on anymore. I'm a grown man with a wonderful partner and a baby on the way, and I've been feeling sorry for myself instead of shouldering my responsibilities.

This time, I've been making things worse by *not* speaking up.

And the next thing I know, I'm most of the way out of the booth, weight on my good leg, raising my glass and my voice as if I hadn't noticed Mom about to speak. Not sure what words I'm going to use, but they're piling up in my brain and my heart, trying to jostle their way out. And I say, "Not to make a contest out of this or anything, but"—that gets some laughs—"I feel like the luckiest person on the planet. I'm so grateful that Andi and I are alive and well, and that Lil Bit seems to be doing just fine in there too. And I'm so lucky to have a big, loving family that would drop everything and come at a moment's notice when I needed them."

I pause just long enough to suck in the breath and the courage I need for this next part, and then I face my folks. Look my mom in the eye. "And I feel so blessed to have had parents who raised us to think for ourselves and to always try to do the right thing, so that as adults my sisters and brother and I would be able to find wonderful partners to help us make our next decisions. Mom, Dad, thank you so much. I will always love and respect you more than you will ever know."

I'm almost out of steam, but I turn to look across the table at Andi. "And Andi, you are the love of my life, and meeting you was my luckiest day so far, in a life full of lucky days. I'm not sure what exact shape our future will take, but I look forward to being your partner and figuring things out together, for ourselves and our baby." I see her wobbly smile and the tears welling up in her dark eyes, and it's all I can do to finish with a "Love you all. Thanks for everything," before my throat becomes too clogged for words to pass.

I sink into my seat, hearing people actually applaud and realizing that I forgot to thank Andi's friends, and then I realize that Andi is on her feet speaking as soon as the clapping dies down.

"I just want to follow up on that really quick to say thank you so much to all of you who have helped us this week, and especially to Amy and Trey for raising a son who would never shirk his responsibilities. Y'all don't know this, but the day we found out I was pregnant, Kevin asked me to marry him. No, no, hold on—We're not engaged. He proposed, and then we had a long conversation about what would really be best. We realized that we needed to take more time and think things through, and that's what we're doing. He's the best guy I've ever known. I'm thrilled and lucky to have him call me 'partner,' and I believe with my whole heart that this baby"—her hand is back on her stomach—"could not possibly have a better daddy than Kevin. Love y'all."

Half an hour later, Andi and I are still looking in each other's eyes and feeding each other choice bits of food across the table. CeCe got sick of us, rolled her eyes and moved to sit with her cousin several minutes ago.

Andi lifts a bit of cider-braised turkey thigh—we're going to have to get *The Sioux Chef* cookbook—to my lips. "You are so dang cool, Mahoney."

I am feeling mighty good, it's true. "Why does that sound familiar?"

"You don't remember waking up in your room at the hospital, do you?" She gives me a smile that makes me wish we were sitting on the same side of this damn booth and that I didn't have to elevate my damn leg.

"Not really, no..."

We're interrupted by my parents, who somehow made it all the way to the table without me noticing. "You two lovebirds." Mom shakes her head, but she's smiling.

Neither Andi nor I contradict her. And my panic of the last few days seems to have evaporated. "Hey, Mom. What did you think of this turkey and the other dishes?"

"I think they're wonderful. I might drop a hint for your dad to buy me that cookbook for Christmas..."

He smiles down on her and we all know he'll do just that.

"I just wanted to say…message received earlier. You're right. You two know what's best for yourselves, and I need to make myself okay with whatever you decide." Mom presses my arm and then turns to Andi. "And, Andi, your message was received too. Thanks for letting me know."

They stand and talk with us for a few minutes and I've never felt so free to offer up my thoughts and opinions. And they seem fine with every single one of them. Despite four-year-old Kev's fearful conclusions, the world doesn't end when you speak up.

Especially when you have a partner who looks at you like you're a hero and who feeds you snippets of food from her own plate, just to have the excuse to touch you. Yeah, I know that's what she's doing, because I'm doing the same to her.

EPILOGUE

JUST OVER TWO YEARS LATER

Kevin

"YOU THINK LILIBET'S OKAY, REALLY?" I frown at the ceiling. It's dark outside and Andi's getting ready for bed but I'm not sure I should undress in case we have to make an emergency trip back to town.

"I think she'll be fine. July says Joe's the baby whisperer. Says he can get her nephew to sleep in under five minutes, no matter how fussy he is."

She's probably right—there's probably no need for me to worry. It just feels weird to not have the baby with us...and to carry on this conversation through a closed bathroom door. Whatever she's doing in there is taking forever.

But damn, it has been a good day. "Salazar, this was the best birthday ever. Thanks." Andi and Lilibet woke me up with breakfast in bed—French toast and a tiny-hand-mangled blossom on a broken stem. We went to the zoo in Asheville, then had lunch before hitting up Malaprop's, where Andi insisted I get all three of the books I was trying to choose between. Then home to

Galway where I was somehow able to hand over our sweet girl to that skinny, baby-charming devil Joe as a smiling July watched.

"I'm glad." Andi's voice has that husky edge that always makes me perk up.

And okay, baby worries aside, I have *really* been looking forward to a whole uninterrupted night with my woman. Maybe we'll fool around and then she'll grant me one last birthday wish and spend the rest of the evening naked so I can look my fill.

I'd want her to wear a little apron while we cook dinner, of course. For safety.

A very little apron. Preferably frilly.

If she ever comes out of the bathroom. What in the world is she—

The bathroom door swings open and the opening drumbeat of "Dangerous Mood" fills the room. In a split second I'm sitting up, wide-eyed, staring at Andi as she was the first time I ever saw her. She's draped against the bathroom doorframe in all her glorious, sexy Andrea glamour.

Her voice keeps pace with my heartbeat as she starts a slow strut over to me, red fringe shimmering and shaking, her beautiful red lips mesmerizing me as she forms each syllable. She reaches the bed and strokes a hand along my jaw as she circles around me. Presses her breasts to me as she slides her fingers down into my shirt, all the way down to my abs and back up to my chest, before she moves back in front of me and steps closer, nearly straddling my knees, her hips swaying and bumping to the beat, her eyes blazing into me as she sings about rubbing my shoulders, and champagne on ice, and how we might just have to mess around twice if once isn't enough.

I am dazed and speechless and mindless with lust, and even

in my current state, I know once will *never* be enough with this woman.

My hands are on her before the song ends. I grip her hip and one thick, juicy thigh, twisting to tip her onto the bed beside me. Throw a leg over her to pin her there. "Andrea…" I growl into her ear as she breaks into laughter and makes a half-hearted pretense of struggling, which only serves to draw my attention to her God's-personal-and-exceedingly-generous-gift-to-us-both breasts. It takes me a minute to remember what I was saying, then I try again. "Please say this dress is a cheap replica of the one from the night we met. Because I'm about to tear it off of you with my teeth."

Somewhere way back in the back of my mind, Vanilla Kev watches closely, only belatedly remembering to throw up his hands in pretend horror.

"No, no!" Andi's squealing and laughing, trying to hold me at arm's length even as she unbuttons my shirt and jeans. "It's the real one! Don't hurt it!"

I tug her up and onto my lap so I can reach behind her to unzip the magic dress. It rides up her spread thighs and, holy moly, she's not wearing anything under it. I am *this close* to rolling over on top of her when she stands and tugs at my jeans. I raise up so she can pull them off of me, but I never break eye contact with her. Of all the many things I love about her, her hungry-for-Kevin expression is one of my favorites.

"Mahoney, I am about to get lipstick *all* over you."

I sweep a hand through her glorious, silky hair. It's almost impossible to keep my eyes open when she puts her mouth on me. I don't want to miss a thing but I can't help it. I tilt my head back on a groan. Suddenly I'm remembering an old song I used to sometimes hear my dad sing quietly in my mom's ear when he'd come up behind her—I think it was Sting and the Police. Something about everything she does being magic.

This, with Andi seeking only to please me, and doing a damn perfect job of it? Magic.

Mornings, when she dances with Lilibet and me in the kitchen, and evenings, when she makes gargoyle faces at us across the dinner table? Magic.

At the shelter, when I catch a glimpse, from where I'm sitting with kids at the picnic tables, of her working at her desk to keep the place afloat? Magic.

Middle of the night, much of last year, when I'd stumble blearily into Lilibet's room to find Andi holding her, nursing her, crooning to her and smiling softly at me from the rocker? Magic.

And days when we go out to eat and she asks if I want fried pickles, just because she knows I *hate* fried pickles but love griping at her about them? Magic.

And oh my lord, if I don't stop what she's doing *right now*, our fun's going to be over too soon.

I touch her face. Pull her up to me for a long, slow kiss. Scoot us back against the headboard. Help her straddle me and slide the straps of her dress off her pretty shoulders so I can touch her bare breasts. Play and lick and suck at them till she's shivering under my lips.

She rises up, one hand wrapping around my ready cock to guide it into her, and I can't look away. She moves like a wave, like a tide, like the pull of the moon, and under her I push up, up, into her, deep and tight. She twines her fingers with mine against the headboard and uses the leverage to take me deeper, her breasts swaying, her eyes holding mine.

We're in sync everywhere, our movements, our rhythm, our intakes of air and our shivering exhalations. The hums that grind in our throats and emerge as moans. The sounds of slick welcome and our bodies joining and increasing desperation. I worship every part of her I can reach, pulling her dark nipples into my mouth one at a time and treasuring them there, treasuring the little sounds she makes—not quite whimpers, not quite words—as I move faster, pushing up deeper, harder. She grips me tight and bucks and bucks and sings her orgasm, a high, giddy, relieved sigh from her beautiful throat. I open my mouth there to feel the sound vibrate through her.

And I feel again what I feel every time with her—disbelief and joy that I am with Andi Salazar. Here in this embrace, here in this afterglow, here in this blessed life with Andi Salazar.

I roll us to our sides and kiss her and kiss her until she's laughing again. "You are the sweetest, cuddliest man!" Her eyes crinkle with her brilliant smile and she scrapes her fingernails lightly through my hair. If I were a dog, I'd be wagging my tail and slapping one back foot on the ground like crazy. I'd be belly up, open and vulnerable and begging for more of anything she wants to give.

She sobers and peers at me. "You always gonna be this sweet, cuddly man?"

I sober too. I don't know what this is about, but I can tell it's serious. I run a fingertip down her cheek. "Andi, you're my happy place. You and Lilibet are my world. Any time I have a choice, I'm always going to choose to be right here with you, holding you, just like this."

"I have one more birthday present for you."

She's already made it one of the best days of my entire life. "Yeah?"

"Well, it's more of a question, really."

I look at her sideways. Her flush of pleasure and emotion gives her a glow, an almost unearthly beauty.

She bites the corner of her lip. Speaks softly. "What would you think about moving in here full-time and letting your apartment go?"

We've been together as a family in almost every bit of our free time, either here or at my apartment, but this is our first mention of this possibility. I was pretty sure having separate places, even if just on paper, made her feel safer, so I never asked.

She's looking at her hand on my chest, pretending this is more casual than it is.

It's huge. This sign of trust from Andi... All my feelings rise up in me, bubbling and fizzing like ginger ale. Like champagne.

I, Kevin Mahoney, inspire this kind of trust. This love I see in her eyes every time she looks at me.

I was right.

Vanilla *is* a valid flavor.

I wrap my arms around her and roll us over and over. When we go off the edge of the bed, I make sure I land under her to break her fall. "Yes. Yes yes yes. Andi, yes."

And then she's laughing and crying and I'm laughing and crying, but I still hear every word when she hugs me tight and whispers, "I love you, Kev. Thanks for being the man who could help me break the Salazar curse."

Read on for a taste of
What She's Having by Laura Moher

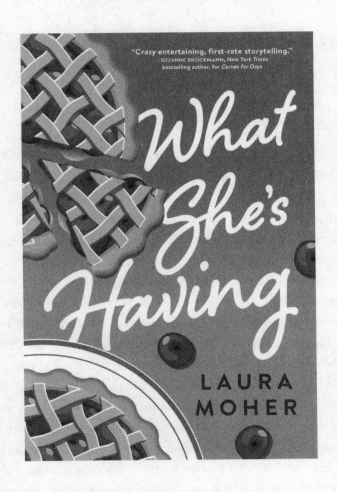

Don't miss the story of how July and
Joe fell in love in *What She's Having*.

Joe

I MUST BE OUT OF my freaking mind.

I peer through the windshield, looking for something—
anything—familiar. Woollybooger's Roadhouse is still in business, its beer-guzzling bigfoot mural more faded than I remember.
The gravel lot has a sprinkling of trucks and cars already, although
it's not quite dinner hour. There are more buildings between it and
the outskirts of Galway than there used to be. A Target, a gas and
convenience station, a small neighborhood. The town itself seems
less changed, brick and stone and wood familiar, the trees taller.

My breath and my heart are doing funny things in my chest.
I could point my truck toward July's on the town square, floor
the gas pedal, and not stop for signs or lights until I'm at the
restaurant. Race inside and sweep her off her feet. Carry her away
to somewhere where we can find our home in each other again.

Or I could act like a normal person with some sense. Follow
the traffic rules, find my building, give some actual thought to
how to approach her now that I'm here.

Because I'm here.

It wasn't untrue, what I told Mom before she died. I really had been restless for a while. I thought opening the second restaurant might take care of that, but soon they were both doing well in the hands of a great group of people, and I was itching to do something else. I came up with a plan to sell the restaurants to my employees and go back to school. Specifically, a social work program.

So the night Mom told me what she and Dad had done, I added Western Carolina's MSW program to my application list. Stayed up late into the night doing my most thorough web search yet for July. No obituary, thank god, and no wedding announcement either. Just a million news tidbits about her being on some board or other. I found the restaurant on Instagram and Facebook, but nothing personal under July's own name.

After Mom died, there was nothing keeping me in Colorado that didn't feel like a burden. I was ready to move on. And July deserves to know what happened, even if her response is, "I'm sorry, who are you again?"

But now, as I ease into Galway, I'm in pep-talk mode. Sure, this change was quick, but that's not necessarily bad. It's *decisive*. And maybe it wasn't wise to commit to this move before I talk to July, but I didn't have a way to reach her except through the restaurant's phone number. I did try calling, twice, but chickened out when I heard the chirpy, definitely-not-my-girl voice call out, "July's!" over lively, clattering background noise.

After two decades of believing she didn't answer my letters, maybe it's understandable that it didn't occur to me until this morning that I could've tried snail mail again.

So I can rationalize or explain away those things.

Buying a building three blocks from July's, sight unseen, though? *That* was nuts, even if it does have empty commercial space below and living quarters above. Don't know what I'm going to do with my MSW—just got a vague idea that I want to work with young people in trouble—but by god, I've got me a building to do it in.

At a stoplight I don't remember, I wonder what my army buddy Gabe would do in this situation. He used to laugh at my impulsiveness, say it was gonna get me killed if I didn't become the boss of it.

Gabe would lay low for a bit, get a feel for things. Make a plan.

It's thanks to Gabe that I got through school and made a success of the restaurants. It's due to him that I'm not coming to July empty-handed. That would've been just great, me knocking on her door saying, "Hey, July, it's me! Sure, I disappeared the day after we made love, and you haven't heard from me in two decades, and well, no, I'm not working right now, but I'm back, baby!"

Chances are she'll murder me outright when she sees me.

Assuming she remembers me.

I have lost my freaking mind.

I count down the street numbers, find my "new" old place, and park.

This would be a bad time to go look for her at the restaurant. It's almost dinner rush. Very bad time.

I fish out the key the Realtor sent me and make my way into my tired brick building. Been empty for a while. Smells like old mildew and dust. The big front window is cloudy with dirt. Cobwebs up high, bits of leftover office stuff on the floors. Plastic trash can, a couple of pens. The fluorescent ceiling fixtures flicker and blink slowly, noisily to life when I flip the switch. That's good. But there are holes punched (*kicked?*) in most of the walls. Shit.

Besides the main room, there's a small office, a restroom, and a storage closet on the ground floor. Up dark, creaky stairs is an equally dirty front room with two tall windows and a kitchenette with ancient fixtures. Behind that, a smallish bedroom and bath. The water pipes groan and spit out rusty water for a minute before it runs clear.

It all needs a good scrubbing, and it'll be night soon. As I step back out onto the street, I can't help glancing toward the square, where I imagine light and laughter and music spilling from the restaurant that was once just my girl's dream.

I'm halfway there, picking up speed, before I get hold of myself and skid to a stop. A young couple passes me on the sidewalk, glancing over, eyes cautious, skirting wide around me.

I can't go to her now. If she's there, she'll be swamped with work.

And I need a plan.

———————

"So you're not here to apply for a grant?" Rose Barnes, the representative I'm meeting with from the Galway Brown Foundation, leans back in her seat with a frown. She's a short, round woman with flyaway hair and big brown eyes in a sweet face.

"No, I'm just at the information-gathering stage." I explain my schooling plans and my desire to work with kids in trouble. "I looked up youth programs in the area, but I couldn't get a feel for what other services might be needed. I'm hoping you can tell me what's here, what's in the works, what gaps still exist... Maybe I can focus my coursework on some of the gaps."

"That's...very proactive of you." She describes the nonprofits working with kids in Galway County. "I've got some materials I can copy for you. Just a sec." She squeezes past me in her little office and goes out to the reception area.

Some wise part of me scheduled this appointment with the foundation before I left Colorado. They fund a lot of nonprofits in this area. Made sense to meet with them right off, to give me something to think about no matter what happens with July.

And it gives me something concrete to do with my morning, because I still haven't come up with a plan for approaching her.

It's a miracle I kept myself from going into the restaurant last night. Walked by when dinner rush was in full swing. Place was crowded, drawing me close, fifty different conversations and laughter I could hear from the sidewalk. I glanced in the windows when I went by but didn't see her.

So I walked around the square, had a beer at Lindon's, went back to my building, and worked on cleaning the living quarters and lugging my stuff in from the truck.

It was weird walking the streets. Didn't see a single person I knew from my few months here before, and nobody seemed to recognize me. Felt kind of like a ghost floating invisible through his former haunts.

Rose Barnes comes bustling back in from the other room and thrusts a fistful of copies at me. "Here you go. This will give you some idea of what we have already. Most of these have websites listed, if you want more information on them." She settles back in her chair. "So you just moved to Galway?"

"Got in last night."

"Do you have questions about the town? Did you find a good place to stay?"

I half laugh. "Actually, I bought a building before I came. Empty retail space on the bottom, apartment on top. Needs work, but it'll do."

She perks up. "What kind of work?"

I haven't given that much thought. "It's got kind of a someone-might-have-been-tortured-under-this-bare-bulb vibe to it. And an old tub with no shower. Gotta have a shower. Also, it's only got a little bitty kitchenette. Appliances older than god."

She glances at her computer screen. "Got time for an early lunch? I can introduce you to my husband. He does reno work, and he knows everybody else in town who does too. We can find you somebody."

"Well...that'd be great. Thanks." I was right, remembering Galway as friendly.

So I get in my car and follow her...and she leads me right to July's corner of the town square.

"I'm taking you to my favorite place," Rose says with a big smile as I climb out of my truck and walk over to where she's parked, just two blocks from my building. "Hungry?" She glances down, and I realize I'm rubbing my stomach.

Having trouble getting my gut to stop doing nervous flips.

"Uh, yeah. Skipped breakfast." Half-true.

I peer in the restaurant's tall side windows as we walk to the corner. No July in sight, but I can sense her there, just like last night. My blood is humming in my damn veins, wanting to burst out of me and go to her with little messages from my heart.

Rose and I round to the front of the building, and I tug open the door with cold hands, pretty sure this is a terrible idea. I'm nowhere close to knowing the right words to say to ease July into seeing me for the first time in twenty years.

Seems to be our pattern, me doing things that will be hard on her without giving her any warning.

Inside there's music and laughing conversation and air scented with fresh baked breads and spices. My empty stomach would be enthusiastic if I weren't scared out of my mind.

"There's Angus!" Rose has been up on her tiptoes, scanning the room, and now she waves at a huge guy flagging us down from a booth on the inside wall.

Dude's a giant. Gotta be nearly six and a half feet tall. A wall of a man with a wild, curly beard. He gives Rose a sweet smile, ushers her into the booth beside him, and then turns to raise an eyebrow at me.

"Angus, this is Joe Anderson. He's new to town. I asked him to lunch thinking you could help him get his place fixed up. Maybe recommend somebody if you don't do it yourself." Rose settles in the booth, and his expression softens again as she drops a kiss on his enormous biceps. "Joe, this is my husband, Angus Drummond."

We shake. I scan the room again before I slide in across from them.

Angus squints at me, his eyes a surprising bright blue-green. "You look kinda familiar. Why's that?"

"Lived here a few months when I was sixteen. Liked it. That's why I wanted to come back."

He nods, points, and shakes one big finger at me. "Yeah... sophomore year? You had long hair?"

One of many things Dad had hated about me. "Tail end of sophomore year and most of the summer, yeah." A flash of movement catches my eye and I glance to the right and—

There she is. My beautiful Amazon. My lungs squeeze up like I just slammed into a wall.

She's still tall and strong and solid, still golden and laughing as she lowers a tray to serve the lucky bastards a few tables over. I hear snatches of her words: "…only bringing this out 'cause it's your birthday, Frank. How y'all doin'?"

I don't give a shit about Frank's answer. My senses devour *her*. Snug orange T-shirt and jeans skating close along her thick curves, her shiny all-shades-of-blond hair caught back in a swinging ponytail, her voice the warm honey I remember. I wonder if she still smells like soap and baby shampoo.

Once in school, before I met July, I heard some dipshit call her fat. Her friends—she's always had good friends—looked him up and down, and then turned to her. "You want to kill him or can we?" July's cheeks were pink, and she could *definitely* have taken the asshole apart with her bare hands, but she just said, "Not worth it. He could probably use an escort back to fourth grade, though…" and swept on by, leaving him sputtering.

Fucking magnificent.

"You know July?"

I'd forgotten all about Rose. She and Angus are watching me, his brow quirked again.

I suck in some air—apparently I also forgot about the body's need for oxygen—and consider my answer. "Used to, yeah," I say finally. "Haven't seen her in twenty years though."

Birthday Boy says something, and July laughs that laugh that always made me feel like I was warming myself by a fire. My gut twists. "God damn," I hear myself say, and realize that Rose and Angus are looking at July now too.

She must feel it. She turns, meets my gaze, and—

All the color drains from her face.

ACKNOWLEDGMENTS

I wish I knew the names of everyone who has had a hand in the creation or promotion of this book so that I could thank you all individually. Besides the obvious folks (my tireless agent Sara Megibow and others at KT Literary, and my editor Deb Werksman and other lovely Sourcebooks folks—looking at you especially, Jocelyn, Alyssa, and Diane) there are numerous others who have worked on and contributed to this and previous books in my Galway series, and I appreciate you all. Thanks also to all the librarians, booksellers and reviewers who have taken the time to stock or recommend my stories, and readers everywhere just for reading.

I've been blessed with a group of lovely friends (Julie, Dawn, and Jennifer), all either therapists or psychologists, who pointed me to good resources on childhood trauma and loss when I was trying to understand how Andi's experiences in infancy might affect her in later life. My critique partner, Mary, blurb fixer extraordinaire, and my other beta readers, Paula and Carol, are wonderful women who always give me enormously valuable and gentle feedback and encouragement. And my favorite child,

William, has been my best cheerleader and all-around support, to the extent that their friends have helped get the word out about my stories too!

Sometimes in the thick of things, writing feels like a lonely, impossible process, and this is where I'm especially grateful for the help and input and humor of fellow writers, including Suz Brockmann, Laura Drake, AE Wasp, members of the Writing While Fat group, and all the lovely people I've "met" and interacted with on social media. You all inspire me and raise my spirits when I need it, and I thank you. And finally, to all the other authors whose works have provided me with pleasure, escape, and/or a higher bar to aim for over the years: Bless you. If/when you need encouragement to continue writing, let me know, because I will definitely give it.

ABOUT THE AUTHOR

Laura Moher is a former associate professor of sociology at the University of South Carolina Upstate in Spartanburg, South Carolina. Her head is full of stories of flawed people who come together to make each other—and their world—a better place. She has deep roots in the South, having grown up in the Louisville, Kentucky, area before moving to the western Carolinas where she taught for eleven years. She has also lived in Colorado and Illinois, and is now happily settled near her son in Minnesota.

Website: lauramoher.com
Facebook: authorLauraMoher
Instagram: @lljzmc